Also by Kate Cann:

Footloose
Fiesta
Shop Dead

And the brilliant prequel to *Shacked Up*:
Hard Cash

The final part of the trilogy will be out soon…

Point

shacked up *n.*

slang living together, whether you like it or not

kate cann

■SCHOLASTIC

To the fabulous Ellis family

Scholastic Children's Books,
Commonwealth House, 1-19 New Oxford Street,
London WC1A 1NU, UK
a division of Scholastic Ltd
London ~ New York ~ Toronto ~ Sydney ~ Auckland
Mexico City ~ New Delhi ~ Hong Kong

First published in the UK by Scholastic, Ltd, 2000
This edition, 2001

ISBN 0 439 99350 4

Typeset by Cambrian Typesetters, Frimley, Camberley, Surrey
Printed by Cox and Wyman Ltd, Reading, Berks.

1 3 5 7 9 10 8 6 4 2

Chapter 1

Bonny's standing in front of the huge windows open to the purple night. I'm sitting on my bed watching her. We're talking about the fact that she's just run away from home and – somehow – it's no big deal. Somehow it's normal.

Some times are like that I reckon. So much weird stuff happens to you you give up trying to make sense of it and you just sit back and let it all roll over you.

Bonny turns and faces me. Her eyes are still wet. "I'm not going back, Rich," she croaks, all determined. "Ever."

"No," I answer.

"She's a – *vampire*. She is. You were right. Mothers are meant to nurture you, help you be who you *are*, they're meant to feed you, aren't they, help you *grow*?"

"Yeah."

"Not try and be some kind of evil twin to you, some kind of *rival*, taking over your life, twisting you, *draining* you. . ."

"What was the row about?"

"The row?"

"You know. Why you left."

"Oh, it wasn't anything special. Just the last straw. I'd been asked to this play – one of the girls at school has a brother in some kind of drama group – and it clashed with this phoney exhibition Mum wanted me to go to. *Anyway.* For once I put my foot down, said I was going to the play, and she was so *scathing*, all 'Oh, darling, *honestly*, amateur dramatics, it'll be excruciating, how *can* you' – and I was . . . I was OK."

"Good for you."

"I was, Rich. I kept calm, and just kept saying I was going to the play. And then it was like I was standing back watching her go through her paces, you know, what she does to manipulate me. I didn't get drawn in, not an inch. I felt like I was standing way, way back, like the other end of a telescope or something, it was weird. But watching her was horrible, really *seeing* her was . . . oh, *God*. Anyway."

"So what happened?"

"Oh – she got furious and shouted and banged about, then she got pathetic and cried and said she needed me with her, then she got really, really *nasty*. . ."

Tears have started to run down her face again. I stand up and think about putting my arm round her shaking shoulders and then I think about making her a cup of tea. Being a coward I choose the tea. "I'll put the kettle on," I say, and I cross the bare boards towards the tiny kitchen.

"Oh, Rich, I feel dreadful," she wails. "Bursting in on you like this. It's just – I had nowhere else to *go*."

"It's OK. Honestly, it's OK."

"I mean – I could've stayed with Barb and Nick. They're so *great*, they'd've put me up – but then Mum would've found me right away. And Barb told me to come here, she made me promise to, and I—"

"Bonny, I've told you, it's OK. It's Barb's *flat*, for Christ's sake. If she says stay here, you can stay. I'm just dossing here too." I'm filling the kettle now, can't hear if she answers. Then I hear: "You were working, weren't you. I interrupted you working."

From the door of the kitchen I watch her get to her feet, bend over the three sketches I did when I felt half insane, half inspired – how long ago? An hour, that's all. It could be a year, the way I feel, the way time's stretching, the way nothing makes sense any more.

The last few weeks have done my head right in. You know the old Wheel of Fortune, takes you up, up, up and then the slow decline? Well, I was on it but for me it was the Big Wheel, the scary Fairground wheel, cranking up fast, so fast I barely had time to draw breath, right to the top, *all right*! And then – crash. Over the top and zipping down even faster, down, down, so fast you're too sick to move at the end.

First I get plucked out of skint obscurity by Nick, telling me he could use my artistic talent to make us both money. He had me all lined up for one of his ad agency clients, alcopops barons wanting to sharpen up their image. I was going to create one of my monstrous creatures for them, and this creature was going to be patented and pasted across billions of bottles of soft booze and make me rich as sin.

So I get given some advance money and suddenly I'm looking good and living the life and then I pull the amazing Portia, and it's heating up between us and I'm squiring her about to all these swishy places, and OK I fall out with my folks but I get to move in here, this amazing flat over Nick's ad agency, and I'm waiting to make it, I'm just *waiting* for the serious money, and then, and then . . . the downslide. The crash.

Nick was sure the deal was going to happen, sure. But it didn't. And everything else seemed to crash down with it.

And now I've got to put it behind me, haven't I? Got to.

Bonny's still stooped over my drawings, engrossed in them. I realize I'm kind of holding my breath. I'm waiting for her verdict. It's the first time Bonny's seen anything I've drawn.

"*God* these are good," she's saying. "These are . . . *amazing*."

"Thanks."

"I'm not just saying that, Rich. They are."

"Thanks."

She turns and looks at me, and I get the feeling she's really happy she likes my stuff so much. "I love the one with the thin people running. It's – *terrifying*."

"Yeah?"

"Yeah. They look like they're just running, you know, not *from* anything, just running 'cos they're too scared to stand still."

I laugh, and carry the tray with the teapot and two mugs over to the bed and put it down. "I was pleased with them," I say. "I was in this weird place when I did them. Kind of – art is all I've got. Art is the reality."

She looks at me like she's waiting for me to explain this crap, but I don't, so she asks, "You got any more?"

"No. Not here. Oh – yeah. Those." And I jerk my head towards the sketches of Portia, propped against the wall.

Bonny picks them up, and holds them away from her and her face kind of sags. "She looks – she looks *gorgeous*."

"She is."

"But not this gorgeous. You've flattered her, you've made her—"

"Yeah, well, I could hardly make her look like a dog, could I."

"I s'pose not," says Bonny, a bit acidly. "Not the fabulous girlfriend."

"She's not any more."

"Fabulous?"

"The girlfriend."

"What?"

"She finished with me. Last night."

"*What?* Why?"

"Because — well, if you want it straight it was because I wouldn't shag her in the lift out there."

Bonny goes a kind of strangled red colour and squeaks, "What, the lift up here?"

"Yeah."

"The *cage?*"

"Yeah."

"You're *joking*. She *told* you that's why she finished with you?"

"No, she just stamped off and yelled 'Loser' back over her shoulder."

"But . . . but . . . she *asked* you to?"

"What?"

"To . . . you know . . . to. . ."

"Shag her. Not in so many *words*, Bonny, no. But it was clear what she wanted and I wasn't up for it and—"

"Oh."

"Don't say 'oh' all knowing like that. I don't mean I wasn't *up* for it. I mean I blew it. She was being all seductive hanging off the bars, and

I – oh, shit, I went and freaked out and *laughed*, didn't I."

"Oh, *great!*" says Bonny gleefully, then she claps her hand over her mouth like she's horrified that the word got out and looks at me with eyes like soup plates.

Idiot, I think. *Idiot*, telling Bonny that. You know she likes you. She asked you out, after all. You should've remembered that, since she's the only girl who's asked you out since you turned thirteen.

"Sorry," Bonny mutters. "It's just – I think it's great you laughed. If she was being all porno queen and everything."

I smile, because that's exactly what Portia was being, and Bonny says, "Sorry – not great. Um. You know. Funny."

There's a long pause, then she asks "D'you think you'll make up?"

"No. For a start, she's got this longstanding boyfriend, Tony."

"Well, that didn't hold you back before."

"No, but – oh, I dunno. She's gorgeous to look at but. . ."

"But what?"

"Look – I *dunno*. I dunno anything at the moment. Let's leave it, OK?"

I pour the tea out and hand her a mug, and she takes it and says "sorry" yet again, then she sits down beside me on the bed and asks: "How come you're here, Rich? In Nick and Barb's flat?"

I shrug. "Same as you, really. Escaping evil parents. Well – parent. My old man."

"What happened?"

"*Uuuurgh.* A row. Things kind of came to a head. It's been bad for years though. I just – I had to get out. That was only about three days ago. And then almost as soon as I'd moved in here I blew it with Portia and then Nick told me the deal with the alcopops people was off."

"Oh, *no*," breathes Bonny – and starts crying again. She's trying to hide it but I can see the tears there. And to tell the truth I feel like crying with her.

"Oh, *Rich*!" she says all trembly. "That was going to be *so good*!"

"I know."

"They're *idiots*. Not to use you. *Idiots!*"

"Yup."

"So what'll you *do*? Now?"

"I don't know. I'm still in college. Just."

"Will you go back home?"

"No. No way. Nick told me I could keep on living here. No rent – for now, anyway. I s'pose I'm going to have to do some cleaning or something. Kill a few rats. I dunno."

"Rats? Are there rats here?" She's looking around anxiously.

"Two or three. It's the canal, it attracts them."

"*Cleaning*," moans Bonny. "You should be paid for your *art*."

"Well, maybe. But no one's lining up with a contract so far."

"I'm so sorry, Rich. I really am."

There's a long, long silence. The huge, empty room has got pitch-black and the great arched windows are opened out on to deep, dead darkness. But I don't suggest putting a light on and neither does Bonny.

"It's weird, really," whispers Bonny, after a while.

"What is?"

"The way we're both – like in limbo. Here. We've both left home, and we're like . . . suspended. Not knowing what's going to happen. What we're going to do."

"Um," I say, noncommittally. It's all a bit too Babes-in-the-Wood for me, this picture Bonny's painting. Like we might have to snuggle down together in a bit, and fall asleep in each other's arms while the canal rats cover us up with leaves.

I stare out of the window, and I know she's looking at me sideways, but I don't look back. And then – shocking as gunfire – there're three loud bangs on the flat door.

"Oh, *God*," gasps Bonny.

"*Portia!*" I go, before I can stop myself.

"It's Mum," Bonny wails. "I know it is."

"How did she get up?"

"The main door was open, I told you –"

"Oh *shit* –"

We're both staring at the flat door.

"Did you lock it?" I mutter.

"No. Did you?"

Then we watch as the handle turns and the door swings open.

Chapter 2

"Hi, kids. Only me."

There's such relief as Barb walks into the room that we both crack out a laugh. "What's so funny?" Barb demands.

"We thought you were Tigger," I say.

Barb's eyes are hooded and tired under her spiky hennaed hair. "*Tigger* isn't going anywhere," she says. "Tigger's slumped over our kitchen table, crying about her daughter and drinking huge quantities of vodka."

"Oh, no," groans Bonny. "Oh, she'd given vodka up, she promised me she wouldn't touch it again, she—"

Barb rounds on her. "Don't you dare get the guilts over this, Bonny, you hear me? You're *not* responsible for how she behaves. Look – you've left, and maybe not in the best way, but it's happened, and *I* think and *Nick* thinks that you've done the best thing – the *only* thing."

Bonny's tear-streaked face is turned up towards her like she's the sun. "You're going to be all right," Barb continues gently. "You've done it. And now it's all about how you go forward from here. Hey – can I put a light on?"

"Sure," I say, and turn on the floor lamp. Barb plonks herself down on the bed the other side of Bonny and says, "Any more tea in that pot, Rich?"

"Yeah," I say. "I'll get a mug."

As I stand up, Barb puts her arm round Bonny and hugs her close, and I'm left feeling like a sterile inadequate – good for providing tea but not much else – as I get up and slope off into the kitchen once more. I can hear Barb murmuring to Bonny, and Bonny crying some more. I have this thought that chocolate biscuits would help, but there're only two left in the packet, so I leave it.

"It's too late to make any big decisions tonight," Barb's saying, as I get back to the bed. "We're all too tired and beat up. I've got this roll-up futon thing in the car, Bonny, for you to kip on."

"She can have this bed," I say.

"Whatever. Look, Bonny – you've jumped, *boy* have you jumped, and now you've got to take your time over getting it right, deciding what to do –"

"I'm not going back," says Bonny.

"No. No, I don't think you should."

Bonny starts crying again when Barb says this, all kind of relieved and hysterical, and Barb hugs her again and I pour out the tea as quietly as I can. Then Barb says: "Look, Bonny, the first hurdle we have to cross is your mum. She's drinking herself into a stupor right now, but pretty soon Nick's going to drive her home and in the morning she's going to come to and realize I know more than I let on."

"What did you tell her?" whispers Bonny.

"I said you'd been to our house. And then you'd gone. I said I knew you were safe. And whenever she started raving about needing to see you *now* I'd fob her off with saying you both needed to cool down, sleep on it, and so on. But that won't work tomorrow."

"Don't tell her where I am!" pleads Bonny.

"Look, Bonny, I'm on your side. You know I am. But she is still your mum. I'm not going to lie to her. I know how I'd feel if Scarlett ran off."

"No, but – Scarlett wouldn't run off!" wails Bonny. "She's only ten! And anyway – you're great – you and Nick, you're brilliant parents –"

"That's not the point, Bonny, love," says Barb. She sounds exhausted. "Tigger's still your mum. I'll back you – you know I will – but we've got to be straight with Tigger too. Anyway – sorting it – making her see your side – telling her you're not coming back home – it'll be good for you. Won't it."

13

"I . . . I s'pose."

"Bonny, she needs to know tomorrow. She needs to know you're safe, where you are."

"Not *where* I am! If she has the address, she'll be right round here!"

"OK, OK, we'll think of something. But you need to *contact* her. Soon as she wakes up."

"I can't," Bonny wails. "I can't face her. Not right now – when I've only just gone – just the thought makes me. . ."

"All right, all right," Barb's saying, all soothingly. "It's just – she'll blame *me*, if I go round. She'll think it's my fault – she won't listen to me. She's never liked me. . . "

"She's jealous of you," sniffs Bonny.

"Jealous?"

"Yeah. 'Cos you've got Nick, and a good life – she's always on about how easy you've got it."

"Hah! She should try living with Nick."

There's a silence, and then Barb says, "Thing is, Bonny, we're both too involved. Too close. To face her I mean. We need someone – you know – more *neutral*."

And then they both turn, and look at me.

Chapter 3

"*No.*"

"Rich, all you'd have to do is *tell* her –"

"No *way*!"

"She likes you. You're male, so she likes you."

"*Jesus!* Even more no way."

"Look, all you're doing is passing on a message. You're like the messenger."

"Messengers get shot."

"*Rich!*"

"Send her a fax!"

"Rich, you are being *absurd*! I can't believe you're being such a baby about this! All you have to do is go round to her flat, and . . . and explain!"

"*All* I have to do? *All?* She'll chew my bollocks off. You know she will. She'll knife me. She'll be hysterical." As I speak, this image of Tigger all hysterical judders in front of my eyes and I say again, louder still, "No way. *No* way."

Bonny slumps forward, puts her head on her knees, and starts crying again, a horrible, thin despairing sound. And Barb reaches out her hand behind Bonny's bowed back and fixes it like a clamp to my arm.

"*Ow!*"

"Look, Rich," she hisses, "I know things haven't gone your way today. I know you're still reeling from that lousy alcopops deal falling through. But this is an emergency. This has to be *done*."

"What about Nick?" I hiss back.

"Too close. He works with her, for Christ's sake."

"Oh, *God*! Can't I just phone?"

"No! Phoning's too casual! Look, Rich, give me a break! I'm shattered! It's been one hell of a day!"

"For me too," I mutter.

"I know, I know. Sleep on it, then *do* it, right? Just say yes, for Christ's sake."

But I don't, I keep silent, and she just about twists my arm off and says, "*Look*, Rich – if you want to keep on living in this flat you'd better start pulling your weight!"

"Oh, *nice*," I whimper, tugging my arm away. "So now you're threatening. . ."

"Oh, sod off. I'm not really threatening you, just. . ."

Bonny's head comes up. "Don't, Barb!" she wails. She looks so desperate it chills me right through. "He'll *hate* me!"

"No he won't," says Barb.

And I hear myself echo, "No I won't. It's OK, Bonny, I'll do it." I reach out, put my hand on her back. "I *want* to."

Pretty soon after that, Barb sends me down to her car to get the fold-up futon and a duvet and pillow splattered all over with moon- and star- shapes that she says Scarlett sent along specially. "I don't know," she murmurs, as I plod back in, "it's like a teenage refuge up here. My two little waifs."

"I'm not a fucking waif," I say before I can stop myself. Well – it's too near that whole Babes-in-the-Wood thing again. Barb looks briefly offended, then laughs.

"OK, OK, you're too big to be a waif. Now come on, let's get sorted."

She sends me off to the kitchen for the broom and a bin bag, and we clear the worst of the rubbish and dirt and grunge away in the bedroom. "Why didn't you clear this room out for yourself, Rich?" she asks.

I shrug. "I wanted to be by the window."

"Ah," says Barb, as though she understands completely. The window is fantastic – huge and arched and elegant, like a cathedral window. Except you can't open a cathedral window, you can't fling

17

the two halves back against the wall and stand right on the edge and feel like you're flying in the sky. Not like you can with this one.

"And I hate those mirrors," I add. The guy who used to own this place had got it all fixed up as a shag pad, and the bedroom's all dark-red walls and mirrors on the sloping ceiling. It's seriously seedy.

"I know," agrees Barb. "Come on, it's clean enough. Let's shift the futon in."

As soon as the futon's been unrolled, Bonny kind of crumples down on top of it. "That's right, love," says Barb, "you get to bed."

"I feel *wasted*," mutters Bonny.

"I bet," says Barb. "You're really white." She fetches the moon-and-stars duvet and pillow, and tucks them round and under Bonny even though she's still got all her clothes on.

"I haven't even cleaned my teeth," murmurs Bonny. Her eyes are half closed already.

"Just sleep," says Barb. "I'll open one of these windows for you, shall I?" She walks over and wrestles with one of the little sloping windows, and gets it open to the night. "God, they're filthy. We'll have to give them a clean tomorrow. Come on, Rich, let's leave her to it."

Then she calls "Night, Bonny" and turns and walks out of the room, and I follow, thinking – clean the windows? How long's she going to be staying, then?

Back in the main room, Barb's too worn out to do much more than wring another promise out of me that I'll go and see Tigger first thing. She says she'll be back here at the flat first thing, too. She *says* she's coming to bring food and stuff and see how Bonny is, but I know it's to check that I've already left for the vampire's lair on the jolly task of telling her her daughter hates her and isn't ever coming home again.

Before I crash down on my bed I pick up the sketches of Portia that Bonny had left on the floor. And I make the mistake of looking at them. The groan that escapes my mouth is very loud in the big, silent room.

A few short hours ago, when I was mad and inspired, I had this revelation that Portia was phoney and fake and all wrong for me. Now I'm looking at the creamy lines of her face, all I can think is how I felt drawing her. All I want is that face made flesh, here in front of me, here in the flat.

It takes me hours to get to sleep.

Chapter 4

I wake up to a great wave of sunlight followed fast by a flood of self-pity. All my money dreams have been smashed, Portia's dumped me, and now Bonny's in the next room and this place isn't my own any more. And all I have to look forward to is a social call on Tigger who'll probably rip my throat out when she hears what I've got to say.

I roll out from under my duvet and stand up, naked and proud, remember Bonny, and dive back under the duvet once more. *Shit.* I can't even wander about starkers in my own place any more, can I. Not now.

I grope beside my bed for the boxers and jeans I discarded last night, and pull them on, lying flat. Then I make my way to the kitchen and put the kettle on, and while it's boiling I shave and shower at top speed. Then I go back in the kitchen, make some tea, and grab a slice of bread and jam and a banana that's only gone squashy at one end. Ever since I've been here, I've eaten breakfast alone in front of the open window. It's magic, and I need some magic right now.

But when I go back into the main room, there's Bonny, silhouetted against the light, still in the clothes she was wearing last night.

"Morning," I say, as graciously as I can manage, which isn't very.

She spins round. Her face is all panicked again, like it was when she first arrived here. "Rich! Are you – did you mean what you said last night?"

"What?"

"About going round to see Mum?"

"Yes."

"Only I thought – if you said I was staying at *your* flat, or one of your *friend's* flats, and then when she demands the address say you absolutely promised me not to tell it –"

"S'pose she demands it over a big knife?"

"What?"

"Nothing."

"She'll accept it from you, if you say that. Just be kind of silent and stubborn."

"Like a donkey."

"Rich – don't go if you really don't want to!"

"It's fine."

There's a pause, then she blurts out, "When are you going?"

"Jesus, Bonny, I've only just got up!"

"Sorry. Sorry. It's just – she'll be up early, I know she will, and she'll start searching for me again, she'll go round to Barb and Nick's and make a big scene, and. . ."

"I'm going, I'm going. Just let me eat this."

I drop down on to the edge of the bed and start gnawing the bread, and Bonny stands there watching me. "D'you want some tea?" I ask rudely.

Bonny flinches, mutters "I'll get some," and scurries into the kitchen. I'm left feeling like a bit of a shit, but I don't exactly care.

Ten minutes later and I'm on my way, with the anxious little map Bonny drew me and Tigger's full address.

I'm quite relieved to see how far away from the flat it is, to be honest. I have to get a bus. I think about getting a cab, but I remember in time that my stack of money which is dwindling fast is not about to get replenished.

It doesn't take me long to find the place. It's an old Victorian house, turned into flats. Bonny told me theirs was on the first floor, which meant they had the grandest rooms but no garden and no view. I walk up the crumbling steps and scan the buttons by the front door; in among the formal printed names there's one in girly twirly script saying "Tigger & Bonny". I take a deep juddering breath, and press it.

And wait.

Thirty seconds later, the big door's ripped open, and Tigger flies out. "O – ooooh!" she wails, in complete anguish. "It's *you*!"

"Yeah, er, Tigger, I—"

"I thought it was my *baby*!"

"I know, I know, it's her I've come about, I. . ." I trail off. I realize I'm gawping at her but I can't seem to get my mouth to shut.

She looks *appalling*. She looks about ninety years old. All her old glitz and glamour has gone, her hair's like a hag's, and she's got this insane, staring, lopsided look. I make myself focus on her face, and realize it's because only one of her eyes has got make-up on. Like Alex in *A Clockwork Orange*.

"Come in!" she hisses. She shoots out one of her hands to grab my arm and I can't help it, I jump back like a scalded cat.

"Richy – come *in*!" she repeats, and this time she manages to fasten her talons on my arm, and hoist me over the threshold. "I'm through here," she says, pushing open her flat door, bundling me inside and then – scarily – kicking it shut behind us.

Then she catches sight of her face in the pretentious golden cheruby mirror in the tiny hall. "Oh my *God*!" she screams, clapping both hands to her face.

"I was halfway through cleaning my makeup off – look – give me a minute, yah?"

And she's off, slamming her way into what I suppose is the bathroom.

My first thought is that she must know I have news of Bonny and yet this is obviously less important to her than fixing her face. My second thought, looking round about me, is that living here must be like living inside Tigger's head and that's followed fast by my third thought: thank God Bonny escaped.

The flat's a mess. A psychotic mess, not a cosy mess. Piles of plates and tureens and fancy dishes, I suppose from her food props company, cover all surfaces that aren't already covered by empty wine bottles, discarded clothes, upturned drawers, over-flowing ashtrays, dirty plates and glasses, piles of papers, stuff, stuff, stuff. There's even a bunch of flowers that's just been left to wither in its wrapping. It's hopeless chaos, and it's all Tigger. Like her ego's spilling out over everything, crowding Bonny out.

I wander over to the end of the room and stand looking out of the window. It's big, but it's shrouded by nasty looped-up curtains, and it's shut tight. I wish I could open it because I'm beginning to think I can't breathe. The air in here is bad news. Sort of stale, and sickly smelling, with a mixture of perfume and fags and alcohol and tension, as if all the oxygen's been sucked out of it by Tigger raging and screaming and wailing over her daughter's departure.

Then the bathroom door swings open, and I turn round. Tigger's still wearing the gold-and-brown lacy nighty thing she opened the door to me in, but she's put some kind of silvery turban over her hag-hair, and she's wiped off the smudged *Clockwork Orange* eye and added a bright smear of lipstick.

She still looks horrible, but not quite so horrible.

"Richy!" Her voice is a thin whine of controlled hysteria. "Sorry! I just – I didn't sleep last night, well, you can imagine, and then I kind of passed out a few hours ago, and then I'd only just come to when you knocked and. . ." She reaches with trembling hands for a packet of fags lying on the table, lights one up, and gazes at me agonized through the smoke. "I've taken it up again. Big time. That's what she's done to me. I was down to only a couple a day, you know, but with this worry, this *torture* –"

I clear my throat to speak, but Tigger shoots out a spume of smoke and says, "Well, where is she?"

"Um . . . *well* . . . she's . . . she's. . ."

"That *bitch* Barb Hanratty wouldn't tell me where she was. How dare she, I could've – I could've – what *right* has she? What right has she to keep my daughter from me? Do you know where she is?"

"Well, I –"

"I have to know. I *have* to see her today. I have to sort it out with her. She can't stay away like this – I'm her mother. She *needs* me. I'm in *hell* here, Richy, you've no idea." She takes another frantic suck on her cigarette, and her voice gets shriller. "We've had rows before, and we've got over them, this doesn't have to be any different. . . She's been working too hard, that's the problem, she's *cracked*. That *bloody* school – sure, it gets results, but it grinds the girls down. . . All that *homework* she gets. She's *always* at it. I'm going to phone the head-mistress. Give her a piece of my mind. No one makes *my little girl unhappy*!"

She ends on this kind of shriek, and I have this sudden overwhelming desire to run. In my mind I'm actually planning how I can make a rush at Tigger, kind of bounce her aside, and get out through the door.

She's mad. She's barking. She hasn't the slightest, faintest idea that Bonny's big problem is *her*. And I've been sent here like a dog to the slaughter to tell her.

"Um . . . Tigger?"

"Yes? Where *is* she, Richy?"

"She's with – she's staying with a friend of mine."

"She *is*?" Tigger's whole face, under its hideous turban, kind of blooms. "With one of your friends? Well – why didn't you say? Why didn't *she* say? I don't mind her having a *boyfriend*! God! I've been desperate for her to find a boyfriend!"

"Tigger—"

"Why couldn't she tell me?"

"She—"

"Who is he? What's he like?"

"She—"

"He does love her, doesn't he?"

"*Tigger*, it's not *like* that. He's just a mate. He has space in his flat – a spare room. He's putting her up for a bit."

Tigger's mouth is twitching, making her whole face jump. "What do you mean – putting her up? Oh – *God*! What's the address? Is there a phone?"

There's a long, long silence. Then Tigger makes a kind of jump at me and gets hold of my arm again, but I can't escape, I can't move. My legs feel like jelly.

"Richy? *Richy!* Why won't you *answer* me?"

'Jesus, Tigger – I don't know what to say! She wants – she wants her own space for a bit!"

"Space? She's got space, here!" And she waves her arm at all the claustrophobic clutter.

"She needs . . . I think she feels . . . I think she wants to be on her own for a bit. Just for a bit."

"*Give me the address!*"

"I don't have it!"

"You do! You must do! You said he was a friend!"

"Yeah, well, we're not that close, we're—"

"Richy stop *bullshitting* me! Give me the address!" Her hand is tightening like a vice on my arm, and her face is so close to mine we're practically rubbing noses. She's breathing panic and smoke all over me and I feel like I want to throw up. "*She made me promise not to!*" I wail.

When Tigger hears this, it's like I've punched her out. She kind of lurches backwards, falls on to the sofa, grabs a cushion, and starts pummelling it, kneading it, like her hands are out of control and moving of their own accord.

It's a grisly sight. I watch, transfixed.

"Why is she doing this to me?" she croaks. "Why is she being this cruel?"

"She just – she says the two of you get too knitted up together, and she wants—"

Tigger raises her shattered face towards me. "But we're *close*! We've got a *wonderful* relationship! Why is she *doing* this?"

This is all too mad for me. I've got to get out. I don't feel angry at Tigger, because she's clearly nuts, but I feel mad at Barb and Bonny for sending me here. I have absolutely no idea what to say, how to deal with this. I feel like some goon in a fairy tale packed off to face the wicked witch without the right charm, without the right spell.

"Tigger, I have to go," I say.

She jumps to her feet, heads towards me.

"I've got to go," I repeat, backing towards the door.

"Are you going to see her?"

"I . . . I . . . probably."

"*Well – tell her the state I'm in! Tell her she has to call me!*"

"I will, OK?"

"*Tell her!* Promise me you'll *tell* her!"

I've got my hand on the door handle, twisting it, praying. It gives. *Hallelujah*. I'm in the hall. I can hear Tigger behind me, I'm waiting for her to jump on my back. I get the front door open. My lungs fill with fantastic cold clean air; I gulp it down. I'm off down the steps.

"*Tell her!*" I hear again, a long frantic scream.

But like in a fairy tale, I daren't look back.

Chapter 5

"**I**t was! It was fucking terrifying!"

"Oh, stop moaning, Rich. It can't've been that bad."

"I'm fucking telling you, it was fucking terrifying!"

"Oh – *God* – is that the only *adjective* you can use?"

"Barb – if you'd been there, you'd *know* –"

Barb fixes me with her powerful, straightforward stare. "What I *know*, Richard, is yes you've had a nasty half hour, but Bonny's spent her *life* like that. And she's in the bedroom now hearing everything you're saying so why don't you stop whining and thinking about yourself and think about her for a bit, *h'm*?"

I fall silent, half sulking and half ashamed. When I got back to the flat and found Barb in the kitchen I just kind of exploded with how grisly it had all been, and I was – I dunno – expecting to be praised, I suppose. Expecting to be thanked at least. But although Barb was concerned with how mad Tigger had been acting, she wasn't that bothered with the effect it had had on me.

The kettle boils, clicks off, and Barb makes me a cup of coffee, which I suppose is something, then she sighs and says, "Oh, dear. She sounds even worse than she was last night. I was hoping she might've calmed down a bit."

"No. I was lucky to escape with my life, I reckon."

Barb heaves another sigh. "Tigger's had these dramatic, horrible . . . *crashes* ever since I've known her. She puts this huge effort into looking good and keeping young and being hugely sociable and running her props company, and you have to admire her for that, but it's – I dunno. It's all run on nervous energy, I guess. Every now and then she just – *breaks*, like a stick."

"She's so desperate to get Bonny back it's scary."

"Yeah, well, it's that that makes me determined to keep Bonny away from her. She's been leaning on her for far too long. It's like – 'be kind to Mummy or she'll crack up again'. No one should have to live under that. Not letting her lead her own life. Using her to keep the nightmares away."

"Yeah, well, the whole fucking flat's a nightmare if you ask me."

"Yeah, you said. It sounds dreadful." There's a

pause, then Barb goes, "Um, Rich – you wouldn't mind if Bonny stayed here for a bit, would you?"

I want to ask, *What's a bit?* but I don't want Barb to accuse me of whining again, so I just shrug and say, "Course not. It's your place after all."

"Yeah, but it won't work if you don't want her here."

"It's fine."

"Just for now. Then – well, I know her dad's not too far away. Maybe she can go to him for a bit. Then she can stay on at her school and –"

"I'm not moving in with Daddy." It's Bonny, standing in the doorway. She's wearing jeans and a T-shirt, and she's looking very different to the way she looked last night, or even first thing this morning when she packed me off to face her mum. She's kind of contained, focused, determined.

"I've thought about what I'm going to do," she goes on. "I'm going to contact Daddy, and tell him I've moved out."

"He'll be quite pleased, won't he?" murmurs Barb.

"Yes. He hates Mum. Well, it's mutual. It was always such a pain to get to see him, Mum always acted as though I was betraying her. . . *Anyway*. He gives her quite a big allowance, for me. My plan is that he just gives that straight to me in future."

Barb lets out a breath like a whistle. "Wow, Bonny."

"What? You think I'm being too hard on Mum?"

"Well – it's a bit of a double whammy, isn't it? She loses you *and* a sizeable wodge of her income, all at the same time."

"Yeah, but that income's *for* me. She got a massive divorce settlement out of him. She owns that flat outright. OK, maybe he can just split the allowance between us. As long as I can afford to live."

"School fees?"

"He pays those anyway. And clothes for school, and trips and things. So that wouldn't change. And he'd be there to help, you know – if I needed it. We'd be able to see more of each other now. But I wouldn't move in with him, because he's got a new family now, and – well, I don't want to." She hones in on Barb, all excited. "Don't you think it would work, Barb? I think it would work. I feel like – *God*! I feel like this great weight's rolled off my back."

There's a long silence. Barb looks as though she's rehearsing something inside her head. Then she says, slowly, "Look, Bonny, it's great you're so up about it all. It's great to hear you so positive, after last night."

"I had a brilliant sleep," beams Bonny. "No dreams."

"Yeah? That's great. Look – I agree with you that one of the first things you do is contact your dad. But you should listen to what he has to say about you living on your own and everything. You're still only seventeen. You've got your A-level year ahead of you. He might want you to live with him, or –"

Bonny's shaking her head. "He won't. His new wife lumps me and Mum together as trouble and she can't stand either of us. Look – it's brilliant, my solution. It's perfect."

"Yeah, but – I don't think it's that simple. I don't think you can just cut Tigger out of the frame and forget about her. . ."

I can hear Bonny breathing, panting almost. "I've got to. Right now, I've got to. *OK?*"

Barb reaches out a hand, lays it on her arm. "Yeah. OK. Sorry. You take it a day at a time, love."

There's a pause, then Bonny turns to me with a smile that's kind of challenging and says, "I haven't thanked you yet, Rich. For going round. Thank you."

"Oh, it's fine, it's—"

"Well, it wasn't fine, was it? It was a sodding nightmare. At least I think that's what you said. Sorry – I should've come out of my room earlier, only you sounded so pissed off I was scared to."

I smirk and nod and can't think of a thing to say. I'm avoiding catching Barb's told-you-so eye.

"I'm really sorry I did that to you, Rich," she goes on. "But there wasn't anyone else. And listen – *thank you* for not telling her where I am." She puts her head on one side, looks up at me, and it's like her whole being is in those words. *"Thank you,"* she says again.

Chapter 6

Pretty soon after that I find myself really needing
to leave the flat. I've got this vague intention of
going into college, but leaving the flat is the main
thing. I'm feeling inadequate and angry both at the
same time and I don't know how to deal with it.
There's Barb being all wonderful and supportive, and
there's Bonny being all wonderful and determined
and strong, and they're both thinking wonderful
brave new thoughts about the future, and all I can do
is feel pissed off someone else is in my flat.

That's the way I see it. *My* flat.

I haven't a leg to stand on, I know that. It's Nick
and Barb's flat, and Bonny is in dire need, far more
dire need than I was when I cleared out. In fact,
compared to Tigger, my horrible angry dad is an all-
round great bloke who's a joy to live with.

35

Thinking that doesn't make me any less pissed off though. I'm having all these raging petty little thoughts like: *I moved in first* and *All right for you, yeah, with Daddy's allowance and Daddy's school fees and Daddy's school trips – go and get your own fucking flat if you're so rich.*

I'm not proud of myself.

I stomp along the road telling myself – you're being an arsehole, Steele. You're pitiful. You know what it is? You're upset that Barb's not putting you first any more. She's stopped being your mummy, started being Bonny's mummy instead. Just grow up, will you. You mincer.

I decide definitely to go into college. It's something to do, and also, at the start of this weird time-warp of a week, on the same day I discovered I wasn't going to get rich after all, I begged the principal not to chuck me out of college, and he agreed, even though I'm badly behind on my work. And as being given that second chance is just about the only thing that's gone right for me this week, I reckon I'd better get down to work.

It's nearly midday, so I can get to Huw's art class then get some lunch and log in at my English session. I've got my manic-inspired pictures with me, the ones Bonny liked. Something to throw to Huw to stop him snarling at me.

The college grounds and steps are pretty empty

when I walk in, and I get to the art room without meeting anyone I know, which I'm glad about. The person I least want to see, of course, is Portia. I'm not ready to handle that yet. But she's bound to be in the art class. Unlike me, Portia doesn't tend to miss lessons.

I walk in through the door, head up, eyes ahead, hoping to slide anonymously behind a table at the side, when Huw catches sight of me from underneath his beetly black eyebrows. "Ah!" he bellows. "Mr Steele! Gracing us with his leather-clad presence, and only a mere ten minutes late! We're honoured, people, aren't we? Strew the flowers – bring out the dancing girls!"

I hate it when Huw goes in for his flights-of-fancy crazy Welsh poetic crap. "Yeah, well," I mutter, heading towards his desk. "Here's some stuff for you."

As I walk towards the front, my whole back's prickling. Somehow, I can sense Portia's presence, over by the window. Somehow, I know she's there. But I'm not going to look round.

In my mind I try to resurrect what happened the other night, when everything had fallen through and I was drawing like a madman in front of the dark sky. When I'd had that feeling like a bolt from the blue that I was glad it was over with Portia because basically she was hard, hard work and basically she chronically pissed me off.

But I can't resurrect it. Not here, not with her

37

spooky green eyes lasering into my back. I can't not care. Oh, *God*, suppose she's told people what happened, the other night in the lift? Or what didn't happen rather. She won't have done, will she? It'd reflect badly on her, wouldn't it? On her sexual talents? Me laughing when I should've been pounding with passion?

Oh, *God*, why did I do it. *Didn't* I do it. I'm an idiot, a total idiot.

"So what have we here, lad?" Huw's saying, pulling my drawings unenthusiastically out of the creased brown envelope I've tucked them into. "More psychotic doodlings? More dark visions of the underworld?"

Then he looks at them, really looks, and his face changes. "Well, well, well, Richard. Well, well, well."

"Well what?"

"You've grown up a bit, haven't you, lad? These are good." He holds them away from him, squints at them hard. "Very good."

"So can I use them?"

"Yes." Sometimes Huw can be brilliantly brief.

"In my portfolio?"

"Certainly. The subject heading we can put them under doesn't quite spring to mind, because as usual they're part of the unique Steele vision of the world, but by God they're going in there. Now go on. Sit down and get on with something."

And I walk away. I'm not going to look at Portia

yet, because I'm sure she'll be looking at me. I'm going to wait until I've been sitting down for a while and I've got well into my drawing and then I'm going to glance up as if for inspiration and glance at her and if she's still looking at me I'm going to bloody well glance down again, fast.

I do all this. And she's sitting exactly where I thought she was, and she isn't looking at me. I decide to look at her until she looks back at me and then do the cunning glancing-down-after-getting-inspiration thing. But this is a mistake. A big mistake.

I'm drawn into her face like a leaf into a whirlpool.

She's treacherous, I tell myself desperately. She's self-obsessed, she's fake, she has as much depth as a sandwich bag. And ... and ... she's *beautiful.* Her perfect feline face is the most fantastic balance of strong and soft lines I've ever seen. I stare at her and I want to draw her again, here, now, forget the abstract I'm supposed to be working on. That pointy, sexy chin, the big weird-green eyes, the way her eyebrows arch up and her cheekbones span out and her mouth, oh God her *mouth.* . . At this point I'm overtaken by a very vivid, very physical memory of kissing Portia and I swear I actually let out a little moan. And Portia looks up and *slam,* I attach my eyes to my work once more and think – oh, *shit.*

Now you've done it, Steele. You idiot. You forgot the first rules of addiction, didn't you:

1. You're never, ever completely cured.
2. Keep well away from whatever you're addicted to because. . .
3. You can always get drawn back in.

Chapter 7

Lunchtime, I run into the usual crowd – Chris, my long-suffering best mate, and Ryan and Ollie, all shuffling through the change in their pockets to see what they can afford to eat. Soon as we're sitting down with our grub in front of us I tell them what's happened, straight out, about the sudden death of my money dream, and somehow, their shrugs and indifference are almost comforting.

"Yeah, well," says Ryan, philosophically. "It was a bit of a long shot."

"It'll happen for you one day," says Chris. "You arty git. It was good to get that far, when you think about it."

"Yeah," puts in Ollie. "Anyway, I can't imagine you with money, mate."

"Thanks," I say.

"No, but – you know what I mean."

"Yeah," I agree dolefully, because I do know what he means.

"So," says Ollie, grinning, "what's happened with the Porsche then?"

"The – ? You mean Portia?"

"Yeah. Fitting name, man!"

I shrug, don't answer. Ollie is black and hench and gets loads and loads of girls after him. I am not about to confess my failures with him listening in.

"Only, I bumped into her this morning," he goes on, "asked had she seen you, she looked at me like I'd stabbed her grandmother. You two had a row?"

"Kind of."

"Shame. She's hot. Bit of a stuck up bitch, but hot."

Chris is looking at me like he knows there's more to all this, when Ryan grumbles, "Shame about your flat, Rich. I was up for a party sometime soon."

"Oh, I'm still in the flat," I say.

The three of them stop ramming food in their mouths and turn to look at me.

"You are?"

"How come?"

"For how long?"

I shrug. "Well – for now. It's just empty, and they like someone being there. Security and stuff."

"Bloody hell, Rich! That's brilliant!"

"Well . . . yeah. But I dunno how I'm going to afford it."

"How much rent?"

"Well . . . free so far."

"*Bloody* hell, Rich – you're squatting in a free penthouse and you're acting miserable?"

"He feels guilty, doesn't he," says Chris knowingly. "That Nick guy. Setting you up for the big one, then dropping you."

"I guess."

"Rich, this is brilliant!" squawks Ryan. "When's the first gig? Hey – we can charge. Ollie can DJ and we can charge. Then you'll have some cash to live on. Hey – you can turn it into a club, man! Every Friday and Sat'day! We can advertise, we can—"

"Ryan, shut *up* will you, you nonce? I can just see Nick standing back smiling while I run a club up there. I'd be out on the street straight away. Prob'ly via the window."

"OK, OK, not a club. But they can't stop you having a party, can they? Jesus, it's not as though there's anything to spoil. It's not as though there's any *furniture*. And we could charge, kind of informal –"

"Well . . . maybe."

"Lights. I can get lights."

"*Ryan!* It's not that easy. For a start – I'm not the only one there any more. This girl's moved in."

"This girl?"

"She's in the bedroom."

There's a pause, then: "Bloody *hell*, man! A girl!"
"In the bedroom!"
"And you're complaining?"
"Shacked up with you!"
"Is she good-looking?"
"What friends she got?"

I make it into English, and Ms Reardon, who looks like a hen and acts like a scorpion, tells me she's glad I haven't quit college (like hell she is) but then acidly reminds me of the vast pile of essays I have to hand in within the next eight weeks if I don't want to get slung out after all. This is depressing but not quite as depressing as it would've been before Barb told me she'd give me a hand because she loved Eng. Lit.

Loving Eng. Lit. is only one of the many weird and sometimes wonderful things about Barb Hanratty. She's like some wiry dynamo, pumping out ideas and energy, gathering people round her, feeding 'em, saving 'em, cutting their hair. If I'm honest I think I'm a bit gone on her, only she's about twice my age, so I can't be. But if the impossible ever happens and I get hitched to someone – well, I want to end up with a relationship like Barb and Nick's, that's all. All fun and open and over the top, not like the make-the-best-of-it scraping-by set-up my parents have got. And I want a house like theirs too. You should see it. It's *style*.

I see the Porsche (Ollie's right – fitting name!)

once more before I slink out of college. It's her back view, as she walks along the corridor. Portia's walk is as fantastic as the rest of her. Let's face it, with a body like hers she could walk like a crab and still look incredibly sexy, but Portia's walk is so elegant, so superior, I find myself having to lean up against the wall just for a minute before she turns the corner and disappears.

Just – *stop this*, Steele, I lecture myself. You've made a fresh start, turned the page to a whole new chapter, and Portia has been written out, OK? You're a visual guy, so you can't help being hoovered into her stunning good looks, but it's *over*. Underneath she's bad news, and you know it.

And anyway – even if you wanted to start it up again, d'you think you stand a snowball's chance in hell? For her it's *mega*-over. She was in the middle of seducing you and you *sniggered into her mouth*. How much more over can it be?

New chapter, new page, fresh start, I'm thinking as I head back to the flat. I'm even feeling quite optimistic in a darkly determined sort of way. OK, so it's all crashed down, but I'm still going to make it. The lads are right, the flat is fantastic. I can get them round, paint it out, whitewash it or maybe go for something darker, and maybe I *can* hold parties there, like Ryan said, parties I can charge for. And then, when I'm out of the woods as far as my backlog of college work goes, I can start doing storyboards for Nick again or maybe work in a bar and I'll be solvent, I'll be *free*.

I'm so busy with these plans I almost forget about Bonny. I'm reminded of her as soon as I head through the flat door, though. She's sitting on my bed, with the windows wide open, and she looks up and smiles happily at me as I walk in.

I can't make myself smile back, but she doesn't seem to notice. "Barb's just gone," she says. "She has been *so great*. Come and see."

She stands up and walks into the bedroom – *her* bedroom – expecting me to follow. Which I do, because I can't make up my mind to be enough of a miserable sod not to.

And she's right, Barb has been great. The whole place has been really cleaned, not just the quick brush-out we gave it last night. The windows are shining, the dodgy sex-den mirrors across the sloping ceiling are gleaming and now they have a whole collection of sharp postcards Blu-tacked across them, softening their nastiness. There's a stylish geometric-patterned rug on the floor and a twirly coat-stand thing in the corner with clothes hanging from it. And the lime-green plant pots that were just about all there was in the room have been planted again. Spiky-looking jobs in the hanging tubs under the light-filled narrow windows, and a little palm in the big pot in the corner.

"Isn't it all *lovely*?" coos Bonny.

"Yeah, lovely," I say. Too fucking lovely, I think. Too permanent.

"She brought the coat-stand and the rug over in her car."

"Great."

"I know the plants are a bit over the top," Bonny says, catching me glaring at them. "But those lovely pots were just sitting there and . . . well, we both love plants, and well . . . it was kind of an impulse. After we'd cleaned the room all up, Barb took me out to Sainsbury's to get some food, and we were saying how we couldn't believe how much lighter the room was now we'd cleaned the windows, and we were by the plant stand, and they had this Buy-Two-Get-One-Free offer on, and she asked me which ones I liked, and she said she was sure plants'd thrive under the skylights, and I said I liked spider plants, because they had such sweet babies, and she put three in the trolley, and . . . and then she made me get the palm too – she said if it was too dark for it in here, it could go out in front of the big window. . ."

Under my expressionless gaze, Bonny dribbles to a stop. I am *not*, I think savagely, having fucking *pot plants* in front of *my* window. But I don't say anything.

I turn and walk back out into the main room, and stand by my bed, and I feel so pissed off I can't move for a minute. It meant so much to me, having a space of my own. After years of cramming myself into the bottom bunk in the tiny bedroom I shared with my

little brother, Sam, it felt absolutely amazing to just
– *be here*, on my own.

It ruins it having Bonny here. How's it going to
work? How can I get any privacy at all out here when
at any time, she can just walk in – through the front
door, to the kitchen, to the bathroom? Even in the
middle of the night, she can just walk past my bed.

There's another room in this flat, a tiny box room,
absolutely crammed with crap, so crammed we
didn't do more than open the door on it and slam it
shut, fast, when we were clearing the place out. But
I could empty it if I wanted to, and sleep in there.
Barb and Bonny would help me like a shot, I know
that. I'm not going to though. Soon as I do that, it's
permanent, isn't it, Bonny being here? It's like flatmates, each with our own room, happily sharing
communal areas. Well, I'm not happily sharing, not
any areas. This space in front of the great windows –
it's mine. I need it. Sole possession. And I'm going to
carry on awkwardly and inconveniently staking my
claim out here, for as long as it takes to get it back.

"I phoned Daddy," says Bonny suddenly, appear-
ing right next to me.

I jerk my shoulders irritably and say, "Yeah?"

"He's coming over. Tonight. Barb's coming over
too."

"*Here?*"

"Well – yeah. He wants to see where I am. You
know."

I grunt, and she goes on "Would you – could you – are you planning to be around tonight?"

"You want me out of the way?"

"No – I want you *here*. Daddy wants to meet you. Barb's been singing your praises, but – you know."

"I dunno," I say rudely. "What time?"

"About sevenish? He said he'd take us all out to dinner."

"I'll try," I say.

"He was pleased, I think," she goes on, as if I'd just asked her what Daddy had thought of recent events. "And he accepted I wasn't going to move in with him. Relieved, I think." She laughs. "And he thinks it'll be fine about the money. Paying it straight to me every month. He says he'll still give Mum some, too – he's having a word with his solicitor, but he says it should be fine because I'll be eighteen by the end of the year."

"Great," I mutter enviously. "So you'll have some fat allowance, eh?"

She shrugs, as though money isn't the issue here, and goes on, "I was so scared he'd say I'd been irresponsible. Running out like that. But I told him how Mum had been recently and . . . we talked and talked . . . it was great. *Anyway.*"

There's a long silence, then Bonny says, "Rich?"

"What?"

"Look – I know you don't want me here. . ."

"I never said that."

"You don't exactly need to. Look – I don't blame you, OK? If I was you, I'd be pissed off. I mean – I've moved in on your space."

There's a pause. Maybe she's waiting for me to contradict her.

"Don't get all freaked by us doing up the room, Rich, please," she goes on. "Barb was just being kind. Wanting me to feel better. You know what she's like."

Yeah, I think, she's kind. Unlike me.

"It won't be for long," Bonny says. "I mean – Daddy'll sort something out for me. It's just for now. OK?"

There's another silence, and she sighs, and walks away into the kitchen, and I'm filled with nasty thoughts again. Like – *Why are you trying to creep up to me, Bonny, when you know I have absolutely no power, no say, in you being here? Why don't you just get honest and say, tough luck, Steele, Barb would side with me, you know she would, so lump it or move out?*

"Want some cake?" calls Bonny from the kitchen doorway.

"What?"

"We got this great fudge-and-walnut cake. Want some?"

I want to be all cool and rejecting, I really want to be, but sheer greed for the sound of this cake propels me slowly towards the kitchen. Bonny's already cut me a massive sticky wedge of it, and she's pouring me out some tea too. I sink my teeth into the cake, and take hold of the mug of tea, and as I do she smiles at me hopefully.

Don't push it, kid, I think, as I chew.

It tastes *great*.

Chapter 8

"So, you're the young knight in shining armour, are you?"

I didn't expect to like Daddy and I'm not disappointed. He's one of these highly groomed supersuccessful businessmen who sum you up and catalogue you very, very fast at the same time as they're doing this automatic, efficient charm-assault on you in case they need to use you.

"I wouldn't call myself that," I say.

"Oh, I think Bonny would."

"Well, all I did was open the door to her," I mutter, but I've already lost his attention.

"I am *so grateful*, Barb," he's murmuring, "you coming to Bonny's aid like that. We knew it was coming, of course. It had to. Tigger is just – *God*, that woman!" And he actually strikes his forehead with his fist. "Still, we're through the first bit. Aren't we. The worst bit. And now it's all down to where we go from here."

"Well, you know she's welcome to stay here as long as she wants," says Barb, looking over at me as though expecting me to chorus my agreement.

I don't, and Daddy says, "That's wonderful, Barb. Wonderful." Then he puts his arm heartily round his daughter's shoulders and says, "Well, come on, gorgeous. Show me your new room."

And the two of them walk into Bonny's room, and I see Daddy kick the door to behind them. Privacy time.

Barb's looking at me, I can sense it, and I can also sense that it's the sort of look that's going to continue until I return it. So I nod to myself a few times, then I glance up at her. I'm waiting for her to tick me off for being such a miserable sod, but she doesn't. She just smiles, and says, "You been home yet, Rich? Sorted it out with your dad?"

I shake my head.

"Well, don't leave it too long, will you?"

"I won't sort it out with him, Barb. He thinks I'm a loser. I won't ever go – I won't move back home again."

"Yeah, but – that doesn't mean you have to stop *speaking* to him."

"I've seen my mum."

"I know you have. That's good. She must want you to make up, Rich."

"She does. I told her I'm going to let the dust settle before I see him again. And get college sorted. So I can tell him I'm not going to get thrown out after all."

"OK." There's a pause, and we both listen to the murmur of voices going on in Bonny's bedroom, just too quiet for us to follow. Then Barb says, "What about money, Rich? Were your folks giving you an allowance?"

I snort out a laugh. "Not exactly. Just regular meals."

"So how will you manage?"

"I've got loads left from the storyboards I did for Nick."

"Oh, Rich – that won't last for ever."

"Well, I know. But you said I needn't pay rent for now, and –"

"Look – just *living*'s expensive. Food and clothes. And toothpaste and washing-up liquid and toilet paper and money for the laundrette and. . ."

"OK, *OK*. I'll get a bar job."

"You're not eighteen."

"No, but I look it. I've had one before."

"But you've got all that college work to catch up on, Rich! When're you going to find the time?"

I look at her, and I can't think of a thing to say, and for the first time it hits me that I'm on my own now, really on my own. It's one thing to play at being in this space with my own front-door key, and it's another to keep on at it. Keep on keeping on at it.

Then it's like Barb senses my despair. She suddenly says: "Look – Nick still owes you. You helped him get that alcopops account. I can let you have—"

"No," I say. "I'm not taking money off you."

"All right. Well – he can give you more storyboards to do. At a better rate than he paid you before. He owes you that."

"That'd be brilliant."

"And you've not got any bills. Not for the time being."

"But –"

"This flat – it's billed with the company. Forget it."

"That's fantastic, Barb. I mean – I don't know what to say."

She shakes her head at me, smiling, and I think: no rent, no bills – surely even an inadequate like me can manage somehow – when the door to Bonny's room opens, and she and Daddy come out. He's still got his arm round her, but it looks less like affection this time and more like control. "So – ready to eat?" he says to us, jovially.

"Sure are," answers Barb.

"Great stuff," says Daddy, and the four of us all kind of shuffle past my bed, heading towards the front door. "So you're sleeping in the living-room, are you, Richard?" he asks.

No, shit-head, I think, I'm sleeping in *my* room,

but before I can say anything Barb goes: "He likes that fabulous window."

"I'm not surprised. Still – doesn't it get a bit . . . awkward? Is there not another room?"

"Just a tiny box room," says Barb.

"Well –" He breaks off, and I glare at him, daring him to suggest I move into it.

"Daddy, it's fine," hisses Bonny. "Honestly. Let's go. Didn't you say you'd booked the restaurant for eight o'clock?" Then she tows him out to the lift, and they all wait by the iron gate as I rather self-consciously lock up the flat behind us.

"Bonny's got some keys, too, has she?" asks Daddy.

"Yes," says Barb. "I got some more cut today."

Oh, great. Oh fucking *great*.

In the restaurant, I order the biggest things on the menu. Not only to get up Daddy's nose but also because I'm very hungry and I figure if I stock up tonight on steak and chocolate pudding I can save money on food tomorrow.

As I chew, Daddy talks, and he fires questions at Bonny, Barb and me. I like him even less now than when I first met him. He's one of these mega-efficient guys who pride themselves on having time for the real human side of life, which I bet means he actually *schedules* family-time slots into his electronic organizer. And seven till ten Wednesday night is Bonny's time. When he must:

1. Check she's OK and sorted and on the right track and assured of Daddy's continuing support.
2. Thank Barb and ensure her continuing support.
3. Check out the nasty flatmate (me) making sure I'm not:
   a) a would-be rapist or
   b) the sort of pervert that might want to dress up in his daughter's knickers.
4. Carry out damage-limitation exercises such as hinting that I move into the poxy box room. *Again.*

He works very hard during the meal and I bet he electronically ticks his "objectives accomplished" box afterwards. The one thing I like him for is saying several times that Bonny really must come and stay some weekends, that her new stepmother – far from hating her – positively insists on it, blah blah. Bonny doesn't look convinced though. And there's been no discussion of getting Bonny somewhere else to live. It's all – "Everything's very new, very raw, let's see how it goes."

As we leave the restaurant, Daddy hangs back with Barb and I turn round just in time to see him trying to force a fat roll of banknotes on her and her refusing.

"Embarrassing," hisses Bonny. "He's trying to pay for me to stay there."

"Not so embarrassing as not being able to offer," I snap. "Like me."

Bonny goes red, and her mouth works as she tries to dredge up something to say. I don't care though. I walk off and stand next to Daddy's car.

Daddy drops Barb off first, and as she exits the car she tells me she hasn't forgotten about my *Macbeth* essay and I agree to go round to hers tomorrow evening, early, to work on it. He then drops Bonny and me off in the office car park, leaving us to make our way up to the flat on our own. You can tell the unreconstructed Stone-Age part of him wants to get me by the throat and threaten me with a gory death if I try anything on with his daughter, but he has to keep me on his side, doesn't he, so he just punches me on the shoulder in this phoney, great-guy way and says, "Look after her for me, OK?"

Bonny and I manage the going to bed routine without too much embarrassment. This is mainly because I stand in front of the window with my back to her and refuse to say one word, not even when she offers me a cup of tea. I feel a bit of a shit but I have to make it clear this main room is *mine*. So she has no option but to retreat, scuttle into the bathroom and out again, and then shut herself in her room – I hope for the night.

Aaaaah. I can breathe again. I open up the windows, and get out my art pad, and start to work. I keep going till three in the morning before I turn in, and this time I remember to keep my boxer shorts on.

Chapter 9

"No, Rich – Jesus! Duncan's the *king*, the one they *killed*. Have you actually read this play?"

I'm handling Barb just fine. She's sitting in front of the word processor, supposedly taking dictation from me, but she's finding some of the stuff dribbling out of my mouth so excruciating she's going ahead and typing what she thinks I should put instead.

If I keep this up I could get an A.

It takes two hours, three cups of tea and a couple of mini-tantrums from Barb, but then my *Macbeth* essay is done, all 1,700 words of it complete with quotes, and it's chugging its lovely professionally spell-checked way out of her printer.

"Thank God that's finished," snaps Barb, checking her watch. "God, look at the time. The kids'll be famished. . ."

"*DOGS BEEN OUT YET?*" It's Nick, yelling up the stairs.

"*WHY ARE YOU BACK SO EARLY?*" Barb yells back.

"*HAVEN'T THE KIDS WALKED THEM?*"

"*WHEN D'YOU WANT TO EAT?*"

It kills me, the way really married couples don't actually answer what they ask each other. It's down to some kind of marital telepathy, I reckon. Barb heads down the stairs, me following, and there's Nick, standing smiling at the bottom. Nick's the kind of bloke who looks really ordinary until he opens his mouth. And then he's transformed; he's this lit-up charged-up mixture that's half theatrical and half sheer energy, and it's not put on, it's genuinely him.

I really like him. Barb does too. She puts her arms round him and says, "You take the dogs out, pooch, and I'll get the dinner on. It's a great evening. Summer's coming."

The two bony lurchers are weaving round Nick, waving their hairy tails, adding their vote to Barb's. "All right," grumbles Nick. "Typical. I get in after a hard day, I'm immediately told to get out again—"

"Ah, shut up," says Barb, warmly. "You need the exercise." And she grabs at the flesh round his waist.

He backs off, yelping, and notices me. "Hi, Rich. You get that essay done?"

"Yep."

"Well, I hope *you* did it, and not Barb."

"Yep," Barb and I lie in unison.

"Great. OK, dogs – get your leads."

And then Scarlett and Freddie appear, jostling each other to be first out of the living-room door. "I'm *starving!*" shouts Freddie. "And *she* won't let me watch my programme, *she* sat on the remote and punched me in the ribs and –"

"*I did not!*" shrills Scarlett, vivid with indignation. She's wearing a bright-blue shiny tiara, baggy shorts, and the red velvet cloak she had on the first time I met her. She spots me, and says, "Hello, Rich."

"Hiya, Scarlett. Love what you're wearing. You should be a fashion designer, you know that?"

"Thank you," she says gravely, then she turns to Barb and hisses, "Mum – we *have* to get another television. I can't *stand* watching television with Freddie. He wants to watch all this baby rubbish, and he makes sucking noises with his teeth, and. . ."

"*No I don't,*" squawks Freddie. "Mum – I'm *starving!*"

"Oh, for *goodness' sake!*" yells Barb, then she sweeps the kids along into the kitchen with her, uttering threats as she goes, and Nick mutters, "*Bloody* hell, don't have kids, Rich, I mean it, mate. God, I suddenly *want* to take the dogs out. I'll drive out to Bannerby Park, give them a real run. Wanna come? We can have a chat."

I say yes immediately, and soon we're tanking down the main road, me in the front of his fantastic old Lotus Elite and the dogs crammed in the back. They're kind of crouched forward, all excited, sticking their wet noses down my neck and breathing dog breath in my face.

"Jesus, Nick, what d'you feed 'em on? Rotten fish?"

"Yup. Rotten fish-guts. They love it. So how're you, Rich? Apart from the alcopops fiasco, I mean."

"I'm shit."

"*Oh* dear. What about that gorgeous girl you were with?"

"She dumped me."

Nick pushes up a gear and says, "Oh *dear*. That's tough."

"Yeah, it is."

"She give a reason?"

"Not . . . exactly."

"They never do. Not the real one anyway. God, I wouldn't be your age again, Rich. Endless heartache. *God*."

I find this weirdly comforting, and laugh. Then Nick pulls over into Bannerby Park. It's the grounds of an old manor house, and it's seriously posh and seriously beautiful. We stow the car and walk through the great iron gates, and I look around at the towering old trees, all in new leaf, and the massive stretch of sky, and I let out this great, deep sigh. "Fab, isn't it?" says Nick. "I love coming here."

The lurchers hurtle off across the grass and then suddenly contort themselves into weird, spiderish, hunching shapes. "What the – ?" I begin – and then I realize. They're crapping. Nick fishes in his jacket pocket, comes out with a fistful of bags, and – worryingly – hands one to me.

"Here, mate – grab a bag. You get that one, I'll get the other."

"Oh, *God*, Nick –"

"It's only shit, Rich. Good philosophical lesson for you."

"What the –"

"In life, there's always shit."

"Oh, sod off," I mutter, but I scoop the poop and hand it to Nick, who bins it, and soon we're off across the grass, heading towards some woods. The dogs are going crazy with the freedom, racing wildly round after each other in great loops. Nick and I stop still for a minute just to watch them.

"It's like flying falcons," Nick murmurs.

"Poetic," I say, impressed.

"I'm a poetic kind of guy, darling. That's what people don't realize about me. Jesus. Look at them *go*."

And as I stare at the dogs this sudden feeling of optimism and hope floods into me, as though maybe life could be quite simple, as though it's just *there*, waiting for me to rush into it, like the grass is waiting for the dogs.

We start walking again and Nick asks, "So how're things apart from your ex?"

"OK."

"You forgiven me yet?"

"It wasn't your fault, Nick. They just didn't want to use me."

"Just 'cos it wasn't my fault doesn't mean you don't want to kill me over it. But I'm glad you feel that way. It's just a matter of time, though, isn't it, mate? You're good. Someone's going to grab you sooner or later. You can wait. You're young."

I find myself smiling. I'm almost cheerful as we stomp across the grass. "You sorted college?" Nick asks.

"Yeah. I have some serious work to do over the next couple of months, but I think I'm back in."

"Good. Keep at it, mate. What about Bonny?"

"What about her?"

"It must be a piss, having a major drama land on you like that. Daughter fleeing mad mother, and that."

"Yeah, it was scary."

"*And* sharing the flat. I'd be really pissed off. Unless you fancy your chances with her, of course. Do you?"

I laugh, and it's with relief. Barb's so nice, so good,

and she thinks everyone else is too, or should be. Nick
– he's more on my wavelength. He understands.

"I am a bit pissed off," I say. "And no – I don't
fancy my chances with her."

"Oh well," Nick shrugs. "Hope she doesn't
cramp your style then. You know. When you get a
replacement for that gorgeous bird you had."

We're on the edge of the woods now, and the
lurchers are prancing in with their ears erect and
swivelling like radar. "They're hunting," he
explains. "Looking for squirrels."

And as if on cue, a grey streak shoots past, off up
a treetrunk, and the lurchers whizz after it. They
miss that one, but another's been flushed out in the
chase, and almost too swift to see, the leading
lurcher swoops down like a pointy-nosed ptero-
dactyl and snatches it up.

"Oh – *Jesus!*" I gasp.

A horrible squeaking fills the air. Then the dog
tosses the squirrel, and the other dog pounces on it
open-mouthed – and there's silence.

Then a couple of twitches, another squeak. And
real silence.

"Oh, *shit!*" I wail.

Nick's looking amused. "Bloody hell, mate, calm
down. It's only a squirrel."

"But they're *nice*!" I say, idiotically.

"Squirrels are just rats with good PR. God – look
at you, all upset! You're as bad as Scarlett. Last time

the dogs killed a squirrel, she insisted on fucking *burying* it. Then we had to stand by the grave, hold an hour-long memorial service."

"You're kidding!"

"Yeah. But only about the memorial service. And she wouldn't speak to the dogs for a whole day afterwards."

"Yeah, well – I can sympathize."

"I'm surprised they got one, actually," he says musingly, as we walk on through the soft green woods. "Spring's not the best time for hunting. You should see it in the autumn. It's like Armageddon out here."

"Aren't you going to say something philosophical?" I demand. "I mean – you managed to get all philosophical about them taking a *dump*. What about *death*?"

Nick shrugs dismissively. "Self-evident," he says. "No need."

On the way back, I'm kind of hoping Nick's going to ask me in for supper, because I want to be around him and Barb and the kids and even the dogs, even though they are murderers. I want to be around their kind of chaotic normality for a while. And I want to get *fed*. But he doesn't ask me in for supper, he just drops me off at the turning to the flat and says, "See you soon, mate, all right?" I trudge across the car park, let myself in the main door, and ride the lift up to the top floor, trying to remember if I ate that tin of baked beans I bought the other day. Then I open the flat door and the smell of cooking meat hits me like a tidal wave. I'm practically drooling it's so delicious, and the hunger I'm feeling clamps my stomach like a vice.

Oh, great. Oh fucking *great*. Bonny's not only colonized my living space, she's going to torture me with cooking smells when I'm dying of starvation.

"Hi, Rich!"

I groan in reply, and she jams her head out of the kitchen door and says, like some kind of wifey, "Had a good day?"

"All right."

"Listen – I've made beef stew."

"I can smell it," I say bitterly.

"With onions and mushrooms."

I groan again.

"If you want some."

Of course I want some! Right now I'd sell my own grandmother for a plateful! But I'm not giving in gracefully. She's not getting round me with all this food on offer.

"Look, Bonny," I say, all kind of world-weary, "I don't think we should start cooking for each other. You're staying here, yeah, but that doesn't make us involved in some kind of cosy flatshare thing, OK?"

There's no answer. I go on, louder: "I don't wanna get involved in *playing house*, you know?

Your-turn-to-cook stuff. Cleaning rotas, splitting the shopping bill, all that kind of domestic shit. I've got a lot going on right now – I haven't got the time for it, OK?"

There's another silence, then Bonny walks out of the kitchen and walks right over to me. She's somewhat worryingly gripping a large serrated kitchen knife in one hand, and her face is very red, and I don't think it's just from slaving over a hot stove.

She takes a deep breath and says, "Look, Rich, I'm not into *playing house* any more than you are. I just need somewhere to stay, OK? You really don't have to be so bloody *unpleasant*. I know why you're doing it – you want me out. Well, it won't work. It'll just make me spend longer shut up in my room. And I can do that anyway, without you having to be a shit about it. I know you don't want me here. I know you want to be left alone. I can keep to my room. OK?"

"Hey!" I spread my hands wide, all innocent. "All I said was—"

"I don't care what you *said*. I know what you want. And you've got it, OK? I'll keep to my room. But for the rest of the time, the times when I can't help passing you on the way to the bathroom or something – well. We can either carry on like this, with this stupid, tense atmosphere the whole time, or we can pretend to be grown-ups, OK?"

"Look – I just meant—"

"My whole life has turned upside down the past few days. I've *got away from Mum*. I've finally *got away from Mum*. And I'm beginning to feel *fucking great* about it. I went back to school today. I told my form tutor what'd happened. I gave her this address, and my dad's number. And it was *OK*. She gave me lots of sympathy and promise of support, and it was *OK*. It's like – official. I've left. I'm starting over, and I'm going to make it. I don't know how long I'll be here. I'm sorry if I'm in your way, but that's not exactly the biggest thing for me right now. The big thing is I've *left*. And you can carry on acting like an arsehole if you like, I don't actually *care*. All I'm saying is – it'd be nicer if you didn't."

There's a long, long pause. Then Bonny pivots round and slams back into the kitchen. I stand there for a minute, a bit stunned, then I walk over and put my head round the kitchen door.

She's dishing up two huge platefuls of fragrant, glistening stew. "That's yours," she says, not looking up. "You can tip it straight down the bog or you can eat it first. I don't actually give a shit either way, OK?"

I get two knives and two forks out of the drawer, then I pick up one plate very humbly, and mutter, "Thanks." She still won't look at me. Then I say, "Eat in front of the window?"

She doesn't answer, just grabs hold of a fat white crusty loaf and carries on slicing it, so I walk over to the window and sit down on the edge of my bed. I'm just weighing up whether to call out, "You gonna sit here, Bonny?" when she stomps across the floor, plonks a plate of bread down in front of me, and says, "I bought some beer."

"Did you?"

"Yeah," she says, sitting down on my bed. "In the fridge. Get one if you want."

I really want. I stand up again, cross the floor, then call back – "Can I get you one?"

"Yes," she answers, through a mouthful.

When I get back to the bed, she takes the beer but she still won't look at me. So we sit side by side with space for two other people between us, silent apart from the noises we make eating, looking out at the rain clouds gathering in the sky.

The stew is completely delicious. The beer goes down like nectar. I wipe up some of the gravy with my third slab of bread and say, "Thanks, Bonny. This is great." Then – making a bid at conversation – I say: "Where did you learn to cook like this?"

"I've been cooking since I was about eight," she says ruefully.

"You have?"

"Yeah. Come on – you've met Tigger. Hardly the housekeeping type, is she? When we didn't eat out, or get take-aways – I cooked."

"Look, Bonny –" I begin.

"What?"

"I didn't mean to be a shit earlier. It's just – well, *I* can't cook."

"Well, there's a surprise."

"And I'm really having to watch my cash."

"Oh, *Jesus*. Look – I don't want to be all formal and get into rotas and splitting shopping bills any more than you do. I told you – *I don't care*. All that – it's not important. I was cooking – I did enough for you. Big deal."

"You're getting an allowance, but I—"

"Oh – you and your *thing* about money. Yes, I've got a rich dad. So I can afford to give you a bit of stew and a beer. Lucky me. I've also got an insane mother. What's your mum like?"

"Lovely," I say, mournfully.

"There you are. Swings and roundabouts. Now stop whinging on, and eat, OK?"

I'm looking at Bonny's profile as she talks. That dull, watery look she used to have has vanished, vanished completely. Her eyes are sparking, her face is full of life. It's like a fire's been lit inside her. I get this impulse to get pencil and paper, to get her down.

"You've . . . *changed*," I venture.

There's a silence. Then at last, she turns and looks at me.

"I bloody hope so," she says.

Once we've scraped out the stew saucepan, Bonny tells me in no uncertain terms that it's down to me to wash up, and disappears into her room. I'm feeling so well-fed and content I wouldn't mind her hanging around for a bit, but I don't say anything. As I slosh the plates about in the washing-up bowl I reflect that now she knows the big room is mine, I can be nicer to her in future. And if she wants to cook – well, that's OK too. Being free, being normal away from Tigger – it's a total trip for her, and who am I to spoil it?

I hear her bedroom door opening. I stick my head out of the kitchen all ready to offer to make her a coffee, when she says, "Rich? Would you do something for me?"

Chapter 10

She comes out of her room and she's clutching a holdall, the one she arrived with the other night, only this time it's empty and that fills me with a horrible sense of foreboding.

"Yeah?" I say suspiciously.

"I just need the rest of my clothes," she says in a rush.

"*What?*"

"The rest of my clothes. From the flat."

"Why are you telling *me*?"

"Oh, Rich, you know why. I asked Daddy and he said he was *never* intentionally coming face to face with Mum again. He offered to buy me new clothes instead."

"Well, why don't you take him up on it?"

"Because – well, it's not just clothes. There's a shoebox of stuff there I really want. And a tortoise-shell hand-mirror my gran gave me. *Please*, Rich. I've got the list here." And she flaps a densely written sheet of paper at me.

"*Jesus*, Bonny, I can just see me working through that list ticking it off while your mum lobs ashtrays at my head!"

"Look – if you go over tomorrow evening, I'm pretty sure the flat'll be empty. Mum's always out on a Friday night."

"So why don't you go?"

"Because it might be the one night she stays in."

"Oh, *God*!"

"But if she is you'll handle it! You're not *involved*!"

"*Uuuurgh!*"

"Please, Rich! I wouldn't ask you if there was anyone else!"

I'm trapped and we both know it. There's a pause, then Bonny ventures: "It's only the clothes from the left-hand side of my wardrobe," as though that might tip the balance and decide me to go.

I think about muttering about how she set out to bribe me with her beef stew, but I decide not to be petty. "You got your keys then?" I ask.

"You are great, Rich," she says.

Very early Friday morning I'm woken by Bonny creeping past my bed and going into the bathroom.

Then she creeps back to her room and ten minutes later she lets herself out of the flat. She hasn't even had a cup of tea.

For some reason I can't get back to sleep, so after about ten minutes I roll out of bed, stagger into the kitchen, and put the kettle on. Then I go into the shower and sing loudly, trying to cheer myself up. Mornings are when I feel most depressed about the whole situation with my folks. Which is weird, because I used to definitely, seriously hate mornings at home. All that shouting, all those stampedes for the bathroom, the crowding, the jostling, yuch. Maybe it's the sheer contrast here, the space and the silence, that's bringing my guilt out. Because in some ways the guilt I feel about doing a runner is growing.

I'll go round, I tell myself, as I towel myself dry. I'll go round next week and see them, make up with Dad, *normalize* things.

The shower's woken me up, made me hungry. I head into the kitchen again, and make a mug of tea. I haven't bought any milk for days, and I finished the last of my Economy Kornflakes the other night, but Bonny seems to have stocked up. I help myself to a large bowl of off-puttingly healthy-looking bran and nut stuff without feeling too ashamed, then I get dressed and head into college. I'm looking forward to seeing the expression on Ms Reardon's face when I lob in my *Macbeth* essay. And I've got some Graphics stuff to hand in too. I'm on *schedule*.

The first sight that hits me as I turn in the gates, though, is Ollie standing very close to Portia on the college steps. It hits me like a sick jolt to the guts. I stop dead and watch them as they talk together.

Ollie has a great body and right now its language is on overdrive. All cool black-guy head jerks and hand-movements, all swaying and sexy. Ollie, like I said, has amazing success with women, like he's some kind of magnet. I watch him focus on Portia and the space between them getting smaller and I feel so mad and jealous I could throw up.

Ollie's got this corny trick he does, of looking straight at a bird's mouth when she speaks, and it works. It's working now. Portia's head is on one side, riveted. And *her* body-language – I don't even want to think about that. She's leaning towards Ollie, looking all kind of intent and sincere, and her arms are spread open, like she's waiting for him to jump into them.

I can hardly bear to watch. Ollie, you *bastard*, I'm thinking. I want to race over there, lamp him, kick him when he's on the ground, but I don't, I start slinking off to the side, heading for the canteen entrance so I won't have to walk past them. But first Portia, and then Ollie glance up and see me. And the look on their faces tells me all I need to know.

I'm in a black fug for the rest of the day. Not even the shock tremors that contort old Reardon's face when

I hand her my classy essay can raise my spirits. It's not just that I want to lamp Ollie for being a betraying disloyal shit-faced *bastard*, though. I'm shocked by what seeing him with Portia *did* to me. I don't ever remember feeling jealousy like it – savage, raging, out of control. Part of me wants to leg it straight over to Ollie and demand to know what he was saying, but I know I wouldn't handle it right. I'd either end up smacking him one, or bursting into tears.

Jesus, Rich, calm down, I tell myself. You and Portia are *through*, remember? You decided she wasn't worth the hassle. Stop . . . *churning* about this!

I might as well tell thunder to stop following lightning.

As the college day is winding down to the weekend, I expect to feel better but I don't. Just kind of numb. Last lesson, Chris seeks me out in the Graphics room. He's got a face like a pitbull on red alert. "Bitch!" he snarls at me.

"Why – what've I done?"

"Not *you* – *Natalie*." Her name scrapes past his clenched teeth. "She has to get *her fucking way* the *whole fucking time* or she thinks I'm trying to *push her around*."

"What happened, mate?" I intone loyally, but I know what happened already. Chris and Natalie are both strong people, and they both like getting their own way. They have this fired-up, on-off, passionate-type relationship that's exhausting to watch from the sidelines, let alone be in.

"There's a house party tonight – Jake Crewe's place," rages Chris. "It looks like being really good. I'm all set to go and I tell her and *she* starts saying he's a drug dealer, she's not going – he is *not* a sodding drug dealer, he smokes a bit now and then same as anyone, but he doesn't deal – not properly anyway – *Jesus*. So we get into a bit of a row about it and she starts saying – you want to go, you go on your own, so I say 'Fine', so then she calls *me* a fucking drug dealer, and storms off, and this time there's no way I'm going after her, I've had it, I'm *sick* of her thinking she can get her own way just by acting *up* all the time."

I leave a sympathetic pause, then I ask: "So you still going?"

"What?"

"To the party?"

"Yeah I bloody am. You up for it?"

"Yeah. You know this morning? I saw Ollie chatting up Portia."

"Yeah? *God*, I'm sick of it. Every little goddam thing has to be this big battle. Why can't she just relax? It's like she's waiting to pounce, waiting for me to put a foot wrong."

"Has he said anything about Portia?"

"What?"

"Ollie."

"What about Ollie?"

"Has he said anything about Portia?"

"No. Why should he? It's up to *her* this time, I swear to God. She wants to make up – she can come to me. I'm not crawling after her."

The party, as it turns out, is not brilliant. We have a couple of beers on the way over, then Chris has a few pulls on this joint going round and sinks into silent despair behind the settee in the corner. "I love her, man!" he's moaning. "I really love her an' she treats me like shit!"

And for the next hour or so he's really boring, and there's nothing much else going on either. Ollie is conspicuously not here; all I can think about is him wrapping himself round Portia somewhere dark and private, getting what I should've got if I hadn't been such a giggling impotent idiot that time in the lift. I look at my watch, wondering when I can call it a night without being reckoned a real loser, when suddenly – oh *Christ* – I remember about promising Bonny I'd go and get the rest of her clothes from her old flat.

I'd completely forgotten. The party, Chris moaning, being eaten up with jealousy over Portia – it'd driven it clean from my mind.

It's ten to ten. I've left it too late, haven't I? But if I don't go now I'll have to go sometime over the weekend, won't I, when Tigger'll almost definitely be there, hiding behind the cupboard door with a long pointy knife in her hand. . . I'm on my feet and heading for the door before I can think any further. I collide with Ryan in the hall, tell him to look after Chris, and leg it down the road.

I do a quick bus-hop to the flat, which is empty (where's Bonny?) and collect the holdall, keys and list, which have been pointedly laid out side-by-side on my bed. Then I do another speedy bus-hop to Tigger's flat.

It's only ten-forty as I stand on the doorstep, summoning up the courage to ring the bell. She'll still be out, won't she? No one comes home before midnight on a Friday night, not even the elderly.

My trembling digit extends, presses Tigger's bell. I can hear it buzz in the distance, and this wonderful silence follows it. In something close to desperation I zap the bell again, harder this time, and once again it's followed by silence.

Now comes the *really* scary bit. I put the larger of the two keys in the lock on the big front door, turn it, push the door open, and step into the hall. Three strides across it, and I'm in front of Tigger's front door. Now it's the *really really* scary bit. I bang on the door, wait. Silence. Then I push in the key, and turn it in the lock.

The hall is pitch-black as I step through. I grope for the switch, and as I pull it I realize I'm holding my breath, as though the light might reveal Tigger hanging by her dressing-gown cord from a doorway or something.

Nothing. I head into the main room, peering around me. I saw this terrifying film once, where this madwoman hid under tables for her victims, and shot out and bit them on the face when they got within range. I figure it's the kind of thing Tigger might do.

I check the whole flat systematically, even though I want to get out of here as fast as possible, because I can't get it out of my head that Tigger might be holed up somewhere. I check under the table, behind the sofa, behind every door, even behind the shower curtain. Only then do I head into Bonny's room.

It's kind of neutral, her room. Painted out creamy white, plain curtains, plain bedspread. Like there's nothing really of Bonny in it. I pull open the wardrobe door. Just the stuff from the left-hand side, she said. One glance tells me this is stuff that Bonny chose for herself and the stuff on the right-hand side – the stuff she's leaving behind – is stuff that Tigger got for her, or made her buy. It's kind of posh, but boring, like Tigger didn't want too much competition. Whereas Bonny's own gear is mostly jeans and shirts with the odd bit of daring club-wear thrown in.

I check the list, make sure I get the right things. I pull out a dark-blue dress that's short and strappy and lowcut, and try to picture Bonny wearing it. She'd look all right, I reckon. She's got enough up top. I bet Tigger told her it made her look fat, though.

Fast as I can, I cram the clothes into the holdall, and then I check the list again. Hairdryer, two pairs of shoes, no underwear – didn't want me to touch her bras and stuff obviously, or maybe she brought it all with her. Dressing-gown from the back of the door. I unhook it and decide I like it, a lot, it's like a kimono, all silky and patterned. Then I'm heading for the little cupboard by the side of her bed, which is where she said her precious shoebox was, but before I can reach it a telephone in the hall outside rings out like a siren and I damn well nearly pass out with terror.

It rings again and again. I stand still, holding my breath, begging it to stop, like I think it might summon Tigger back to answer it. Then it clicks off, and Tigger's voice shrieks: "*Hi – yee! You've reached Tigger and Bonny's home! But we're out having fun – or soaking in the bath – anyways, we can't speak right now! Leave your name and number, all righty?*" Then there's a *beeeep* and a low, concerned female voice responds, leaving her message, and even though I can't hear what she's saying, the relief that she got the machine and not Tigger is more than audible.

Then there's silence.

I wait till my pounding heart has slowed just a little bit, then I slither over to the bedside cupboard. There's Granny's old hand-mirror on the top, just like Bonny said it would be. And inside the cupboard, behind a little raffia basket full of pastelly coloured nail varnishes, is the shoebox.

I pull it out. It's tied up with about a million different bits of string and ribbon, all very elaborate, and the thought comes into my head that they're there to let Tigger know that Bonny would know if she ever opened the box up.

I check my watch. Five past eleven. That's still early, isn't it? Suddenly, I'm dying to know what's in the shoebox. What Bonny considers so precious she's prepared to send me back to the vampire's lair to fetch it. I push at the ribbons near one of the corners, and they slide off, taking a good proportion of the rest of the string and ribbons with them.

Oh, shit, that's done it. I bet the ribbons and string are in some kind of code-order. However I try to put them back it'll be wrong, and Bonny will know.

Still, she won't know it's *me*, will she? I'll tell her I found it like this. I mean – wouldn't Tigger go through her daughter's stuff as soon as she disappeared, looking for clues and addresses?

I slide the box-lid off. I flip aside two babyish Valentine's cards, three letters, the top of a box from a Smarties Easter egg, an old kids' hanky with "Wednesday's child" embroidered on it. Then I come face to face with myself in eye-makeup.

What?!?

My brain's got the answer while my face is still contorted with shock. It was that bloody barbecue, wasn't it, at Barb and Nick's, a couple of weeks ago.

When Scarlett forced me to let her make me up seventies-style with glitter and eyeliner, and Bonny bet me four quid I wouldn't walk around like that.

And then took two photos of me.

The second photo is underneath. This one's in half profile, and it's better, less camp.

Weird. That barbecue – that was when Bonny asked me out, and I said no 'cos of Portia. But she still kept the photos. Even though I look like a poofy mime artist in them. Even though I said no.

I scoop out the rest of the box's contents – three shells, an empty perfume bottle, two theatre programmes, a notebook, some birthday cards and letters, a blue-grey pebble, two photos of Daddy, one of a baby, and one of a girl I've never seen before. I open a couple of the cards and read them and suddenly I feel really shitty for poking about like this. It's her life, her memories, I've got no right. . . I shove all the stuff back in the box, and wrap the ribbons round as best I can, then I stow it in the holdall with the clothes and the hairdryer and the hand-mirror.

I check my watch. Eleven-fifteen already – *shit.* I'd better go before the vampire crawls back to her crypt. I switch off the light and head for the exit, and I'm reaching out to twist the catch on the front door when it clicks all on its own and – like in a nightmare – swings slowly open towards me.

Chapter 11

" *W* hat the bloody hell are you doing here?"

"Tigger, I know how this looks. . ."

"*Jesus* you scared me! *Jesus Christ!!*"

"Tigger, I—"

"*Is Bonny with you?*"

"No, but she sent me, she gave me her key and—"

"*God* – look at me, I'm trembling! *God*, I thought you were a burglar! *God!!*"

"Tigger, I'm really sorry, I—"

"I need a *drink*!" she shrieks. Then she pushes me backwards down the hall into the living-room, and once inside she heads over to the sideboard where there's a row of sticky-looking bottles and glasses. She pours out two glasses of clear silvery stuff and then – bizarrely – hands one to me, saying "Cointreau."

I take it, because I don't know what else to do. Tigger plonks herself down on the sofa and absent-mindedly pats the cushion next to her. I take a big gulp of Cointreau, choke on it, drop the holdall, and sit down.

This is weird. I'm waiting for her to start ripping into me, and instead she's pouring me drinks and generally cosying up. "Bonny just needed some stuff," I croak out.

"I have had the most *amazing* night!" she replies, as if I hadn't opened my mouth.

"Bonny asked me to—"

"I've met *the* most fabulous man in the *history* of the *world!* Oh – *God*, he's gorgeous. Well – we really met at the beginning of the week – he was at the gallery Cathy works at. He was helping put up this exhibition. And we hardly exchanged two words but there was just this – you know – this *spark*. So I badgered Cathy to have one of her little dinner parties. I absolutely *bullied* her, I was shameless. It was worth it though. He came!"

She turns to me, all open-mouthed and googly-eyed, inviting me to share her delight, so I go all open-mouthed and googly-eyed back and say, "Wow!" I feel like an idiot, but to be honest I'm so relieved she's not screaming at me I'm happy doing just about anything.

"It *was* 'wow', darling – it was fab! Cathy sat us together of course. And he was really shy at first and wouldn't say much but I kept filling up his glass and in the end – *well*, it was like we were the only two people in the room!" She snatches up her bag, starts furiously rummaging. "They had one of these instamatic cameras. Cathy took one of us, and I grabbed it just before I left – ah! *Here* it is!"

And she lurches sideways, leans on my shoulder, and sticks the photo between us so we can gaze upon it in unison. It's a standard fast shot. There's a pepperpot in close-up, and behind it Tigger with a big phoney grin, holding up a wine glass, nestling up to this boring-looking guy. He has this dazed, fearful look about him, a bit like a rabbit trapped in headlights.

Suddenly Tigger snatches the picture away from me, looks at it closer, and lets out this scary wail. "Oh, *God* – I look like his *mother*!"

Grandmother, I think, while I say, hastily, "Nah, you don't – don't be ridiculous!"

"Oh, darling, you really think I don't?"

"Course not. You look a few years older, yeah – but that's good."

"Is it?"

"Yeah! He probably likes you 'cos you're mature and all."

She's a hand's width away from me. I'll say anything to keep her sweet.

"You think so? We got on *so* well. He was asking my advice about decorating his new flat, and he just *hung* on my words – well, it's another one of my things, interior design. I offered to come round and see his place, give him some real advice, and he took my number. . ."

"There you are then. Bet it was just an excuse. I mean – yeah, he wanted your advice, but what he really wanted was your phone number."

"Darling, you think so?"

"Sure I do. Oldest trick in the book."

"I just – I *adore* him," she sighs. "It's just – I don't know. All these gorgeous young things around – how can I expect him to be interested in *me*?"

"Oh, but guys love mature women," I gargle. "They don't just want girls with all their insecurity and everything. They want someone who knows where she's at. And if she looks as good as you – *well*. . ." She's lapping this up like a starving cat laps up gravy, and I'm finding it very hard to shut up. It's like all this verbal gunk is being sucked out of me by the sheer force of her need. "You look great together," I say. "In this photo. Really great."

"Oh, darling, you are a *gem*," Tigger's purring. "The girl who ends up snaring *you* is going to be a very, very lucky girl indeed." And she edges a bit closer to me. Oh, *shit*. I have this sudden all-out-panic-alert thought that she might think *I* fancy her.

Oh my God. With Tigger, anything's possible. Anything.

"The first time I met you, you know," she's

saying, "I thought – wouldn't he be perfect for Bonny."

"Yeah?" I say, relieved.

"But you had that other girl – what was her name?"

"Portia."

"That's it. What a beauty. And such *style*. Bonny never quite. . . I used to say to her, listen to *me*, darling, style is my thing, I can help you with what to wear, but I don't know, she *would* insist on –" She breaks off and sighs, and then she suddenly looks at me as if she's just woken up and remembered she's got a daughter and demands: "Did you say Bonny sent you here?"

"Yeah. She wanted some of her stuff, that's all."

"You've *seen* her?"

"I – no. I just got this message through the friend she's staying with."

"But you had her key!"

"Um – she . . . she posted it to me."

Tigger must know this is a load of crap, but she doesn't challenge me. "Did you tell her the state I'm in? That I *must see her*?"

"Yeah, yeah, I did. And I know she's worried about you. I mean – that's partly why she wanted me to come round. To see how you are. And you seem – well, you seem a hell of a lot better, Tigger, don't you?"

Tigger rounds on me. "No!" she shrieks, right in

my face. "No, I am *not* better! I can't sleep, I can't eat. . . *When*'s she going to get in touch?"

I flinch away across the sofa. "I . . . er . . . look, I'm just the messenger!"

"But you've *seen* her! You must have *seen* her!"

"Only once," I lie. "After that first time."

"And how is she? What's she doing? When's she coming home? *What's she told you?*"

I feel this huge need to deflect the conversation away from me, so I say, "Well – she's seen her dad."

It's like lobbing a match into a petrol tanker.

"That *BASTARD*! Oh – *GOD*!! I might've *known* she'd go running straight to him! I bet she's going to move in with him! She is, isn't she – she'll live with him and that cheap slut he picked up, and say *this is my new family* and play big sister to those stupid brats and she'll have a huge new bedroom in that massive house he bought, even though he could only afford this rabbit hutch for me. . ." Tigger leaps to her feet, snatches up a packet of fags from the table and lights up. Then she exhales violently and shrieks, "*GOD* – I can't believe she'd betray me like this. *She* knows what it was like when he left us. What I *went* through. And now she's going to go crawling back to him, playing happy families – she'll be sitting across the table from that *bitch*, that home-wrecking *bitch*, eating her *macaroni cheese* and telling her all about her day at school and then she'll be reading to those blobby brats and helping them with bathtime and putting them to bed, all terribly cosy while I'm just *withering* away here. . ."

There's no point in trying to interrupt this, so I have another little surreptitious slurp of Cointreau. It's quite good. Tastes of orange.

"*How* can she do this to me? Doesn't she know what I'm going through? *How* can she be this disloyal? *What have I done?*"

She seems to be waiting for an answer, so I swallow hard, then I look up, all sincere, and croak, "It's not you, Tigger – it's nothing you've done. It's Bonny. Where she's at right now. Look – I'm pretty sure she's *not* going to move in with her dad. From what I heard. She likes that flat she's in. She wants her space. It's like – it's a stage she's at. You know. A teenage thing."

Tigger looks appeased. Actually, my skills at lying and invention are beginning to impress even me. "You are a sweet boy," she says, taking another hard drag from her cigarette. Then she comes and plonks herself down on the sofa beside me again.

"I'm sure she will get in touch," I gabble on. "I'm sure of it. Just give her a bit of time."

There's a long pause, during which we both drain our Cointreau glasses. Then she suddenly announces: "I've been having such nightmares!"

"Yeah?"

"Last night – I was wandering around in this great, desolate place – and I was looking for something, but

I didn't know what it was – and then I found it. It was a box, and I just *knew* it was what I was searching for. When I opened it up, it had my head in it."

"Urgh! What – all bleeding and everything?"

"I can't remember if it was bleeding!" she snaps. "What does that matter? It was my head – looking back at me – and my eyes were so sad, so desperate. . ."

"What, your eyes in the box?"

"*Yes.* And do you know what I thought?"

"How come I can see this if that's my head in there?"

"*No!*" Tigger's getting quite pissed off with me. "No, I didn't. I thought – I *never realized* before how . . . how *pretty* I am!"

Oh – my – God. Time to go. I hope that soft-sounding woman who left a message on the answer machine is a friend, and I hope she drags Tigger off to serious psychotherapy soon, but there's nothing I can do.

I stand up, and mutter, "I better go now. I'll miss the last bus." Then I stoop down, and pick up the holdall.

"That's Bonny's!" she says.

"Yes – I told you, she wanted me to pick up some of her clothes –"

"You've got Bonny's clothes in there?" she screeches, like I'd just told her I was toting Bonny's dismembered body.

"Yes, Tigger – *Jesus*! I told you!"

Her hand shoots out, grabs one of the bag's handles. "You're going to see her, aren't you! You must be! Well, I'm coming too!"

"Look – you can't. I don't know where she's staying."

"Stop *bullshitting* me, Richy! *I'm coming with you!*"

I'm very tired, and wound up, but even so I'm still a bit ashamed about what happens next. I kind of yank the bag sideways, and Tigger stumbles and lets go and topples on to the sofa, and while she's still sprawling face down I leg it at top speed out of the flat and away into the night, leaving both the doors open.

Chapter 12

"Never again, Bonny, OK? That's all. Never again."

"OK," she says, cradling the holdall in her arms.

"I mean – she needs help. Serious help. She—"

"Rich – don't tell me, all right? Maybe I'm being selfish, but I just can't hear about her right now, OK? It's someone else's turn."

"Yeah, OK. So long as it's not mine."

"She's got this cousin, Maisie. I phoned her tonight. Maybe she can help. I felt awful phoning her but – well. Mum's got no real friends."

"I think the cousin might've phoned when I was there. Left a message. Scared the shit out of me."

"Yeah? I hope so. I hope it was her." Bonny wanders over to my bed, sits down on the edge of it, and starts to unzip the holdall. She pulls out the shoebox, and all the string and ribbon falls off in a great, accusing heap.

"It was like that!" I say, hastily.

"Mum's been poking about in it. Of *course*. I'm surprised she hasn't ripped up those photos of Daddy." Then Bonny looks up at me and demands: "Did you look in it?"

"No," I lie. I'm quite glad it's dark in here 'cos I think I go a bit red. "Christ, Bonny, I didn't have time to look at anything. I just wanted to get *out*."

Bonny shrugs. "I bet. Anyway, it doesn't really matter. It's just some stuff from the past I want to hang on to." She looks up at me again. "As well as some junk I should've thrown out."

Hey – does she mean my photos? I feel almost hurt for a minute, then I say, "Well – things are looking up anyway. Tigger's got herself a new man."

Bonny looks unimpressed and slightly sick in equal measure. "Was he there?"

"No. But he had her phone number and stuff. Maybe if she gets involved with him, it'll take the pressure off you a bit –"

"Rich, she's not going to get *involved* with him! Soon as he finds out what she's like, he'll run a mile!"

"You don't *know* that."

"I *do*. She's always been great at picking men up, but it never lasts. She kind of dazzles them, all her glitzy energy, they think she's great at first, but it's like a firework going up, you know? She fizzles out pretty soon and then she's *awful*, needy and nasty and demanding and – well, they take off." Bonny sighs, and pushes the shoebox back into the holdall. "She makes out she wants it that way. That she's a big success, picking all these guys up. 'Ringing the changes' she calls it. She's always sneering at people like Barb – 'God, I'd go *mad*! The same man all the time – I need change!' I dunno, maybe she really believes it."

There's a pause. Bonny can imitate her mum's voice so well it's not funny. "So these men she picks up," I ask, "she brought them back to your flat?"

"Yeah. I'd go to bed early, stick my pillow over my head so I wouldn't hear her screwing them."

"Oh, gross."

"Yeah, it was a bit."

"I mean – that is *gross*. Completely *gross*."

"Well, it wasn't *that* bad. The worst bit was if I bumped into them in the morning. They'd always look dead shifty, and 'just have coffee', and slope off, fast."

"Hearing them though – *yuch*."

"Why *yuch*? Just 'cos she's over forty?"

"'Cos she's your *mum*!"

"Oh, Rich, how *sweet*! Your mum does it too you know! Or *you* wouldn't be here!"

"Yeah, but that was a long time ago."

"You mean you've never heard your parents at it?"

"No I bloody haven't! The whole thought makes me want to heave!"

Bonny bursts out laughing. "You know, it kills me the way the average bloke is such a buttoned-up prude when it comes to anyone *else* getting their rocks off."

"That isn't true!"

"Yeah it is! You all go, 'Woah, yeah, her, she's gagging for it, wouldn't mind giving that one one' – but if anyone *else* gets their end away you act like a vicar in a porn cinema!"

"*Yeah?*"

"Yeah!"

"I don't mind *other* people doing it!" I say, all indignantly. "I just think it's disgusting if you're *old*!"

"So you're going to give sex up, are you? When you get too old for it? When's that going to be, eh? Thirty? Twenty-five? *Next year?*"

She's really ripping the piss out of me, and the thing is, I'm quite enjoying it. "You're being ridiculous," I go. "I'm not saying old people should give it up. Just – be a bit discreet that's all. Not rub everyone's noses in it."

"Maybe you'd like to give old people a *curfew* too."

"Not a bad idea, Bonny."

"I mean – they're pretty offensive, aren't they, hanging around on the street."

"Yeah, they are. Sitting on park benches with their shopping bags an' all. They should be inside before nine o'clock at night."

"Not hanging around chatting on street corners."

"Right."

"Taking up seats in pubs."

"Right. And they should only have limited use of public transport. I'd take back their bloody bus passes for a start."

"God, *Richy*! You're such a fascist!"

"I know. It's the uniforms made me join up."

We both laugh, and then I say, "So where were you tonight? Did you have a good time?"

"Yes," she says, then she stands up without another word and walks into her room, calling back, "Night."

I'm sort of sorry to see her go. All the drama with Tigger and everything, and chatting it over – it'd taken my tortured brain off Portia and Ollie. Just for a bit.

Before I drop off to sleep I tell myself it's Saturday tomorrow so I'm going to seriously sleep in. Trouble is, I can't get to sleep, and you can't sleep in if you're still awake, can you? I'm tossing and turning the whole night, with images of Ollie and Portia storming through my head, and I swear I'm not properly asleep when this weird buzzing on the wall wakes me up. I can hear all these disconnected words: "*Footy*. . . need the . . . PRACTICE . . . still *asleep*? . . . lazy BASTARD. . ."

It doesn't take me long to realize it's the flat's malfunctioning intercom, so I stagger over to the wall and press the button, then I stick my head out of the flat door to see if the intercom's actually worked for once and opened the main door.

It has. For once, it has. The lift is rattling its way down and within minutes it's rattling its way up again, with Chris and Ryan standing inside. They're all kitted up and they're looking depressingly energetic.

"Get your gear on," orders Chris. "Footy practice."

"No way. I never said I was up for—"

"You don't get a choice, mate, OK? Not after we've come all this way to get you. Come on. We all got shit-faced last night. We're gonna work it off. *OK?*"

"OK, OK," I grumble. "Don't take it out on me."

"What?"

"Just 'cos you've bust up with Natalie."

"Don't mention that *name*, man. Let's just get out there."

"Give us a cup of tea first though," says Ryan.

"Where's Ollie?" I ask suspiciously.

"Wouldn't get up," says Chris. "Too tired."

Too tired? I bet he was, the bastard! I'm going to kill him! "I'll put the kettle on," I say.

"So," mutters Ryan, when we're in the kitchen with the kettle on, "where's this bird then?"

I jerk my head towards the bedroom door. "In there."

"In bed?" says Ryan wistfully.

"Yes, probably. Jesus, Ryan, you are one sad bastard, you know that?"

"Yes," agrees Ryan, dolefully, and just then,

Bonny's door opens and she walks slowly out. She's wearing the silky kimono thing I bought back from her old flat, and she's looking all sleepy and soft and curvy and . . . well. Lovely if you want the truth.

"Hi," she mumbles. "Sorry."

"Want some tea?" I ask, casual as hell, while Ryan gawps.

"Yes please," she says. Then she turns to Chris and says, "Hi. We met at that party – remember?"

"Yes," says Chris. "I do."

I pour out four mugs of tea and Bonny says, "So you're going for a football practice, are you?"

"Yep," says Chris. "Five-a-side. There's this tournament coming up, and I want us to go for it like a proper team. Which will be difficult with losers like these two on the side, but there you go."

Bonny giggles at him, and he grins back. "I haven't had breakfast," I say sulkily.

"I got some muffins," says Bonny, pulling a packet down from the cupboard. "Anyone else want one?"

"I mean, Jesus, mate – what more do you want? She likes you, she feeds you – she looks *great*—"

"She's not my type, man."

"And she's got money. You said she's got money." We're nearly at the park, and Ryan's been bleating on the whole way about how I'm looking a gift-horse in the mouth.

"Jesus, Ry, shut up will you? Change the track."

"OK, I will. What would you do if one of these chat-show people – you know, like Jerry Springer – phoned up and asked you to be on his show 'cos your girlfriend or someone had a Sexy Secret they had to tell you?"

"A *what*? What the fuck are you on about *now*, Ryan?"

"It's these Confessions Shows. They do my head in. I mean – yeah, I watch them, just for a laugh, but I just don't get how they get *anyone* to agree to go *on* them. I mean – what kind of guy gets up there in front of millions of people and lets his bird tell him she's really a bloke? Or she's been shagging his best mate? Total humiliation. Especially when the best mate comes on, and the bird says she can't help herself, 'cos he's about twenty times better in the sack than you – I mean, *Christ,* if someone asks you to go on a show, you know you're getting set up to get made an arse of, don't you?"

I don't answer. In my mind I can see me one side of a chat-show stage, and Portia on the other, and her saying, "I never meant for it to happen! It's just he's such a stud!" and then Ollie walking out, all smarmy and apologetic and hey-Rich-I-hope-we-can-still-be-friends. . . "Why are you asking me this, Ryan?" I say, all suspicious if not paranoid.

"Asking you? I'm not asking you."

"You are. You asked me what I'd do if someone tried to get me on a show so my girlfriend could tell me a Sexy Secret."

Ryan guffs out a laugh. "I was only *theorizing*, mate. Why're you so uptight? You and the Porsche back together or something?"

Footy practice is not up to scratch. Chris has to retire to throw up after only ten minutes; Ryan and I just can't seem get moving. Andy, the fifth member, doesn't show, and neither does that treacherous cheating bastard Ollie. After one hour and ten minutes I announce I've had it, and I head back to the flat. I'm planning to pull the covers back over my head and go back to sleep, hopefully till nightfall.

I let myself in and I can tell straight away that the place is empty, which is a big relief. I wander over to my bed, which has never looked more inviting. On the pillow there's a white, square note, and I grimace when I spot it – I bet it's Bonny telling me I've got to clean the bog or something. I pick it up, yawn, unfold it and read:

Why are you avoiding me? I need to see you. I've finished with Tony.

Portia.

Chapter 13

U nderneath Portia's note, there's a number. It's only her *mobile* number, isn't it?

I AM ECSTATIC. I'm rocketing. I'm in another *dimension*. I can't do anything for the next five minutes, just roam about the flat going "*Yes! Ye-ess!*"

So she's finally dumped old Tony, has she? The boyfriend she forgot she had when she got together with me. And now she wants to *see* me. I'm going to come face to face with that *face* again. I'm going to talk to it, watch its mouth make all those sexy, squishy shapes as it speaks, watch those eyes burn, I'm going to be up close, close enough to inhale, I'm going to reach out and touch her, I'm going to get to. . .

I'm going to get to kiss her again. Pull her close to me, touch her, I'm – *oh* – *my* – *God*. This could go far. This could go anywhere. I feel like I might blow apart at any minute.

I throw myself back on my bed and let out a long roar like a stag going for the rut. Then I jump up and do what I should've done twenty-four hours ago. I leg it down to the phonebox at the end of the road by the garage and dial Ollie's number.

"All right, mate? What? Sorry. Your mum said you were up – look, don't wank on, Ollie, I'm in a payphone – I want to ask you something. I saw you yesterday. With Portia. At college. What were you talking about?"

"You," he says.

"Yeah? *Yeah?* What about me? Come on, man, give, tell me."

"She been in touch with you yet?"

"Yes. A note. And her mobile number."

"So why you phoning me and not her then, eh?"

"*Ollie*, I swear I'll – look, just tell me what she said, OK?"

"OK," he laughs. "Woah, she was intense. She was intense, man."

"About what?"

"Oh – you. Life. That is one intense chick."

He's enjoying this, playing me like a haddock on a line. "Just tell me what she *said*," I groan.

"She was asking about you. Asking did I know

what you felt about her. I said you felt OK. Wasn't going to give too much away, was I?"

"Did she say – what did she tell you?"

"Said it was your fault she'd bust up with her boyfriend. Said she liked you best."

"*Yeah?*"

"But she was going on about you not treating her right. *Backing off.* What you done, Rich? When did you back off?"

"Nothing – I didn't."

"So what she mean?"

"Look – I'm gonna phone her now, OK? Thanks, Ollie."

"My pleasure, man. And hey – Rich?"

"What?"

"Don't back off this time, OK?"

I put down the receiver and stand in the phone booth for a bit, trying to make my breathing steady. My mouth's gone as dry as dust. I think about legging it down to the nearest shop and getting some Coke or something but I know I'm just Delaying the Moment. So I unfold Portia's note, take another deep breath, and punch her number into the phone. Two rings, then: "Hiy-*eee*!"

"Portia – hi."

There's a brief silence then – "Richy? Hi."

"I got your note."

"Did you?"

"Yeah. Thanks."

"S'OK. Thanks for . . . calling."

"S'OK."

"So – um?"

"You wanna meet up?" I garble.

"Yeah. Yeah, I'd like that."

"When – now?"

"Where are you?"

"Just outside my flat."

"Can we meet in that pub near you then?" she asks breathlessly.

"What – The Ship? By the canal?"

"Yes. I don't want to be anywhere near my place. I wouldn't feel safe. It's Tony. He's gone apeshit, I mean I'm quite literally scared for my life, he's – oh, *God*. I'll tell you when I see you, OK?"

I can feel my mouth splitting in a grin. It's Portia the drama queen back on the scene. I can't wait.

"Half an hour?" she says.

"Sure," I reply.

Then I *run*. I burst back up into the flat, stripping off my disgusting, sweaty footy gear as I go. Then I'm into the shower and out again in five minutes, and pulling on my good gear, the gear I bought a couple of weeks ago when I was rich. *Shit*, I wish that hadn't all fallen through. How can you keep a bird like Portia without money?

I kick that thought aside. Like I'm kicking aside all the other thoughts, such as: *You made up your mind she was bad news* and *She pissed you off* and *What's happened to your brain?*

Right now my brain isn't getting a look in.

When I get to the pub, Portia is already there. Which is an all-time first. She's even got a drink in front of her.

I almost seize up with the pleasure of seeing her, just sitting there waiting. Waiting for me. "Hi, Portia," I say, trying to sound macho. Trying to stop my smile goofing out and taking over my entire face.

She looks up at me, knowingly. She looks even more gorgeous than she did in the agonized fantasy I had about her last night. "Hi, Richy."

"Can I get you another drink?" I ask.

"Sure," she says, all breathy and intense. "I'm not planning on staying sober. Not the way I feel right now. White wine spritzer. Please."

I race up to the bar, order her drink, and only a half for me because I want to keep my head in gear. Then I sit down opposite her.

"Well," she says.

"So," I answer.

"Yeah. I – look, Richy. I want to apologize."

"You *do?*"

"Yeah. For overreacting. The other night. At your flat. Storming out on you like that."

"Well, I—"

"The thing is, Richy, things had been going

really weird for me. I mean – things with Tony. And I like – I felt you – *well*. I kind of wanted you to take control, you know? Make the decision for me."

I can feel my hands sweating. If she means – she *must* mean –

"I was totally confused," she goes on. "I didn't know what I wanted. I just – I just knew right then I wanted you."

My eyes swivel sideways. Partly 'cos I don't trust my face enough to risk looking at her, partly to see if the group of guys on the next table have heard this. I kind of want them to hear.

There's a silence. It's my turn to speak. "Portia," I begin, "if you knew how *bad* I felt about what happened, how I messed up I mean –"

"Look – I don't want to talk about it, OK? It's in the past. And maybe we both messed up. It's just – when you *laughed* – well. All I could *do* was walk out. I just felt so totally *humiliated* and *rejected*." She blinks over the table top at me, trying to evoke those emotions. But Portia doesn't easily do humiliation. Or rejection. In fact she looks about as humiliated and rejected as a lynx on a rock.

"Say something," she murmurs.

"I – God, Portia, what d'you want me to say? That I've spent every waking minute since then wanting to kill myself for being such a jerk?"

"Have you?"

"Of course I have. You were being so . . . *fabulous*, and I just. . . I just. . . The thing is, Portia, with you, it's got to be mutual, you know? I couldn't do anything I wasn't sure you really wanted. You know?"

Masterstroke! Portia's glowing and smiling, leaning across the table top towards me. "That's what I like about you, Richy," she says. "You're so sensitive."

I smirk, kind of hoping the guys at the next table haven't heard that one. "What happened with Tony?" I ask.

Theatrically, Portia flings herself backwards in her chair. "*Don't ask!!*"

"That bad, hey?"

"*Worse!* I got a cab home. And he was waiting for me, outside my house. In his car. He looked so mad, Richy, I can't tell you. He was all – where have you been, why did you turn your mobile off. He said we had to talk. He made me get in his car, and we drove off – he was raving on about how he wanted to trust me but he couldn't, he never felt sure of me. I made him pull over and park. Honestly, Richy, the way he was driving, I was scared he'd kill us both. We talked and talked. Well – *he* did. *God*. He's so insecure – all this crap was coming out about how he just wanted a woman he could trust and how it was destroying him because he knew I didn't love him as much as he loved me. . . *God*. It was so *tedious*."

Silently, I pledge never to bare my soul to Portia. "So how did it end up?" I ask.

"I dumped him."

Nice. "What – just like that?"

"Course not. I needed a lift home, didn't I? I said I had to get back, and when we stopped outside my house I did the whole 'I need some space to think' bit."

"And did he buy it?"

"He *cried*. It was disgusting. If I hadn't already decided to finish with him, that would've done it. Honestly, he was *abject*."

Not for the first time, I find myself feeling seriously sorry for old Tony.

"He just *smothers* me," Portia's going on. "All his stupid jealousy, and his checking up, and his possessiveness. I feel like I'm being *buried alive*. And it's got worse since . . . you know. You."

"Me?" I ask, innocently. Delighted.

"Yeah, since I've been confused about you, since – *anyway*, he agreed to leave me alone for a week. To think. I'll phone him up in a day or two, say I've thought, finish it for good."

The casual way she says this – it half horrifies me, and half really turns me on. Which is weird. But I tell myself I'll think about the psychology later.

"Wouldn't it have been better to finish it for good there and then?" I ask.

"Richy, I didn't *dare*. You should've seen his *face*. I mean – he looked *insane*. And after he'd finished crying, he got really nasty, angry – he started smashing the steering wheel with his fist, saying he couldn't stand it, demanding to know if I'd met someone else, saying if he saw me with someone else he'd *kill* him. . ."

I can feel myself going a bit pale. "Did you tell him?"

She makes a little kissy shape with her mouth, and says, "*No-o!* I don't want to see you hurt, Richy. Anyway – we're not exactly an item, are we?"

"We could be," I say.

"Is that an invitation?" she asks.

"You want another drink?" I ask.

And she looks at me and says, "No. How about showing me this flat you've moved into?" Then she picks up her mobile phone from the table, and I watch her flick it off.

Chapter 14

I close the wrought-iron gate on Portia and me, and the lift clanks into action. As we ascend, at first I can't look at her, then I make myself. She's smiling at me, all lopsided and ironic and sexy.

"All *right*," I say, because I know she's thinking about the last time we were in the lift. "All right."

She hasn't got her hands anywhere near the bars this time. She's got them on her hips, like someone listening to a lame excuse. I walk over and stand right in front of her. She laughs up at me.

"What's so funny, Portia?"

"You are. You're funny."

"Yeah?" I'm bringing my face down. I'm corny and I don't care. I'm in range of her mouth now, breathing in while she breathes out.

"Yeah," she says, waiting.

I put one hand on her shoulder, all kind of I'm-in-control-here, then I bring my mouth down on to hers. She doesn't move for a second or two. I'm kind of nudging at her lips, trying to get them to answer me.

And then she does.

God, I've missed this. I have missed this *so much*. She's such an expert. She responds, and then she leads, and then she slows down, and it's all so *right*. She's got her arms wrapped tight round my neck, her body pressed up against every inch of me, her leg pushing between my legs.

We come up for air, but we don't let go of each other. "The lift's stopped," she says, into my neck. I keep my left arm round her waist, and I pull open the iron gate.

With my razor-sharp grasp of female psychology I've processed what she said about me taking control and making the decision for her and I've decided this time I'm going to go for it, I'm going for it till she slaps my face. So I half lift her off her feet and kind of pivot her round, swing her round to the flat door, and she's laughing, and I get the door open, and then I wrap both arms round her and half lift her again and do this kind of weaving shuffle towards the bed. And then I topple down on to it, pulling her with me.

I can't let it stop. If it stops, if I say *Hey, want to look round my place?* or *Can I get you a coffee?* it might never start again. We fall side by side, but in one smooth move she turns on to her back and I cover her and we start kissing again. Oh, God I want this. I shuck my leather jacket off and dump it on the floor. I'm pressing down on her, I'm propped on one forearm and the other's working its way up and down her fabulous body, not believing the speed of this, not believing its luck – then I feel this scrabbling at my chest.

She's only undoing my shirt buttons, isn't she.

I kind of suspend reality after this, and everything moves very fast. She gets my shirt off, I get her shirt off, I get her bra off, I can't believe how beautiful she is. I fall on her, kissing her, and she starts this weird bucking beneath me, and I realize she's struggling out of her jeans. *Condoms*, I think, frenziedly. *Christ*, condoms! I've got some. I bought some. When this whole thing with Portia really got going I bought some and put them in the inside pocket of my jacket.

"Hang on," I croak. I roll across the bed, grab my jacket and find the condoms, and when I turn back Portia's lying on her side completely naked watching me. She is brain-meltingly beautiful. It takes me about three seconds to shed the rest of my clothes, and throw myself on top of her again.

We're both kind of laughing now, with excitement, and recklessness, and she's pulling me down on to her, and I can't help myself, I'm making all these groaning and moaning noises of sheer pleasure as I kiss her and touch her and inhale her scent. I've got the condom gripped in my hand, and Portia discovers this and prises my fingers open, then she expertly rips off the top and pulls it out and puts it on me.

And then too soon almost for me to let the wonder hit me we're making love. I can't believe it, I can't believe how great it is and how free and fabulous she is, moving with me. Oh, *God*, hold on, hold on, don't let it happen too quick. I fix my mind on blackness. When I was with Emma, the one real girlfriend I've ever had, I worked out this way of holding back. Let me still be able to do it. *Let me.*

I last and I last. And even though I've switched off part of my brain it's the most fantastic thing, it's fantastic . . . she's beginning to make noises now, little, greedy, impatient noises, and they're so unbelievably sexy they tip me over the edge and . . . *wham* oh, *Christ.* I try not to yell out with the sheer brilliance of it. I keep moving with her. And then she gives a kind of groan, and lies still.

I don't want to speak to her. I don't want her to speak to me. I'm afraid it might spoil it all. I start kissing her hair, and down her neck, but she's gone very still.

I deal with the condom. I want to ask if it was OK for her, but I can't.

Then she suddenly gives out a big sigh, rolls over,

buries her face in my chest and says, "What have we *done*?"

I stroke her shiny dark hair. All I can think of is a crap joke. "You mean you don't know the name for it?"

She butts my chest with her forehead. "Don't be stupid! God, I don't know how that happened. I never meant for that to happen."

I go kind of cold. "You mean you're sorry?"

"*No*. Yes. I don't know. Where's the bathroom?"

I point, silently, and she swivels round and out of bed, picking up her shirt and slinging it on as she stands up. Then she picks up her bag. Then she disappears into the bathroom.

I'm left in bed, crushed. I don't understand. That was *fantastic*. It was so fantastic it had to have been good for her too, right? How can she snap back to reality so fast? I'm still floating up in the ether. I've forgotten everything – I've forgotten – *SHIT!! I've forgotten Bonny!* Who could've at any time marched in through the door and – *shit*!

I scramble off the bed, pull on my boxers and jeans, shake out the duvet. Then I look up at Bonny's bedroom door. She could be *in* there. She could've heard *everything*. A bit better than actually walking in on us, but only just . . . I swallow hard, head over to her door, knock, get no answer, and open it. The room's empty. Wonderfully, blessedly empty.

I shut the door again and exhale, long and shaky, standing there half naked in the middle of the huge room. We got away with it, this time. But how am I going to work it if there's a next time?

Don't count on there being a next time, Steele. Portia didn't seem too impressed, did she? I can hear the sound of the shower coming from the bathroom. Washing me away. I gather up Portia's clothes and go over to the bathroom door and rap on it.

"Portia – you want your gear?" I figure I can't explain about Bonny through the door, but I needn't have worried. Three seconds later the bolt's snapped back and a wet hand shoots silently out and takes the clothes. Then the door's bolted again.

Oh, *shit*. Something major is wrong here. I mean – why's she locked me out? Why can't I go in there and help her soap up?

I stomp into the kitchen all anxious and upset, and for want of something to do, fill the kettle. Then I hear the bathroom door open again, and Portia walks into the kitchen. I'm too scared to look round. I'm too scared of what it might say on her face. Then like a miracle two hands make their sinuous way round my chest and she says, right into my ear, "So how's the ace lay then?"

"*What?*" I'm so happy my voice comes out like a squeak.

"You heard. And you *know* you are."

I turn round, grin at her. She's looking all

polished again, hair brushed, clothes done up, lipstick on, almost like nothing's happened. "You look *fabulous*," I say. I can't believe I've just been in bed with this creature. I can't believe my luck.

"Well, don't let this go to your head, but I feel pretty fabulous. Hmmm. Are you making coffee there?"

"Yup. Or tea. Anything you want."

"God, I'm hungry. Got anything to eat?"

"Well, there's bread. I think it's a bit stale but I could toast it."

"What you got to put on it?"

But before I can answer, there's a rattle at the flat door and then it opens and Bonny walks in.

Chapter 15

"**S**he's got a *key*!" squeals Portia.

"Yeah, she's um – she's staying here—"

"*What?*" Portia turns and glares at me, a distillation of rage and indignation.

"Portia, it's nothing – she's staying in the bedroom over there – she ran out on her mum and—"

Bonny's crossed the room, she's standing in the kitchen door, laden with glossy bulging carrier bags.

"Oh," she says, when she clocks Portia. "Hi."

"Hi," says Portia, frozen as an ice storm. "I was just going."

Then she sweeps past the pair of us and out through the flat door, slamming it behind her.

I'm after her like a shot. *No way*, I'm thinking. *No way. You're not running out on me for a second time. Not now we've – not now we're –* I get out the door just in time to see the roof of the lift cage sinking out of sight, and I helter-skelter off down the stairs. I hit the ground floor the same time as the lift and I reach the iron gate just as Portia is heaving it open. I grab it, stop her opening it up any further, doing this hench Samson thing with my left arm, filling the gap with my body, keeping her caged.

"Get out of my *way*," she spits, pushing at me, but I don't budge.

"Not till you've heard me out," I go. "God – d'you always overreact like this, Portia?"

"*Overreact?*" she shrieks. "A girl lets herself into your place just after we've made *love* and you say I *overreact?*"

"Look – can we go back upstairs?" I hiss. I'm suddenly aware I'm standing there in the main entrance, barefoot, bare chested.

"No! Let me past!"

"God, Portia, you're being completely fucking imbalanced! D'you always have to believe the worst or something? I told you – Bonny ran away from her mad mother, and she had nowhere else to stay, and this place belongs to Nick and Barb, it wasn't up to me whether she stayed or not –"

"Yeah? Yeah? Well if it's that innocent, how come you didn't tell me, eh?"

"I forgot –"

"Oh great. You *forgot*. She could've walked in at any time while we were on your bed and you *forgot!*"

"Yeah! I forgot! I forgot because *you* were completely filling my mind, OK?"

Another masterstroke. There's a brief pause. "Believe me, Portia, I'd've forgotten if I'd had a fucking *army* staying with me," I say, just to make sure I've got the point across. "Now can we go back up? I'm getting cold."

"You sure she's not your girlfriend?" Portia sniffs.

"Oh, come on. Look at yourself. Then look at her. D'you really need to ask?"

That was a bit of a shitty thing to say, but it works a treat. Portia sniffs again, and I risk letting go of the gate and putting my arm round her neck. Then I rest my forehead against hers and say, "I'm sorry. I'm sorry I forgot about Bonny. You made me forget. OK? *OK?*"

"OK," she mumbles.

I'm quite glad that Bonny's still in the kitchen when we get back, making herself a mug of coffee. I say "Hi, Bonny. You've met Portia, haven't you? My girlfriend?" and Bonny does this frozen lopsided smile at me and turns to Portia and says, "Yes. Hi."

Crisis over. There's a long pause. Bonny's staring at my chest, no doubt wondering why I'm flashing it about. I sidle over to the bed, collect my shirt from the floor, put it on.

"So how long are you staying here?" Portia asks Bonny, in this queenly voice.

"Not sure," shrugs Bonny.

"It must be a bit awkward," says Portia. "Sharing with a guy."

"Compared to what I've been used to it's heaven," Bonny says.

"*I* thought your mum was really great."

"Yeah, well, you saw her *once*. At a party. She is great at parties. It's all the other times she's poison. Anyway – I'll leave you to it, OK?" Then Bonny picks up her mug, collects her glossy carrier bags from where she dumped them by the kitchen door, and goes into her bedroom, shutting the door just a little more loudly than she needs to.

Portia turns to me. "She *fancies* you," she hisses.

"What makes you say that?" I ask, preening.

"The way she was looking at you. The way she was with me."

"Yeah, well – I think she does a bit."

"A *bit*? *God*. Talk about an atmosphere."

"I expect she felt embarrassed. I mean – it was a bit *obvious* things had been going on."

"Only because you forgot to get dressed properly."

"Nah – more than that. It's in the vibes, Portia."

"Don't talk shit."

"OK, OK – it was the way you acted when she walked in."

"Oh *fine*. Blame *me*. How d'you expect me to act when I find out you're living with another girl?"

"Keep your voice down – she'll hear!"

"And why should you care if she does?"

"'Cos – 'cos it's *embarrassing*, OK, Portia? I mean – whether I like it or not, she's here. Look – d'you wanna go out or something?"

"Why should we let *her* drive us out?" spits Portia. "Anyway, you promised me coffee. And *toast*."

"OK, OK, let's do it."

"Actually I'd sooner have a beer."

"I think there's some in the fridge – Bonny got some the other night when—"

"Oh, how *sweet*," snaps Portia. "You share food. D'you have a *kitty* or something?"

She's jealous. *She's jealous!* I try to keep this humungous smirk off my face, and say "No. Nothing like that. Portia – if you *knew* how much I wish I still had this place to myself. . ."

"Look – your domestic arrangements aren't my business. Have you got any cheese?"

I know there's some in the fridge, and that's Bonny's, but I don't say anything, because I'm knackered with the effort of just trying to keep the whole situation sweet. I just get a couple of cans and a slab of cheese out, telling myself I'll square up later. Then I make the toast while Portia hacks great slices off the cheese and lays it on the toast. Then we take it all over to the bed and I open the big windows because the afternoon has got really warm.

"Oh, *God,*" squeals Portia. "How can you do that – how can you stand so near the edge there?"

"It's great. Come and see the view."

"No," snaps Portia, "I'd faint."

"You won't fall – I'll hold your hand."

"I don't trust you. Come and sit down over here." And she sits on the far side of the bed, away from the window, and pulls the ring on her can of beer.

I sit down on the bed next to her and this fantastic, sleepy, relaxed feeling comes over me. It's been one hell of a Saturday. I lay myself down, propped on one elbow, and the memory of making love with her rises up and engulfs me. I take a bite of toast. I don't want the toast, I want to make love to her again. Maybe she does too. After all, she called me an ace lay didn't she? I sit up again, lean up against her, nuzzle into her neck.

"Gerroff," she says through a mouthful.

"Aw, come on, Portia. Isn't it great here in the sun? I could get back into bed, couldn't you?"

"What, with your boring little flatmate about to burst in on us any minute?"

"We could just sleep. We could just get into bed and sleep here in the sun, and when we wake up it'll be dark and we can make *fantastic* love again. . ."

I'm just trying to get Portia's ear between my teeth when Bonny's door opens again, and she walks out. Portia snorts, pushes me away, takes another long swig of beer.

Bonny's *transformed*. She usually has her hair all drooping round her face, but she's clipped it up and it's looking all stylish, and she's wearing these sharp silver earrings and a rusty-coloured jacket, some great trousers and high-heeled boots. She looks full of energy. Sparking with it.

She hurries over to the front door like she thinks we wish she'd disappear, and opens it, then she turns and says, "I'll be back really late, OK? Bye!" and shuts it behind her without waiting for an answer.

"So *that's* what she had in those expensive carrier bags," says Portia sourly. "Lucky cow. Where's she get all her money from?"

"Daddy," I say.

"*God.* It's *so unfair*."

"I don't think she's that loaded. I think she's just been on a bit of a spree, celebrating her new freedom."

"*God.* Some people have *all* the luck. Although that jacket didn't really suit her. Did you think?"

"It'd look better on you. *Everyone's* clothes would look better on you." I'm nuzzling into her neck. "Or off you."

"I'm so *sick* of my old gear."

"Portia you've got stacks of clothes!"

"I haven't had anything *new* for ages."

"You've got me," I say, taking her plate away from her. "I'm new."

"Don't be stupid. Give that back, I haven't finished."

"*No.* How can you think about food?"

"Give it back!"

"She's gone. We've got the whole place to ourselves. You heard what she said. We can get back into bed, and we can sleep and then make love, or we can make love and then sleep. . ."

Portia leans over me, snatches up her last bit of toast, and I grab her and roll her backwards. Then I start this thing I do that's sent her crazy before, kissing her fast all up her neck, and she laughs, and I think – I'm winning, I'm *winning* – she shifts to the side, puts her arms round my neck – I'm *really winning* – then I move forward to kiss her on the mouth but before I get there she lets out a horrible shriek like a parrot having its tail feathers ripped out.

It damn nearly does me *in.* "*Jesus,* Portia, what the *hell* –"

"I just caught sight of my watch!" she cries. "*Oh – my – God!* It's nearly six o'clock!" And she chucks me off her and wriggles off the bed and jumps to her feet.

"So? What does the time matter? *Jesus.* Did you have to screech like that? *God.* It's like aversion therapy. I won't be able to kiss anyone ever again. As soon as I'm close to their lips I'll hear that noise in my head and –"

"*Look*, Richy, stop *blithering*! You've got to shower. And change. Wear that gorgeous blue shirt, the one that makes your eyes look sexy. And your leather coat. And pick me up – *no*. Tony's probably staked out the house. The Rose and Crown, yeah? That's where you boys meet up, isn't it? And it's quite near the golf club. Eight o'clock."

"*What* are you going on about?"

"I have to go. I've got less than *two hours* to get home and get ready and get back to meet you again . . . And I don't even know what I'm *wearing* yet!"

And she grabs her bag and stalks off towards the door. "*Portia!*" I wail.

She spins round like she wants to slap me one. "Look, just *be* there, OK? I told you about the party didn't I?"

"No!"

"Oh. Look – it's Sondra's eighteenth. She's booked out the golf club. *Everyone's* going. It's going to be *fa-abulous*. Except I'm going to be in such a *rush*. See you around eight, OK?"

And she's gone out the door without even kissing me goodbye.

Chapter 16

"Why don't girls care about the real things in life, huh?"

"You mean like sex?" says Ollie.

"Yeah. No. I just mean – they've got their priorities wrong. They really have."

I've really enjoyed the last half-hour in the Rose and Crown. When I turned up, just Ollie and Ryan were there, and Ollie guessed immediately that this time I hadn't backed off from Portia. So I didn't feel too disloyal filling them in on some of the details. Nothing sleazy – I'm not that sort of a bloke. Just things like her saying I was an ace lay. But when I get round to telling them about the party tonight, I realize there's this dissatisfaction niggling at me, and it's rooted in the fact that Portia seemed to be far more excited at the thought of the stupid party than she was about the thought of making love with me for a second time.

Or even – if I'm honest – for a first time.

"That's birds, man," says Ollie, all world-weary and knowing. "They have different priorities to us."

"I don't know what you're moaning about," moans Ryan. "Bloody hell. She *slept* with you didn't she?"

"Yeah," I agree, "it's just – *God*. We had the whole place to ourselves. Why couldn't she give this stupid party a miss?"

"Girls like to parade, man," says Ollie, mournfully. "With their friends. They like to dance and stuff."

Ollie likes to dance too, but with him it's not parading, it's foreplay. I smile at him, all sexually-experienced man to sexually-experienced man, and Ryan (who isn't) stands up and heads off to the bog. I lean across the table and mutter, "You ever had a girl who wanted to shower the minute you'd finished?"

"God, man, is that what's bugging you?"

"She came out all lipsticked up, like we hadn't been doing anything."

"She just wanted to look good for you. Relax. Enjoy it."

"Yeah. Yeah – I will. But she seems – I dunno. She said how great it was, then she seemed really ratty, really touchy. . ."

"Birds sometimes do that, too," says Ollie, nodding sagely. "You tell her you love her?"

I'm gobsmacked at the thought. "*No!*"

"You ought to've done, man. After, and everything."

"Well, she didn't give me *time*. . ."

"And then when this other bird Bonny turns up – *well*, that'd sour her, wouldn't it?"

"I s'pose."

"You said you thought she was jealous. That is *good*." Ollie sits back, grins at me. "You just want to enjoy it, Rich-*ard*! When's she supposed to be arriving?"

I check my watch. She's only ten minutes late. Which for Portia is nothing.

I've followed her instructions to the letter – I've even had another shave. I'm a bit worried that this is the third time I've worn my best shirt without getting round to washing it but it's OK under my jacket with an extra load of aftershave. I'm geared up for the night all right. It'll be the first time we've been really out together. Boyfriend and girlfriend. *Lovers*, I think, and I go all gooey and hot just at the name.

Then Ryan gets back to the table, and the pub door swings open, and Andy and Matt walk in, followed close by Chris and Natalie, whose relationship is clearly on again. Natalie is wound round Chris likes she wants to take root on him and Chris is looking kind of pleased and proud and embarrassed all at the same time.

Natalie is one of those raunchy, slightly geezer-looking girls Chris has always gone for and I haven't – which is useful, seeing as we used to do a lot of pulling together. I like Natalie though – she's a laugh. She's got a blistering tongue when she gets going, and it cracks you up – unless it's turned on you of course.

We all call out hello and how you doing and fight about who owes who a drink and pretty soon the seven of us are crowded round the little pub table discussing our plans for the night. My announcement that I'm off to Sondra's eighteenth birthday party causes a great gale of derisive laughter from Natalie.

"Not *Sondra Harvey. God.* What a complete Barbie. The party'll be *crap*, Rich. All cocktails and balloons and crap music. I can't *believe* you're going there."

"It's his woman," Ollie explains, fatalistically. "The Porsche is taking him along."

"Well, blimey," says Matt, impressed despite himself, "you finally pulled her did you?"

"Yup," I say, and I exchange a meaningful look across the table with Chris which means – *talk later*.

"Well, where is she then?" asks Natalie.

"She'll be here," I say, and I check my watch. It's eight-twenty. The first fingerings of fear clutch at my guts. Suppose she doesn't show?

Natalie turns her attention to Chris again, grabbing his hand and rubbing her face against his shoulder. "Christopher, why has your friend got such *crap taste*," she says, "when you've got such *brilliant* taste?"

"Dunno," says Chris, smooching back at her. "Something in his childhood I reckon."

And then the pub door swings open again, and Portia makes her entrance, and it seems like most of the noise in the pub evaporates with shock.

I'm pretty shocked too. Even more shocked than relieved that she's shown.

Portia has gone all-out for major glitz and glamour. She's gone all exotic with her eye make-up, and her hair is slicked back from her face. But it's the dress that's the real killer. It's *tiny*. It covers up skin you expect to see – like her throat and her forearms – and reveals prodigious amounts of bits usually kept hidden. She's got very high-heeled shoes on and her legs look amazing, unreal, like they've walked out of a strip-cartoon.

"Bloody hell," mutters Ryan.

"That's underwear!" grins Ollie.

"What – a – *slag*," Natalie breathes. "Like she's going to the Rubber Ball."

"What's the Rubber Ball?" gasps Ryan. He's goggling like a maniac.

"A fetishist's convention," snaps Natalie. "Don't look so excited, they wouldn't let *you* in."

I stand up, and walk over to claim Portia. I know enough about Portia's mindset already to know she likes being *claimed*. Publicly, passionately, showily. I do this, without smudging her lippie too much, which I know she hates, and lead her over to the table.

I tell her she looks absolutely great, but I'm still too stunned to know if that's true or not. She looks so *extreme*. I've always had fantasies about squiring about the kind of girl that makes every guy's head turn, but now it's actually happening it's kind of weird. I decide we should get to the party as quickly as possible, where she might not stand out so much, or at least not so many people will know me. "You want a drink?" I ask.

"Sure!" she says loudly, generally, as though she expects everyone to be listening to her answer. "Just one, yeah? Then we must *rush*, Richy – I don't want to be late – she'll've opened all her prezzies."

"What have you got her?" I ask loudly, to drown out the vomiting noise Natalie's making behind her hand, and I nod at the little pink-wrapped box Portia's put down on the pub table.

"Oh – the most a-*dor*-able silver bracelet. It cost a *heap*. Well – it's from Jenny too. But I chose it. I wanted something that would last, you know? And remind her of *me*. Us. You know – for *ever*."

I daren't look at Natalie and Chris. I slide up to the bar, get Portia her drink. When I get back she's taken my seat but she jumps up and pushes me on to it, then she perches on my knee. She's showing off, but it's still quite a turn on. I put my arm round her waist and look down at her perfect cartoon legs lying against mine.

"So – what are you all up to?" Portia says, wriggling back against me. "Just a boring old night in the pub?"

"Why d'you assume that?" asks Chris, needled.

"Well, you're not exactly dressed for anything more interesting are you?"

"I've got a frock a bit like yours in my bag, actually," says Natalie. "Thought I'd change in the bog—"

"*Why?*" shrieks Portia, not realizing Natalie's taking the piss. "God, I couldn't be bothered to get dressed twice. If people want to stare, that's their problem."

Natalie's looking at Portia like half of her wants to laugh and the other half wants to lay her out.

"Come on, Portia," I say, "drink up and let's get to the party."

I veto catching a bus. I can't face it. Well – the footie crowd might be on it, mightn't it? I lend her my leather jacket but that looks even raunchier, like she's got nothing on underneath. About ten different guys whistle her as we're strolling along, and I kind of spin round loose-fisted to glare them out, but as they're obsessively ogling Portia's legs they don't catch the impact. I shout "Fuck off!" at the ones on their own but the big gangs I leave alone. Portia doesn't seem to care or even notice. It's probably all just background music to her.

As we walk, Portia tells me that Sondra's dad is a member of the golf club which is why she's pulled off the all-time scoop of hiring the big Events Room for her bash. Portia's dead excited. She can't really walk very fast in her towering shoes, but she totters along as speedily as she can. As we go she answers her mobile twice and says "Sorr-*eee*! I'm on my way!"

As I expect, the golf club is all up-itself and pompous with a big, space-wasting entrance lobby covered in dark wood panelling and portraits of old men. Over to one side there's a display stand holding up a board with *Sondra's Party* written on it in fancy rainbow lettering, and an arrow pointing the way. Underneath are pasted two big photos: one of Sondra as a frilly baby and one of her as she is today in a sultry pose that makes her look dim-witted and pouty.

"Oh *sweet*!" coos Portia, towing me past. "God – I can't believe it – she's *eighteen*!"

What I can't believe is I'm here as Portia's *boyfriend*. Me. The guy who used to cut his own hair. I try and contain my excitement as I lope along the corridor after Portia's stunning form. Although – aside from being with Portia of course – I've got the strongest feeling the whole party is going to be a colossal drag. All I can think about is how I can get Portia on her own. Whether we can slope off somewhere and make it together again. Whether I can get her away early and back to my flat and maybe barricade Bonny out until at least two in the morning. . .

We reach the party room. Jenny, Portia's sycophantic best mate, is lurking just inside. Jenny screams, "Porshy you look *GORGEOUS*!" and then they both kind of fall on each other and kiss each other on the face a lot, and then Jenny looks up and sees me and screams again.

"I *KNOW!*" Portia screams back at her. "Tell you later!"

"Oh – my – *God*!" Jenny's going. "Oh – my – *GOD*!"

"I know, I KNOW! It all just – HAPPENED!"

"Is this why you're so *late*?"

"Yup – blame *him*!" she shrieks, and giggles suggestively. I want to say, "Hang on, Portia, we were only in the pub," but I can sense this would not fit with the impression the Porsche is trying to create, which is one of unbridled lust and uncontrollable passion. So I raise one eyebrow, Bond-style, and try to look like I've been slowing things up by ravishing her all along the high street, and Portia giggles again and takes my arm and presses up really close then she turns to Jenny and says, "Come on – let's give Sondra her prezzie," and we move on into the guts of the party.

For the next ten minutes or so I'm Silent Escort Man. All Portia's friends mob her and scream *"What's happened to TONY?"* and Portia kind of winds herself tighter round my body and rolls her eyes and acts like I'm such a stud she just couldn't help herself, and I have to remind myself to *breathe*. Nobody talks to me, they just goggle at me and scream at Portia. I'm mainlining on Portia's body pressing up against mine. I've got my arm round her waist in this casual-possessive way and this *grin* on my face. The whole thing is one big all-out massage to my battered old ego, but it's a bit unreal too. We're really hemmed in and I'm starting to need a drink. After a bit we move on in and find Sondra and there's a lot more screaming and kissing when she gets given her little pink box, and then more when she pulls out the little silver bracelet and then it takes both Portia and Jenny and two other girls to fasten it to her wrist. . .

I'm beginning to get a headache. I'm beginning to *really* need a drink. I'm just about to interrupt Portia to tell her this when the crap phoney DJ at the end of the room says "OK, everybody, we're all here to have FUN – the party starts HERE!" and sticks some very loud music on.

"Come on," carols Sondra, "I want *everyone* to dance!" And *everyone* moves off in a jolly group en route to the dance floor. On the way, I manage to steer Portia off sideways to get a drink at the bar.

We're served by a very bad-tempered old man, and I have to *pay*.

"God," I grumble, as the old git chucks very little change from the fiver I gave him back on the counter, "you'd think they'd at least *subsidize* the drinks."

"Oh, don't be so miserable," snaps Portia. "You can't expect Sondra to pay for *everything*."

Or Portia for anything, I think, as I glug into my beer. But who cares. Then Portia takes my half-empty glass from my hand, slams it down next to her glass on a nearby table, and tows me on to the dance floor. I can't dance – I'm no good at it, never have been. Portia doesn't seem to care though. I sway about a bit while she goes into this amazing, sexy, twitchy routine all round me. A bit like pole dancing with me as the pole. It's one hell of a turn on. Everyone near us is watching her, keeping their eyes on her. She dances on and on. And I'm getting thirstier and hotter by the minute.

She won't let me take my leather jacket off. "Oh, Richy, keep it on, you look so *great* in it," she hisses, and starts gyrating all round me again.

Two records go by, three. I'm going to pass out with heat and horniness if this doesn't stop. I'm eyeing my beer in desperation now, left alone on the table up against the wall, getting as warm as I am. "Hey," I say, reaching out to catch her by the arm, "hey."

"What?" she asks. And she dances up so close you couldn't get a Rizla between us.

"Let's move off to the side for a bit, ay?"

"Don't you like my dancing?"

"The trouble is, Portia," I say all smooth, "I like it *too much*. Isn't there anywhere we can be alone here?"

"Rich-*ard*! We're at a *party*!" she squeals, but she lets me propel her over to my beer, which I finish in double-quick time, and I'm just about to suggest a wander outside in the cool night air when a whole gaggle of her friends surround her and I'm shoved off to the side as Silent Escort Man again.

Once more, Portia's centre stage. She keeps leaning in close with everyone, whispering, then she pulls back and laughs out loud. Everyone's going on about how great she looks and how *terrible* and *daring* she is to dump Tony and grab me, and then telling her how great she looks again. I stand there like a stupid shop-window dummy watching her being gorgeous, watching her move and laugh and being idolized, and I want her even more.

Sod it. Sod this hanging about. She's *mine* now, isn't she? And I still can't quite believe it but I've got the right to touch her whenever I want to now, haven't I?

'Hey – Portia?" I call, in my deepest voice.

She flicks her head round at me. "Yeah?"

'Come on – I need some air."

It's worked before, when I've pulled the domineering hard man, and it works now. I knew it would – she's on this trip about being blown away by me, atomized by the passion between us, so she can hardly tell me to sod off can she? She undulates through her gaggle of friends and winds her arms round my neck. "*Sowwy*, darling," she says in a Tweetypie voice. "Was you getting bored?"

"Very," I say. "Come on." And I put my arm round her shoulders and steer her towards a little green illuminated exit sign at the back of the big room.

"I don't want to go out there," she says peevishly. "It'll be *cold*."

"It's not. Just for a minute. Come on."

A few other people have had the same idea, which means the door's already ajar and it's easy to hustle Portia through it. We step out on to a broad terrace, lit up by some poncy lamp posts and the lights from a window upstairs.

"What d'you want to be out here for?" she moans.

"Why d'you think?" I go, all romantic hero, and I kind of scoop her up into my arms. I can tell she's irritated but she's decided not to show it. She lets me nuzzle at her neck, she wraps her arms round me and I smell her hair and I'm swamped by the memory of how she'd wrapped her whole body round me only a few short hours ago, and I'd pushed inside her, and moved with her, and I want to do it again so much I'm rigid with it, I can't speak.

"Oh, God – don't you want to?" I mutter.

She kisses me to shut me up.

"Don't you?" I say again.

"Yes," she says, unconvincingly. "But we're at a *party*, Richy."

"Let's go for a walk," I mutter. "Down that path there." It leads into some trees. Maybe we could . . . maybe. . .

"No," she snaps. "Come on – I'm going in. I'm *cold*."

And she flounces back through the door, confident I'll follow. Which I do, of course. She turns back to me and smiles when she sees me following her and holds out her hand for me to take. Which I do, of course. Maybe I was being a shit, trying to hustle her for sex. It's just – how can I want her so much it's like some kind of fever affecting my brain and all she cares about is strutting about in here? We could've at least *kissed* for a bit longer, couldn't we?

She tows me back on to the dance floor, waving hi to just about everyone as we weave our way through. The crap DJ has put a slow number on because it's getting near going-home time, and Portia goes into overload again, right up close to me, reaching up and putting her arms round my neck and drawing my face down to hers, and then we're kissing like our lives depend on it, and I'm appeased, I'm happy, except somewhere at the back of my mind this voice is going – *Portia's got her audience back.*

The end of the party is real crude and abrupt. The clock hits twelve-thirty. The music stops. The DJ makes some creepy announcement about hoping we all get home safely. And then all the lights go on.

Everyone blinks round as their eyeballs dilate, and heads for the darkness of outside. Portia's group of sycophants surround her like the tide coming in, and then all the girls flow over to Sondra standing glowing on the golf-club steps to tell her what a brilliant, *brilliant* party it's been.

"My *dad*'s here," says Jenny, apologetically, waving half-heartedly at a large Ford just rolling into the car park. "He insisted. Anyone want a lift?"

Among a chorus of "Yeah please!", Portia turns to me. "How are we getting back?"

"I dunno. We can walk into town, the last bus might not've—"

She spins back to Jenny. "Yes please, Jen! Hang on!" Then she grabs me, chews my mouth briefly and says, "You don't mind do you, Richy? Only these shoes – if I walk one more inch in them, I swear I'll die. It's been *fa-abulous*, yeah? Phone me!"

And without waiting for me to answer she scrambles into the single space left for her in the wide back-seat, and like an idiot I shout "Take care, yeah?" while she's shutting the door, and she smiles and flips her hand at me through the window, and the car pulls slowly away down the long gravel drive.

Chapter 17

I feel like shit. I feel like someone in a desert who's just had a brimming glass of cold water snatched from his crusty lips. I think briefly of running after the car, jumping on the back of it, hammering on the window shouting "PORTIA, COME BACK!" I don't, of course. I set out instead to walk all the way back to the flat. I reckon if I walk fast it'll be a bit like a cold shower on my libido, plus all the stuff mushing about in my head will sort itself out and I'll feel clear about things, I'll feel better.

I made all these assumptions, that's the problem. I thought – no, to be honest I *didn't* think, not at all, not once Portia told me she'd ditched Tony and we ended up back at my place in bed together. I mean – blimey – what's there to think about? I just assumed that now we'd be girlfriend and boyfriend and *involved*.

I don't *feel* involved though. Not walking home at one in the morning all on my own I don't. Not when we hadn't exactly *been together* at the party. And I don't mean made it together, although I wanted that so much it kind of skewed my brain, I mean . . . I mean . . . shit, what *do* I mean?

I scuff along and I wonder what my mates would make of it. I think of Ryan's face all screwed up with disbelief at the fact that I'm pissed off and that cheers me up a bit. "Bloody hell," he'd say. "You get to go to bed with one of the classiest girls at college and she takes you along to her friend's party and she's all over you in front of everyone and you're *pissed off*?" And Ollie would say, "That's real status, man. Enjoy it."

And I did enjoy it, I did, the whole day, the whole night, but . . . but . . . oh shit. I might've slept with her but somehow I haven't got through to her, I haven't rattled her self-containment, I don't figure in her life.

I might've slept with her, but she's still Portia, isn't she?

The car park in front of the flat's pitch-black when I trudge up to it. The canal looks snaky and sinister, like a waterlogged face might rise to its surface any minute. I hurry over the gravel, getting my key out as I go and then I look up and jolt with shock because there's someone standing there, a black shape, just standing there motionless in the shadows by the big glass doors.

It's Tony, I'm sure it's Tony. He's followed me, he's seen me wrapped round Portia with my tongue in her ear and now he's going to beat me to a bloody pulp with the metal bar he's got stashed behind his back and then scrape me up and tip me into the canal. . . I stand stock still, heart hammering, mouth drying, and then the black shape speaks.

"Rich?" it says, in a tiny quaver. "That you?"

"Yeah?" I reply, while everything in me kind of sags with relief. It's Bonny. The shape steps out from the wall. Definitely Bonny.

"*Shit,*" she's saying. "Oh, *shit,* I was scared. I'd just got my key out and then I heard you coming up behind me and I couldn't *move.*"

"*You* were scared? I thought you were Portia's jealous ex-boyfriend."

"Well, *you* sounded like Frankenstein's monster, coming towards me."

"Well, *cheers.* You saying I've got big feet?"

"God, I'm glad it's you. God, I was scared."

"What you doing coming back all on your own?" I say, putting my key in the lock and pushing the big glass doors open. Bonny follows me into the hall, watches as I turn on the lights and de-activate the security system, but she doesn't answer me.

"You ought to get someone to see you back, Bonny, it's dead isolated out here. Suppose it had been Frankenstein's monster? Or some *real* monster?"

I turn to the lift, press the button. I suddenly get

the feeling she's really upset about something, trying not to cry. "You all right?" I gruff out.

"Yes," she whispers.

"You're not, are you." The lift clanks to a halt, and I pull back the gate and usher her in the cage, and then we're clanking off up to the top floor. She won't look at me. We get inside the flat and I lock the door behind us and say, "If I make you some of your hot chocolate can I have some too?"

She smiles at that, says yes please, and we plod into the kitchen. I don't put the big overhead light on, just this little glowy one at the top of the cooker, because I reckon she won't want to be all lit up if she's in a state.

"Going to tell me what happened?" I say.

"Nothing," she says, in this choky voice. "Just a crap evening."

"Join the club," I say, before I realize what I'm saying.

"But you're back with Portia!"

"Yeah, yeah, I know. I didn't mean – we went to a crap party, that's all. What did you do?"

"Oh – this guy I met, ages ago. We'd been out once or twice, but nothing serious. . . He's quite a bit older than me. He got in touch via one of my mates, he was all concerned 'cos he'd phoned and got Mum and she'd told him the whole drama. . . *Anyway*. He said he'd take me out to dinner. Which I thought was really nice."

"But it wasn't?"

"No."

The kettle clicks off, and I start making the hot chocolate, only I'm doing it wrong apparently because Bonny silently takes the spoon off me and finishes it off herself. "Why wasn't it?" I ask.

"Because he was a prat, that's why. We started to talk and I thought – wow, this is amazing, he actually cares about what's happened to me. And then a whole group of his friends came in the wine bar we were in. And they start all this "wow you old dark horse, you cradle snatcher" stuff. And I'm waiting for them to clear off but they don't, they buy more wine. So then I'm waiting for him to suggest we go, but he doesn't, he asks for the sodding *menu,* and suddenly everyone's glugging back wine and all this food arrives, and they're all talking and I'm totally, completely out of it, and he keeps putting his arm round me and hugging me as though that's all I need to keep me happy, and then they all want to go to a club, and he does too, and I say I don't want to, so he calls me a cab."

"Bastard," I say.

Bonny looks at me. "You think?" she says.

"Yeah. Letting his friends bust in on you like that."

"Maybe he was trying to cheer me up."

"He didn't ask you, though, did he. It was all what *he* wanted."

There's a pause, and we both pick up our mugs and take a sip. We're standing very close 'cos there's no space to do anything else, me leaning against the fridge, her against the kitchen counter. I think about suggesting we should go into the big room, but I don't want to stop her talking.

"It really pissed me off," she says, "the way he changed when his mates turned up. It was like he was just using me to show off then." She sighs, and I can't see properly in the dark kitchen, but it looks like her eyes are filling up. "I really needed to talk, too," she said. "It had all suddenly . . . *got* to me. About Mum and . . . and everything. I suddenly feel so *fucking* guilty about running out like I did. . ."

"Hey – what d'you mean? You did the right thing. You know you did."

"Yeah. Maybe. It felt right, at first. It felt fantastic, like getting out of jail, like having my head straight for once. But . . . I dunno. I've been thinking about her. Worrying."

I take another slurp of chocolate and say, "Bonny, if all this is leading up to trying to get me to go and see your loony mother again –"

Bonny groans out a laugh. "No. No, Rich, I wouldn't *dare*. This next stage is down to me. I mean – I've got to see her again sometime, haven't I?"

"Yeah, I s'pose. But not yet. You know – you're only thinking this way 'cos you've got it all sorted."

"What d'you mean?"

"Well – you've *done* it! You've escaped. And it's OK at school, and you've sorted the money with your old man, and you've found yourself a fantastic flat with an amazingly fabulous flatmate –"

"Who'd like to chuck me out –"

"Now don't exaggerate! What I'm saying is – everything's OK. Which means you've got nothing to fight for. Which means you've got time to feel guilty. But don't."

Bonny smiles across at me. "You're really quite intelligent, aren't you?"

"Yup."

"You hide it, but you're intelligent."

"Don't take the piss. What I'm saying is right."

She laughs. "Yeah, I think it is. It's like I've paused for breath and – *wham*. All this comes in. But – I dunno. I am going to have to face her one day. Right after I cleared out I thought – that's it, never again. But I can't do that. I do love her. And even if she was hopeless, she did care about *me*. . ."

"Bonny, I don't think she *saw* you. Not *you*. Not who you really are."

There's a weird silence then, and I feel like I've crossed some line, some boundary, and I feel very uncomfortable, and I pick up my mug and turn and wander out into the main room, saying as I go, "I've got to sort things with my folks too. I can't let another week go by."

Bonny follows me. "What you going to do?"

"I dunno. Go round. Tomorrow. My old man goes to the pub Sunday lunchtime, every bloody week he goes, I'll go round then, see Mum, see what's what." I'm a bit amazed when that exits my mouth, because it's the first time it's occurred to me. But it makes sense. I ought to go.

"You could stay on with them, for lunch," Bonny says, a bit wistfully.

"That depends on whether Mum thinks it's reconciliation time or not. I said some pretty shitty things to the old man the last time we spoke. Well – yelled."

"I've never shouted at Mum," says Bonny, even more wistfully. "I've never let myself get out of control with her, you know? I knew if I did I'd . . . *God*, I'd. . ."

"Well, maybe you should. Maybe that's what you ought to do when you next see her. So she really understands why you ran out on her, and everything."

Bonny's shaking her head. "I couldn't. It would be too – it would be *terrible*. Totally destructive."

I shrug, and suddenly the conversation's over. Bonny says, "Look, I'll be five minutes in the bathroom, OK?" and I nod, and throw myself down on my bed to wait for my turn.

I'm kind of kicking myself for being so nice to her. I'm thinking – if I'm this nice, when's she ever going to go? Still, I didn't tell her how good she looked in her new clothes, did I.

And I'd sort of meant to, because she really did.

Chapter 18

I wake up early the next day, and I'm all in on myself. I've pushed Portia aside as altogether too churning-up and complex to deal with, and I'm dwelling instead on the basic things in life. I check my wallet, feel sick at its emptiness, decide I've got to get Nick to give me some more storyboards to do. Then I check my college diary, feel sicker at its *fullness*, realize if I don't get back down to work I'll be yanked into the principal's office by the scruff of my neck to watch him tear up my time extension. So what I do is pull on some clothes, swipe some more of Bonny's horrible muesli stuff, get a big mug of sweet tea, lie down on my stomach on my bed with my books on the floor in front of me – and get down to it.

Try to get down to it. Lying on the bed like that

brings Portia back full force. I don't see my books, I see her, her face underneath me. I twist round, lie on my side. I get up, go to the bathroom. Then I get down to it.

It's great, with the windows wide open and this weedy, reedy canal smell coming in, and no weekday noise down below. After a bit, I actually concentrate. I read round, and make a few notes, and then I get this adequate draft put together that I reckon Barb will help me pull into shape.

I'm on a roll now. I pull out my graphics file, find some big sheets of paper and then I actually read through the assignment properly and do something that fits the description, which is a bit of a first for me. I usually can't be bothered, or even if I can I still go off on a tangent somewhere else. Huw's pretty liberal about this – "*More of your deranged doodlings, lad? Still, not completely without talent, are they? They'll do*" – but the graphics guy is much more of a stickler. This time though, he won't be able to accuse my stuff of "*bearing absolutely no relation whatsoever to the topic set*". This time, he'd better give me an A, the bastard.

I'm just finishing off some ideas for different sorts of packaging when I get this prickly feeling along my shoulders, and when I look round Bonny's standing there in the door of the bedroom. She's got this slightly scary intent expression on her face.

"Hi," I say, grumpily.

"Sorry," she goes. "Don't let me disturb you."

"I won't," I say, and turn back to my work. "Oh," I call out guiltily, as she heads into the kitchen. "I had a bit of your muesli, OK?"

She comes straight back out of the kitchen and says, "I really don't mind. In fact if you knew how little I minded, you'd eat the whole box."

"Yeah? Well, that's good, 'cos I think I nearly did."

"It's OK. I mean come on – we've talked about this. You nicking my food is the least of my worries."

"Yeah? Well, in that case can I open that packet of choccy biscuits you've got stashed away in the cupboard?"

She laughs, disappears into the kitchen again, and a few seconds later the packet of biscuits whizzes past my left ear and lands on the bed beside me.

"You're a star, Bonny!" I call out, tearing the packet open. "I've worked up a real appetite, being brilliant and all."

"Can I see?" she says.

"Sure." I hold out the sheet of paper for her to see. "It's just packaging designs."

She walks closer, stares at them, and laughs, shaking her head. "*God.* You don't really have to try, do you? You're . . . *effortlessly brilliant*."

"Yeah?" I laugh, pleased. "You reckon?"

"Definitely. Don't you ever think of having another go at the big time, you know, getting Nick to tout your stuff round the ad agencies?"

I shake my head. "Once bitten..."

"Oh, come on, Rich! Everyone has things fall through on them!"

"Yeah but – it was the *energy* it took up, you know? I felt wasted just *hoping* for it. I hate to agree with that smug git Huw but I think I've got to concentrate on getting through college, getting off to art college . . . then we'll see."

Bonny pulls a quirky, piss-taking face. "Very sensible, Richard."

"I *am* sensible," I say. "A lot of people don't realize that about me."

She turns to walk off, then she turns back and says, "Getting back with Portia – was that sensible?"

I kind of blank her, expressionless. There's no way I'm getting into a discussion about Portia with her. *God.* Sometimes girls just don't respect your *privacy.*

"Sorry," she goes. "Sorry. Not my business. Hey – *if* you're so sensible – can you do something about the rats up here? I'm sure I heard them again last night. They're in the roof."

"Na, that's pigeons."

"Look – they're *rats.* You *said* there were rats here. *And* I saw some last night, jumping into the canal."

"Yeah, but they're not actually in the flat, are they?"

"Give them time. And the way you spill my muesli all over the floor."

155

"Did I? Sorry. We could get a cat I s'pose."

"To kill them?"

"Apparently just the smell of a cat frightens all grotty rodents off."

Bonny's glowing. "Oh, shall we? Get a cat? I love cats. I've never had a pet, and I always wanted one..."

"It wouldn't be a pet. We'd have to treat it mean, so it got savage enough to kill."

"You just said its smell would be enough!"

"Yeah, well. I fancy seeing a few kills too. A few blood fights."

"You're sick, Rich, you know that? Gimme one of those biscuits."

She takes one, then she wanders back to the kitchen and I think – Bonny and I get on really well together. How come I always get on better with girls I don't really fancy?

Nature sucks, that's why. Nature ... Portia's perfect sexy cat-face rises up behind my eyes again. Work stops again.

I *finally* stop work at midday. I know Dad leaves the house to go to the pub at twelve-thirty and gets back at one-thirty on the dot to carve the Sunday joint. It drives me crazy the way it's all so rigid in our house, but in this instance it's quite useful. I'm outside my house at twelve-forty-five. I've still got my key, of course, but I reckon it's better to knock first this time. Almost immediately, my little brother answers the door. "All right, Sam?" I say, jovially. "How you doing?"

He doesn't answer. He's glaring at me and the corners of his mouth are turning down like they used to when he was small and on the verge of an all-out screaming session. He lowers his head, balls up his fists.

"Mum in?" I ask – and then *whumph* – the little bastard head-butts me in the stomach, and then he just stays there, kind of jammed against my guts.

I grab him by the back of his sweatshirt and haul him off. "What the *fuck* are you doing?" I demand. His face is all red and scrunched-looking. The minute I let him go he shouts "YOU – PISS – OFF!" then he turns and pounds up the stairs.

Mum's appeared in the doorway of the kitchen. She's not smiling, just staring at me like she's desperate for something, some kind of answer. "Hi, Mum," I go.

"Hello, Richard," she says.

"What's up with him?" I ask, jerking my head towards the stairs.

"What d'you think's up with him? He doesn't know what's happening with you. He hasn't *seen* you for a week. Over a week."

"So? You'd think he'd be really chuffed, having the bedroom all to himself. . ."

"Don't be stupid," Mum says in a monotone,

then she turns and disappears back into the kitchen again.

Great. Not exactly a brilliant start. I follow her into the kitchen and say, "Aren't you going to give me a kiss then?"

I know that'll melt her, and it does. She lays down the wooden spoon she was holding and turns to me and smiles, all kind of ruefully, and I wrap my arms round her and kiss her on her forehead, and she says, "Oh, *Richard*. What are we going to do with you?"

"So how are you, Mum?" I ask. "How's it been?"

"How d'you think it's *been*? We've all been worried sick about you. No way of contacting you, or anything."

"You can reach me anytime through Chris."

"I know. He's a good lad. But it's not the same as being able to contact *you*, Rich."

"Well – that's why I'm here now. To tell you how it's going." And I let go of her and take a deep breath, and tell her all my non-Portia news: that I'm not getting kicked out of college, that I've started working, that my dreams of mega-riches through the world of advertising have been cruelly smashed.

"Oh, luv," Mum says. "Oh, I'm sorry."

"Well, Dad won't be, will he. He'll be pleased he's been proved right."

"Rich, that's not fair."

"Might not be fair but it's true, isn't it?"

"He'll be really glad about college. He'll be really glad you're working at it."

"Yeah, well, I didn't have anything else left, did I?"

"Oh, don't say that. You'll get your chance again."

"Maybe. God, Mum, that smells good. Beef, is it?"

"Lamb. Richard – do me a favour."

"What?"

"Pop up and see your little brother."

"What? Why?"

"Because he's upset about you, that's why. He said last night – 'D'you think we're going to see Rich again?' You might not realize it, but he looks up to you."

"Oh, *bollocks* –"

"Don't talk like that, Richard."

"Sorry, Mum."

"Are you going up?"

"Yeah. OK."

I stick my head round the door of our old bunk-bedroom and it's weird, like going back in time, although it's only just over a week ago that this was my space, the only space I had. "All right, Sam?" I say.

He won't answer me. He's lying on his back on the top bunk, rhythmically kicking into the wall.

"Must be good having this room to yourself, eh, Sam?" I go. "Have you had any mates to stay in my bed?"

He still won't answer. Then he gives the wall an extra hard kick and says, "When you coming back?"

"Well, I've got my own place now, mate. Can't live at home for ever."

"You're only *seventeen*," he says, scornfully.

"Eighteen, nearly."

"Not for *ages*."

"Five months."

"That's *ages*."

"Look – you want to come and see this place I've got?"

"*No.*"

"It's cool. Got its own lift."

He refuses to answer again. I'm getting fed up with it. "Look – I'll see you, OK?" I say. "And we can fix up a time for you to come round." Still no answer. I turn, go back downstairs.

The minute I stick my head round the door again, Mum goes: "How was he?"

"Didn't say much. I said he could come to the flat."

"Did you, luv? That's lovely."

"Sulky little sod didn't answer though."

"He'll come round. Thanks for trying. Um – look Rich, I really don't think it's a good idea for you to stay for lunch, all right? I mean – not with your dad not expecting you and everything. I'll tell him you've been and I'll tell him your news, and then maybe next week we can arrange it properly. . ."

It seems to me pretty fucking sad that you have to *arrange* to sit down and eat a meal with your family, but I don't say anything, just nod. She checks her watch, and I know she's anxious about me clearing out and not giving the old man a heart attack.

"I'd better be off, Mum," I say.

"Look – there's something. . ." She hurries over to the sideboard, pulls open the centre drawer, pulls out a cheque book. "I opened you an account," she says, awkwardly.

"What?"

"A bank account. We still get child allowance for you 'cos you're in full-time education. I'm transferring it to an account, with a bit extra. It's every month. I've spoken to your dad, he agrees. Here's the statement."

And she hands a sheet of paper to me. The balance line says £150.

"That's going in every month," she repeats.

I ought to be pleased, but I'm not. It feels so final. Like being paid off. Like a fucking divorce settlement.

"Um, thanks, Mum," I say. "That's—"

"You won't be able to live on it, luv," she rushes on. "Are you working?"

"I'm going to be," I say. "More storyboards. Look – thanks, Mum. This is great."

She's turned her back on me, and now she's bent over and rummaging at the bottom of the cupboard she keeps her flour and pasta and stuff in. "I got some food for you," she says, pulling out a square cardboard box and standing up. "I worry about you not eating properly. It's just a few tins." And she shoves the box into my arms.

I look into it. Lots of cans of tuna, lots of cans of baked beans. A jar of coffee. A packet of tea. A packet of spaghetti. Cans of sweetcorn, cans of soup. Like I'm going on a long camping trip or something. I look at it and get this feeling I want to cry and I put everything I've got into making sure I don't.

"You remember how I made that tuna sauce, for pasta?" Mum says. "It's easy, just an onion and some tinned tomato. . ." She trails off, checks her watch again.

"I'd better go," I croak. "Thanks for this, Mum. See you soon OK?" And I hook my arm round her neck and kiss her again, and then I leg it out of the door with my cardboard box.

Chapter 19

I head back to the flat, surfing along the road on a
great wave of self-pity. I know Mum loves me,
she'll always love me, but it's like she's putting me
second now, after Sam, after Dad, after the general
well-being of the rest of the family who'll be more
at ease tucking into their Sunday lunch without my
destructive presence lurking there like Banquo's
ghost or something.

(Hey – some of that *Macbeth* crap must be pene-
trating my skull after all!)

Sunday lunch-times though. They're the pits.
The last sad, gravy-soaked bastions of family life. I
need to talk, I need to have a pint and a good old
moan at someone, but who can I talk to on a Sunday
lunchtime? Ollie, Chris, Ryan . . . they've all got
these old-fashioned mums who insist they're there

for their dinners. "The only time we all sit down together," they say. "You be there, son, or else."

I don't want to phone Portia. Why don't I want to phone Portia? I don't know, but I don't. I'm all down, confused, my head's like porridge, and in that kind of state I'd cock it up, I'd say the wrong things, I wouldn't handle her right.

I mooch back to the flat, and I'm taken aback by how disappointed I am when I find it empty. Bonny's gone out. Probably also for Sunday lunch. She's probably right now round at Daddy's tucking into a great slab of meat carefully roasted by trying-hard stepmum . . . the whole family'll be there, healing and bonding, chewing and swallowing. . .

I'm hungry. Seriously hungry. I can't believe how much the need for regular food dominates my life since I've moved out of home. How much energy it takes just to keep providing this body with sustenance. I dump the box of tins on the floor and hook out a can of beans and pull the ring on it, then I grab a fork from the kitchen and start shovelling beans into my mouth straight from the can. Cue more self-pity. I mean, solitary cold baked beans – I ask you.

I feel quite desperate if you want the truth. Really down. Then I remember what Barb said, about coming round any time I felt low, and suddenly all I want to do is be in the Hanratty household. In among all their easy-come, easy-go chaos and noise. And I've got two excuses to go, too. I need to ask Nick about doing some work for him, and I need Barb to look at that essay I drafted out this morning.

I pick up the essay from my bed, and head for the door.

"Rich! Hi! Come in! What you here for?"

Barb looks happy and a bit tight and very busy, all at once. She turns immediately on her heel and heads back along her stylish sea-green hall to the kitchen at the end, and I follow her, shutting the front door behind me.

"You're not still eating are you?" I say anxiously as I round the corner into the kitchen.

"Still eating? We won't be eating for hours. Not unless I get some *BLOODY HELP ROUND HERE!*" She says the last bit really loud, and Nick's voice comes back all cajoling from the next room: "Aw come on, doll! This is *work!*"

"Work my arse," snorts Barb. "He's got half his team in there, they're s'posed to be brainstorming for this new account, but all they're doing is getting sozzled and telling jokes." She turns, focuses on me. "So – is this just a social visit or what?"

"I wanted to ask Nick about storyboards. My cash is running out."

"Cash does tend to do that," she says wryly. "Yeah – I'm sure he can find you some. He's always moaning on about how much stuff he's got piling up. You got time though? With your college work and everything?"

"Yeah, I think so. I've made a good start on it."

"Good for you, Rich."

"In fact – I've got another essay – if you could bear it, I wondered if –"

Barb looks unenthusiastically at the creased-up papers I'm holding and says, "Yeah, sure. At least you've got something written down this time."

She turns and whips open the oven, and pulls out a cooking pot big enough to bath a baby in. Then she lifts the lid, releasing a fantastic garlicky smell, tastes what's inside, says "Mmmmm" and follows it up with "You had your lunch? Stay if you like. Lamb casserole – there's loads."

I'm drooling already, despite the can of beans I ate. "You sure, Barb?"

"Sure I'm sure. Tell you what – you could do me a *big* favour in return. While I do the veggies. Take the dogs out, I asked the kids, and we got into one of these it's-not-my-turn sessions, so I told them to forget it, and the dogs have been making me feel really guilty ever since."

Ten minutes later I'm in the park more or less across the road from the Hanratty house, with the two lurchers pulling impatiently on their leads. I'm a bit nervous about being solely responsible for them, but

Barb told me to "know I'm in control" and they'd know it too.

She didn't tell me what to do about other dogs though. A stupid little shaggy mutt has approached one of the lurchers, and is doing that indelicate dog thing of trying to ram its nose up her arse. I stoop, and let the lurchers off their leads, and they both bound off across the grass with the shaggy mutt in determined pursuit.

"Is your bitch in season, dear?"

I pretend I haven't heard this, and walk on. But then it's repeated, right at my left elbow, shrill, insistent, and a bit out of breath: "*Is* she in season, dear? Only, my Teddy won't leave her alone if she is."

"Well, they're not my dogs," I say, stiffly, turning round to see this dumpy, beaming, sixty-ish woman with a horrible green hat on. "But I'm pretty sure she's not."

"Not that it would make a lot of difference, if I'm honest," she goes on. "Teddy just loves the ladies, I'm afraid."

The male lurcher cocks his leg on a rubbish bin, and like the worst kind of pervert going, Teddy races over and sniffs in ecstasy, then lifts his leg up too. "Oh, here we go with the leg-cocking competition," the woman carols. "Got to wee wee higher, haven't you. One wees there, the other wees higher. Have a boy's competition."

Oh, *Jesus*. I quicken my pace a bit, and Teddy

starts barking. The lurchers bark back. "Oh, having a barking competition now are we?" she says. "Oh yes, barky barky."

Barky fucking mad, I'm thinking, speeding up even more. But she's following.

"I may as well walk with you. As he's taken a fancy to your dog. Oh I *love* these little creatures, don't you?"

"What – dogs?" I mutter.

"Yes of course, dear! Although actually I love all little creatures, squirrels, rabbits, all of them – don't you?" I refuse to answer and she says, "They're so contented, so happy. We want to go to America and Barbados and Spain and all they want is a walkies to the park. Oh, Teddy – leave her alone! Are you *sure* she isn't in season, dear? He *does* like the ladies. The bigger the better, isn't that right, Teddy? He went after an Alsatian last week. He'd need a step-ladder to actually achieve anything but that doesn't put him off, does it, Teddy?"

Oh, bloody hell, she's talking doggy intercourse. Beam me up, someone. Save me. I'm practically running now but she's keeping pace *and* still managing to talk.

"People tell me I should get him done, you know, but I think that's cruel don't you? Have your two had their bits off, dear?"

Oh my God, please.

"Teddy's still got his bits," she pants. "Well, it's

cruel, isn't it? Chopping them off. I mean – how would *you* feel if someone chopped *your* bits off? Not that they do him any good, do they, Teddy? All the ladies have had their bits off. Or out rather. Poor old Teddy. Still, he lives in hope, don't you, Teddy? Teddy – *stop that*!"

I break into a run. I start legging it across the park, and the lurchers race happily alongside me, and Teddy follows, evil randy little hopeful rapist git that he is, but he's no match for the lurchers, and soon he's just a nasty little blot on the horizon, he and his crazy owner both.

When I get back, Barb smiles at me all grateful. "Thanks," she says. "Nice walk?"

"Yeah," I say. "OK. Apart from being stalked by this madwoman and her *gross* little oversexed dog."

"*Gross*," echoes Barb, smirking into her pan of carrots. "Dogs can be so basic can't they?"

"Yeah," I mutter.

I think she's taking the piss but I'm not sure. Then she looks up and says, "Um – Rich?"

"Yeah?"

"Tigger phoned this morning. She *knows* I know where Bonny is. She got really nasty with me."

"Yeah?"

"Yeah. Look – while you were out, I was thinking. Well, OK, plotting. If I set up a meeting here – for her and Bonny – kind of neutral ground – would you come too?"

I can feel the blood seeping out of my face. "Me? *Why?*"

"Because I thought we might own up about you two flatsharing."

"Ah."

"I thought it might set her mind at rest."

"Barb – *nothing* could set Tigger's mind at rest. She's a fucking psycho."

"Well . . . maybe. But it's not just that. You'd give . . . I thought you'd give Bonny courage. To face up to her, I mean."

I gawp at this, but before I can think of any kind of answer Nick blasts into the kitchen saying "OK, sweetheart, what you want me to do?" and then all the serving up and carrying in starts and soon we're all sat round the big table in the conservatory, and Barb's dolloping out great platefuls of posh-looking stew. Four other people are there, three guys and a girl – I've seen all of them before at Nick's office. They're all gushing with gratitude about being given such good food and they're really relaxed, really friendly with me. Nick's holding court as usual, still talking about the new account, until Barb tells him to stow it and get the mashed potatoes dished out and then she goes to the door and shouts for the kids.

Scarlett and Freddie trot in, Freddie heading for his plate like a heat-seeking missile. Scarlett gives me a lovely smile when she sees me, and plonks herself right next to me. She's got one of her black, droopy, spidery outfits on, with a red feather boa and this time a gold tiara.

"What do you wear for school, Scarlett?" I ask.

She curls her lip. "*Uniform*. But I've got two tiaras that look like headbands, and I wear them too. How's Bonny?"

"Bonny's fine. Bonny's great. Did you see what your mum did in her room?"

"No, but she told me about it. Are you in love with her yet?"

I choke on a bit of carrot I've just forked into my mouth. "Am I in *love* – ? No, Scarlett – we're flat-mates, you know?"

"Yes, but I thought if you got to *know* her, you'd fall in love with her. She's lovely."

"Yeah, I know she is. I really like her. But I've got a girlfriend."

Scarlett bridles. "Who?"

"This girl called Portia."

"What's she like?"

"She's really pretty. Gorgeous."

"So are you in love with *her* then?"

"Er – no. Not really."

"Why not?"

"It's . . . difficult. I can't . . . I can't really *talk* to her, for one thing."

"Well, what's the point of *being* with her then?" asks Scarlett, her voice ringing with scorn. Then her face changes and she looks at me in disgust and says, "*Oh.*"

And luckily, then, Barb intervenes by filling up my wine glass and Nick slams some more casserole on my plate, and I get drawn into the general flow of chat once more. One of the guys asks why I've stopped doing storyboards for them and that leads neatly into Nick offering me some work and Barb says (again), *as long as it doesn't interfere with his college work*, and I say it'll be fine, after all I'm on the doorstep now, aren't I, I can do a couple of hours a night, no problem.

And so it's settled, and Nick clears the plates, and then Scarlett heads self-importantly out to the kitchen and brings out this great-looking pudding, all chocolate gunk and cream, and Barb announces that Scarlett decorated it, and everyone claps good-naturedly and Scarlett goes all red.

I tip myself back in my chair and listen to all the chat going on around me, and I realize all my angst has gone. I'm feeling good again. It's the wine. It's the company. It's the red meat. It's being given work. I feel great. I feel ... I feel *horny*.

And suddenly all I want to do is get out of here, get to see Portia. I sit there feeling randy and having philosophical thoughts about the way thoughts and desires have this rhythm about them, ebbing and flowing like the sea. All the doubts and the criticisms and the disappointments of last night have been washed clean away, and my feelings for Portia are at high tide. Flooding.

Barb is standing up, yawning, and people are passing their dishes towards her. "So Rich – you want to do some work on that essay now?" she asks. And then she yawns again.

"Oh, no, let's leave it, eh?" I mutter. "You don't want to do that now. Maybe I can just leave it here for you to look at. I've really got to go. I need to phone someone."

Chapter 20

"Hi – Portia?"

"*Rich*–y!"

"How you doin', darlin'?"

"Great, I'm great. Wasn't last night fab?"

"Absolutely fab."

"I'm sorry about leaving you stranded, I just was *so* tired..."

"It's OK, it's OK."

"*God*, I'm glad you phoned. I mean – I wanted to speak to you, but I've got no way of contacting you, have I?"

"You could come round to the flat."

"Yeah, but you might not be in."

"Portia – if you're coming round, I'll guarantee to be in." She giggles, and I say, "So are you?"

"Am I what?"

"Coming round?"

"What, for a cosy threesome with Boring Bonny?"

"Bonny's out. She told me – she's going out." I'm lying of course, but I'm sure I can fix it. "Come on, Portia. I've got some wine in."

"What sort?"

Oh Jesus, what does it matter what sort? "What sort d'you like?"

"Chardonnay."

"That's what I got."

"Honestly, Richy, you are such a *li-*ar!"

"You come round, Portia, and you will see the best bottle of Char-don-nay you ever *drunk* just waiting here for you. How is that a lie?"

"Stop it. *Honestly.*"

"What time you coming?"

"I've got work to do."

"So've I. But we need some relaxation and pleasure, don't we?"

"I guess," she giggles.

"What time?"

"Eight," she says duskily, and clicks the phone off.

"A bottle of cheapish Char-don-nay, please," I say at the offy nearest to the phone box. I'm pretty smug about my pronunciation.

"Hm," says the shop man.

"Hm?"

175

"Chardonnay," he sneers. "The wine-drinker's lager."

I reckon he means this as an insult but I don't give him the satisfaction of rising to it. "That's right," I say. "One bottle please. Cold if possible."

He shows me a bottle and I ask, "Got anything with a better label?"

"A better *what*, sir?"

"A better label. You know – a bit more flash."

He doesn't answer, just snorts and delves into the fridge and comes out with a bottle with a label with a silver fairy-tale castle on. "Oh that's great," I say. "How much?"

Back at the flat, I jam the bottle of wine in the fridge and then go straight over and knock on Bonny's door. I know she's in 'cos of the light seeping out.

"Bonny, I've got a huge favour to ask of you," I say into the door. "*Huge.*"

"What?" she says. Then: "It's OK, come in."

I open the door. She's lying on her bed, all cosy, a book in front of her, papers spread around. "Working?" I ask.

"Yup. History."

"Clever. Er – Bonny?"

"Yeah? What's the favour?"

"Portia's coming round."

"Oh."

"Tonight. In about an hour's time."

"And you want me to promise not to come out of my room until she goes away again."

"Well, actually, Bonny – I was kind of hoping you might be able to go out. Kind of."

"*Out?* Why? Look – I'll stay in here. I'll even promise not to use the bog."

"Well. . ."

"Rich – it's Sunday night! I've got *school* tomorrow!"

There's a pause. She's lying on the bed looking indignant, I'm standing in the door looking pathetic and hopeful.

"It's a bit *awkward*, isn't it, your *bed*room being so open," she says finally, bitterly.

"Yeah," I agree.

She sighs, shifts about, and finally she says, "OK, I'll go. I'll go back to Dad's and pick up the cat. He'll give me a lift back. No later than ten-thirty, OK?"

"OK! Bonny – you're a star. I'll do the same for you, honestly." Then it hits me. "*What* cat?"

"We talked about getting a cat, remember? Well Ellie – that's Daddy's new wife – she knows this old lady, and she's got this tom cat, and he's causing all this trouble with the neighbours, killing birds and stuff, and I said that's just what we need, a fierce cat for the rats, and I said I'd talk about it with you. We can have him on a kind of a trial basis, see how it goes."

"You mean we can give it back?"

"If it doesn't work out, yeah. But I hope it does work out, I saw a rat running along the ledge outside the window just before you came in, and –"

"OK, OK, Bonny. Trial run, yeah?"

Bonny grins at me knowingly, and what she knows is I'm so keen to get her out of the flat I'd agree to a trial run for a fucking rhinoceros.

Bonny exits the flat a good fifteen minutes before Portia sweeps in, which is good because it gives me time to get something groovy playing on my little cassette player and find a couple of wine glasses without chips.

"Boy-*friend*!" coos the Porsche when I open the door to her. She looks terrific. Just jeans and a tiny jumper, not too much slap.

I stand there and grin at her for a second or two, then I take a step back and she walks into the flat. Then I don't step back any more and she collides with me. I grab her, put my arms round her waist, kiss her on her hair just where the parting is, move down, kiss her forehead –

"He-ey," she breathes, "let me get *inside*, OK?" She sashays past me, turns round and asks, "So – we got the place to ourselves?"

I nod. "Definitely."

"Where's that wine you promised me?"

"Chilling," I say, so smooth you could polish me. "You want some?"

"Please," she says, and wanders further into the room, looking all around, smiling.

I leg it into the kitchen and hook the wine out of the fridge. Then I remember something awful. *We don't have a sodding corkscrew.* Shit, how could I forget? How smooth am I going to look now?

"You know – you could do so much with this place," Portia calls out. "It's *fa-abulous*."

"Yeah," I call back. "I know."

My desperate brain hikes up this vague memory of a boozy party a while back, and Chris opening some red wine with a knife. He kind of plunged it in the cork and then jabbed the cork down into the bottle, and the wine spurted crimson all over the walls like he'd just stabbed someone, but there was at least two thirds of the wine left behind. . .

"You ought to paint it out," calls Portia. "Freshen it up. And get a sofa or something."

"Yeah, I know." Frenziedly, I yank open the cutlery drawer.

"And *curtains*. Those big windows – they're really cold-looking."

"Yeah, I –" Oh, *hallelujah*. There, nestling next to the teaspoons at the front, is a brand new, shiny corkscrew. And not some cheap job either, but the real McCoy with arms on it. Bonny must've got it. Bonny's a saint, a saviour. I didn't even think she drank wine.

"And a rug," the Porsche says. "These floor-boards are very *stark.*"

I open the bottle in one smooth motion, fill the two glasses to the brim, and swagger out of the kitchen, a glass in either hand. "Actually, Portia, I like stark," I say. "There is no way curtains are being hung on those amazing windows and nor am I having some crappy IKEA rug covering up these fantastic floorboards."

Portia raises one of her sorceress eyebrows at me and I hand her a glass of wine. "Cheers," I say.

"I was only making *suggestions*," she says poutily.

"Yeah, I know. And I was rejecting them."

"Well, there's no need to be so aggressive about—" She breaks off then and makes this little melty noise – "*Ooo-ooh*". She's spotted one of the drawings I did of her way back at the start of our relationship, propped strategically against the wall. "You *kept* it!" she purrs.

"Course I did. I kept all of them."

"That is so *sweet*. You know, Richy, I *lo-oved* you drawing me."

"Did you?"

"Yeah. You want to draw me again?"

"Sure."

"Now?"

Drawing her wasn't exactly what I had in mind, but I can't think of a good way to say *no let's go to bed instead*. She puts her glass down on the floor, turns and faces me, and then matter-of-factly pulls her jumper over her head. She's got one of those really sexy low-cut bras on underneath.

"Portia, are you –"

"I thought you could do a life-study," she interrupts, and peels down her jeans.

I stand there gawping like someone's just hit me over the head with an ironing board, and she says, "Come on, Richy! Anyone'd think you hadn't seen my body before."

And then she takes everything else off.

Chapter 21

First I take in a deep, shuddering, ecstatic breath. Then I turn away, head for my bag, root out my pad of paper and some pencils. Then I draw. My hand's only shaking a little bit.

Oh, God, everything's right. I'm getting her down. Her leg, there . . . and the shading underneath her back . . . this is doing it, it's right. This is Portia. I'm working fast but I'm good. God, this is cool. God, wait till I tell the guys about his. Wait till I tell Ollie. Her nose, her mouth, the way it opens . . . I could be Rossetti, couldn't I, up in his studio with that fabulous red-headed mistress he had. This is so cool.

I finish the first sketch, tear off another sheet to start a second. Portia shifts position, reaches out to pick up her glass and take a slurp of wine. And I draw her again.

She's only the second nude I've ever drawn in my entire life. The first was in this special session Huw ran, about six months ago. The model was a strong-looking, bulky woman, late twenties maybe. Before she stripped off she got us all to hold her hands, stroke her arms, feel the texture of her skin, feel who she *was*. It was an incredible experience. I drew like a demon that day. The woman was hardly a stunner but by the end of it I was half in love with her just 'cos I'd got her down so well.

And now Portia. I'm drawing like a demon again, working without stopping, without hardly breathing and I feel like I'm making love to her over and over again. And I want to, I want to make love to her so much, but I know that's coming, and there's something so deadly erotic about drawing her, drawing all the beautiful shapes and lines of her, knowing that *soon*. . .

I finish my third sketch and she says, "Let me see." So I flop down beside her on the bed, her all naked and me not, and show her the sketches one after the other. I've got my arm round her shoulder cuddling her up to me, feeling so horny I could explode, and I'm wondering what to do first – kiss her or start taking off my clothes – when something makes me glance at my watch. And I see it's five past ten. *Shit!* Bonny said she'd be back no later than ten-thirty! Does that mean *earlier* than ten-thirty? *Shit!*

"These are *fa-abulous*," Portia's purring. "You've made my leg look too fat, here, look, but –"

I *pounce*. I twist round and land my mouth on hers like I'm so transfixed by lust I can't help myself. And then I'm half on top of her stripping off my gear and she's laughing, and that drawing, that posing, that looking, that waiting, it was all we needed, and very very soon we're making it again.

I feel like I know every inch of her body now. We make love with the pictures getting creased all around us.

And then it's over, and we're safe, we're still alone.

"Portia," I say, into her neck, "we should get up."

"Hmmm?" she murmurs.

"We should get our clothes on. Bonny'll be back soon."

"Oh, *for God's sake!*" she snaps, and the wonderful after-glow feeling sputters out, like she's chucked cold water on it. She twists angrily, snatches up her pile of clothes.

"I'm sorry," I say, retrieving my jeans from the floor. "It's just—"

"When are you going to get this place back to *yourself*?"

"Soon. Really."

She snorts, hooks up her bra. "*God*. I'd like a *shower*."

"Well, have one. It's fine."

"I hate being *rushed*. I mean why – actually –

should we worry about it? We ought to just stay in bed."

"Wouldn't you feel a bit of a prat when she walks in?"

"*No*. Why should I? You think making love together is something to be ashamed of?"

"Oh, *come on*, Portia, you know what I think about making love to you."

She snorts again, yanks her jumper over her head. The mood's gone, it's smashed, shattered. "You want a refill?" I say desperately, picking up her glass. She shrugs sourly, pulls a brush out of her bag, runs it through her hair.

I pull on my jeans and T-shirt and pad out to the kitchen to fetch the bottle of wine. When I get back she's fully dressed and sitting on the edge of the bed. I fill us both up, then I sit down beside her and put my arm round her shoulder, trying to get back some of the good feeling, the close feeling. "What's the latest on Tony?" I ask. "Isn't your trial separation week nearly up?"

"Yeah, it is," she says. "Tomorrow." She takes a long swig of wine, then she says, "He's kept to it too."

"Yeah? You didn't phone him then?"

"What?"

"You said you were going to phone him, finish it for good."

"Well – no. I thought I'd stick to the agreement. I mean – *he* has. Apart from sending me flowers the other day. Freesias. I *lo-ove* freesias. They smell so heavenly. I suppose I *should* phone him."

"What – to say thanks?"

"No, dummy! To end it."

"You still want to then?" I murmur smoochily, nudging my face into hers.

"Yes. You know I do. Stop that – it's not just 'cos of you! I'd finish it anyway." And then she struggles up off the bed, all peevish, and says, "Look – I'm gonna go. Waiting for that boring cow to come back is doing my head in."

"Oh, Portia, at least finish your wine!"

"Give it to *Bonny*."

"Look – she won't be living here much longer. I swear it."

"Good. 'Cos it's really cramping my style, OK?" And with that she blows a somehow insulting kiss off the end of her fingertips, and flounces out of the door.

I drain her glass and collapse back on to the bed, dribbling wine out of the side of my mouth, exhausted with the effort of trying to please her. The sketches are all falling off the side of the bed, fanning out on the crumpled duvet like a jagged sort of V-sign. I pick one up, melt just at the memory of drawing it. And then I hear this furious yowling noise, about a metre from my head.

Chapter 22

"Hi! The door was open!" says Bonny, guardedly. The yowling continues. "So I came straight in." It's coming from the little crate thing she's carrying. "I saw Portia leaving, anyway. She didn't see me though. Well – she didn't say hello anyway. She just walked straight past the car. Daddy asked who she was and I said she was your girlfriend and—"

"*Bon-ny!*"

"What?"

"Why are you jabbering on when there's a noise like something getting skinned alive in there?"

Bonny puts the crate on the floor. "This is a pet-carrier," she explains slowly, as though I'm a particularly thick child. "You use it to carry –"

"– pets in, yeah, yeah, I know. Is that the cat you were going on about?"

Bonny unhooks the crate door and says, "Yes. This is Petal." And Petal steps out of the crate and fixes me with a look of concentrated loathing.

Petal is ginger, angry and *huge*. If he were a bloke he'd be the skinhead leaning up against the end of the bar with the loud voice you're very, very careful not to make eye contact with. The one you make sure you don't leave the pub at the same time as. The one who – if you knock his arm and spill his beer – you just hand over the contents of your wallet to, straight off, no question.

"Petal?" I say. "Pitbull more like."

"I don't think he liked the lift," Bonny says, tenderly. "It was the clanking. He was fine in the car."

Petal raises his bullet head, *sneers* at me, stalks past, heads straight for the open window – and disappears. "Oh *no*!" wails Bonny. "He's fallen *off*!"

"Don't be daft," I say, anxiously, heading over there fast. "There's a fire escape."

We both reach the window, peer out. No sign. "He's *fallen*!" wails Bonny again.

"He *hasn't*. He's a cat. Sure-footed. Pawed."

Then from below comes the sound of frantic scrabbling and scuffling. "He's clinging to the fire escape!" Bonny whimpers. "Trying not to slide down! Oh, God, Rich – save him!"

I practically fall out myself, trying to see, but it's too dark. Then, ominously, the scrabbling stops.

"Pass over the floor lamp," I grunt. "Let's get some light on it."

Bonny dashes off, tows over the lamp. Its flex is just long enough to let me position it on the edge of the window and shine it out.

Two bright cat's eyes shine malevolently back at us. Then they swing away like headlights, and disappear. "Well, he's still alive," I say.

"Where's he gone?"

"Round the side. There's a whole warren of little roofs and ledges and stuff round the side. It's a cat's playground."

"Suppose he doesn't come back?"

"He will. We'll leave the window open. You know what I reckon that scrabbling was? It was a rat. He was after a rat."

Bonny kind of swells with pride when I say this. "You think? God, I bet you're right. What a clever *baby*!" She stands up, heads over to the carrier bag she left by the door when she came in.

"What's that?" I ask.

"His stuff. Food, and cat litter and stuff. If I leave a dish of food over by the window, maybe it'll lure him back."

"And *if* you leave a dish of food over by the window, maybe *I'll* throw up! Trying to get to sleep with the smell of it."

"Oh, Rich, don't be stupid. It's top quality."

She opens the bag, pulls out a nasty-looking cat

litter-tray. "Don't even *think* about putting *that* next to my bed," I grouse.

"I'm *not*. I'll put it – well, I'm not sure where I'll put it. The thing is, we were s'posed to keep him shut in for a couple of days."

"What – shut in with us? Oh, great. What happens when he gets cabin fever and goes nuts?"

"He *wouldn't*. You're just s'posed to keep a cat in until it gets used to its new home. Look – I'm gonna put some food out. See if that attracts him back."

She gets out this little dish and this can of cat food and a fork, and soon she's scooping brown gunk out, rattling the fork as loudly as she can against the dish. And then, as if he's doing us one enormous favour, Petal's skinhead head appears over the ledge, and he jumps in and starts gorging.

Bonny clasps her hands together in delight and watches him gorge. It's not a pretty sight. "I thought cats were supposed to be elegant," I sneer.

"He's just *hungry*," coos Bonny.

"That's no excuse. I'm calling him Pitbull."

"Don't be so *horrible*. D'you think we should shut the window now?"

"No. Give him his freedom. He'll be back now he knows this is where the grub is."

Bonny has gone very still, very quiet. I glance over at her and see she's looking at the three sketches I did of Portia, fanned out on the bed. Then she looks away, and stands up. "I hope he'll sleep in with me tonight," she says. She won't meet my eyes. "But d'you mind if I leave my door ajar when I go to sleep?"

I say no, and she picks up Pitbull who's too stuffed with food to protest, and hurries off into her room with him.

It has been one *hell* of a weekend. I decide to crash immediately. While I'm scrubbing my teeth I find myself thinking about Bonny going all quiet over the sketches of the Porsche. What was that about? She *knew* I wanted her out of the way so we could . . . well. Maybe it was just being faced with the evidence like that. Maybe it was a shock.

Because I'm pretty sure Bonny doesn't fancy me any more. Not since she's been living with me. Familiarity breeding contempt and all that. Plus we're so relaxed together now. She doesn't *act* like she fancies me.

I hit the bed and I'm asleep in seconds.

Until Pitbull wakes me up by walking over my face.

Monday morning, we're both up early. I collide with Bonny in the kitchen and say, "Your sodding cat woke me up about a hundred times last night!"

"Oh dear," she laughs, guiltily.

"Tramping all over me to get to the window. And then he started *kneading* me. With that steam–engine noise cats do. Wanted to sleep on my chest."

"So did he?"

"No he bloody didn't! I shoved him off. Then he waited until I was nearly asleep and jumped on my head."

"He likes you!" she says, reprovingly.

"He's a raving sadist. Who wants to be liked by a raving sadist?"

"Oh, stop moaning. We had a deal, remember?"

"Yeah, OK. Look – I meant to say thanks for that. Last night. If ever you want me to clear out for you..."

Bonny grimaces. "I doubt it."

"Oh, go on, you might get lucky."

I'm not prepared for this next bit. She rounds on me, eyes blazing. "That's how you see it, is it?"

"What?"

"Sex. Getting lucky?"

"Jesus, it's just a phrase, it doesn't mean anything."

"Like sex doesn't mean anything?"

"Bloody hell, Bonny, what you being so touchy for? All I said was I'd clear out for you if you ever—"

"Well, I don't suppose I will. *Ever*. OK?"

"God, don't be so touchy. I thought you'd be more relaxed about it – the way your mum is and all."

Bonny's hackles are well up now. "What d'you mean? You thought I'd naturally be an old slag like her? Or you thought I'd have her cast-offs or something?"

"No – *Jesus*. Just – oh, forget it. Forget I said anything."

"As a matter of fact, I've hardly ever slept with anyone."

"Look, Bonny, this is none of my business, this is –"

"And I shan't again until it's really *right*. I was stupid to do it the first time to be honest. I just do not know what the *big deal* is, about losing your virginity. It's not like it's a big achievement, a big effort. For a girl, anyhow. You just go out on the street and announce you're up for it and you'd find someone willing in about ten seconds flat. It's not like guys are exactly *discriminating,* is it?"

"Yeah, well, for a girl maybe –"

"It seems to me it's lot *harder* to stand up against all the sniggering and my-God-are-you-still-a-virgin crap from tossers like you than it is to go out at fifteen and get laid. And get *disappointed*. And maybe put off sex for life. Some of my friends've been put off sex for life, the way they talk. Seems to me it's a bigger achievement all round to *wait*. Until it's right, you've met the right guy, and you're so turned on by him you think you'll explode if you don't have him. . . *God*." Then she slams the kettle on and I exit the kitchen. Fast.

I'm beginning to think I don't understand women.

* * *

I find Portia as soon as I can after getting into college. Firstly, because I want to make sure that whole weekend wasn't just some lurid fantasy I had and secondly, because I've got something to ask her.

It wasn't a fantasy. She's with Jenny and a couple of her other friends and she turns on the Girlfriend Act full power. Which is great but maybe a little too much for a Monday morning. When she's finished chewing my mouth I say, "Portia – you know those pictures I drew of you?"

"Mmmm?" she asks all sultry, looking up at me from under her luscious lashes.

"Would you – could I – what would you say if I asked you if I could, like, *show* them? Submit them?"

"To Huw you mean?" she shrieks.

"Yeah. Look – bad idea. Sorry. They're just brilliant, and there's three of them, and – forget it. Sorry."

"Go ahead," she breathes.

"What?"

"Go ahead! You're right – they're fabulous."

"But people might – I mean, it's pretty clear it's you in them. Well – two of them."

"So what? I'm not ashamed of my body. You got them here?"

Silently, I hand her my art folder. She whips it open, and whips out the three sketches. Then she starts holding them up to Jenny and the others, who all practically pass out in awe and amazement and envy. "They got a bit screwed up," Portia husks out. "We made love on top of them."

"She doesn't care," I say to Chris later on that day in the cafeteria. "She's not a bit embarrassed. She was waving them around like flags. And if Huw accepts them, they could be up on the wall for everyone to stare at, part of the next exhibition."

"Well, that's appropriate 'cos it's what she *is*, mate," says Chris, sagely.

"What, an exhibition?"

"-*ist*. An exhibition*ist*. She's gotta have attention, hasn't she, or she'd wither up and die. All those creepy friends she gathers round her, up her arse the whole time."

I look glumly down into my coffee. He's right. It's something I noticed from the start about Portia – that she has to be at the centre the whole time. Getting compliments. All the time her creepy sycophantic friends tell her she's gorgeous, fab, wild, losing weight; their envy comes off them in waves. And she preens herself under this barrage of compliments; she glows and grows and battens on it.

Portia never gives compliments though. She'll say something like "yeah, fine" to a direct question about a dress or hair – but she won't really give out. It's like compliments are a kind of currency, and to get them makes her rich and strong, and to give them makes her poor and weak. There's something witchy about it, this one-way traffic, this collecting, this guarding. Like she's the priestess in some cult and all her friends have to lay offerings of words in front of her and she's got such power that no one ever questions why.

Because she has got power, Portia. And over me most of all.

"Don't brood, mate," says Chris. "Makes you look daft."

"I dunno," I sigh.

"What? You've finally pulled the Porsche after dribbling round after her all last term and you don't *know*?"

"It's just – it's weird. I mean – she's dumped Tony and got off with me the same week. And she's really *proud* of it."

"Hm," says Chris. "If she wasn't so good-looking she'd get a real name for herself. As in slag."

"Yeah, well, I'm not complaining."

"Aren't you, mate? Cheer up then for Christ's sake."

Huw is not as bowled over by the Porsche Pictures as he should be. "Hm," he goes. "Well, they're very gorgeous, obviously. Yes, they're good, the set – it's good. But they're a little – what shall I say – *sterile*, aren't they, lad?"

"Sterile?" I squawk.

"Yes. A bit girly. Glam."

"She's a *great*-looking bird," I splutter.

"I know she is. I recognize the face. But – well. I presume you have a *relationship* of some kind with her? Feelings? Thoughts? Where are they, lad? You haven't brought them out."

He turns, chucks them down on the table behind him. "Did she mind you giving them to me?"

"No, not at all. I asked her."

"Good. Well, they're good, Richard boy, of course they're good. But – you haven't made her *real*, somehow. I think your other nudes were better." Then he grins at me. "Have you ever tried drawing a man?"

Portia collars me just as I'm leaving at the end of the day. I ask her to come back to the flat and she declines, then she says, "Can you get off early tomorrow. Only, I've made this appointment. In town. I want you to come with me."

Oh my God, an Appointment I think, in panic. And she wants me to go with her. It's the Family Planning Clinic, it's got to be. She's going on the pill. I have to be with her. As her *partner*. *Oh my God*. I'm half delighted, half kind of trapped and cornered and terrified and – "Appointment?" I croak.

"Yeah. To get my tummy-button pierced."

Chapter 23

The next day Portia and I are seated side by side in the front seat on the top of a bus making our way to the other side of town. I love riding the tops of buses but Portia's making it quite clear public transport is below her. She mentions Tony's car at least twice as we sway along.

"Did you phone him?" I ask.

"Yes," she snaps.

"And finish it?"

"*Yes.*"

"What did he—"

"Look, it was awful, OK? I don't want to talk about it."

The bus pulls into the main street and stops, and I'm kind of hugging myself with the knowledge that she's all mine, now. Just about everyone on the bus but us clumps off. I reckon we've still got another five minutes up here, swaying along like a galleon. So I put my arm round her and try and get into a bit of a session.

She's not having it though. She pushes me off like I'm a badly trained dog and I sit back, deflated.

"You sure you want to get this piercing done?" I ask, for the tenth time.

"*Yes*," she snaps.

"I just don't know why you want to *mutilate* yourself this way."

"Oh, for God's sake."

"Couldn't you just get your ears done again?"

"Oh, Richy, stop being such a *drag*."

"I just think –"

"Look – I asked you along for moral *support*. Not a non-stop lecture." She turns, glares at me. "I'd've asked Jenny, only she's so *squeamish*."

We find the place without too much trouble. It's called "Magda's" and it's got all this weird runey dungeon-and-dragon crap in the window.

"God, you have checked this place out, haven't you?" I mutter, as we head in through the door. "Only you can get all kinds of shit from dodgy needles and –"

"Richy, *shut up*!"

There's more dungeon-and-dragon stuff inside – shelves of bleeding-skull candles and writhing wizards and spooky-looking voodoo stuff with lots of feathers and beads. There's even a glass case full of gothic-shaped dope pipes. The woman behind the counter puts my mind at rest a bit though. She's a down-to-earth Londoner and she raps out about how utterly *safe* and superior Magda's methods are and then she runs through taking care of the healing process.

Then this guy appears out of the back curtains. I say guy, but he's actually a great white ape. The kind of guy who hits you straight where your most frantic fears are. The kind of guy you hope won't be coming the other way in the long, dark alley you have to walk through. The kind of guy who survives all-out nuclear attack and carries on surviving by scaring the other survivors to death and then eating them.

He's got a bleached half-shaved head, a torn, sleeveless vest, armies of piercings, studs and tattoos, mad, glaring eyes and hands like malevolent baseball mitts. "Coming round the back then?" he says to Portia.

Oh – my – God. "The back". Oh my *God*. He's going to rape her. He's going to rape her then strangle her.

Then eat her.

I'll never see her again.

I've got to do something. I've got to protect her. I've got to be a *man*.

"Um . . . mind if I come too, mate?" I whimper. "Only – um – she's a bit nervous, you know."

Post-nuclear apeman leans across the counter towards me, like he might be about to bite off my nose. "We don't allow no one out the back with the clients," he growls.

Oh, *right*, I think hysterically. And why not? So there aren't any witnesses, that's why not. So there's no one to help YOUR VICTIMS. Oh – my – *GOD*!

"Why not?" I squeak, heroically.

"'Cos we had a punter in a coupla months back with his girl, and when I put the needle into her, he fainted, right? Fell across her. Fucking dangerous. Right?" And he sneers at me, like I was the kind of bloke to faint too.

I'm feeling pretty faint right now. I turn to Portia, expecting to see her pale and terrified, and looking to me for protection. I'm gearing up to shouting "Forget the whole thing!" and steering her manfully out of the shop.

But Portia's looking just fine. She's got the tip of her tongue pushing sexily against her top lip, and she's gazing at the Armageddon tattoos on post-nuclear apeman's massive muscly forearms.

"Portia. . . ?" I croak.

She snaps her head up, like I'd caught her out. "Yeah?" she says.

"You want to go through with this?"

"Sure I do."

"But – you heard what he said. You gotta go back there alone."

Portia looks at apeman, and they exchange a brief, knowing look. Suddenly I'm the outsider. "Oh – I'm going to be *fi-ine*," she coos. "I'll be in very capable hands."

And she wriggles her way round behind the counter, and disappears under the apocalyptic curtain that apeman holds courteously back for her.

Oh, shit. Oh, *shit*. I pace the shop floor, from the glass case with the dope pipes to the display of bleeding-skull candles and back again. My ears are straining to hear the sounds of a struggle, or a mutilation, or Portia trying to scream through apeman's massive mitt, and my heart's pounding with what the hell I do exactly if I do hear something.

"Oh, calm *down*," bleats the woman. "Stop walkin' up and down. Anyone'd think she was 'avin' a baby in there!"

"I can't hear anything!" I wail.

"Well, what d'you expect to hear, eh? Blood spatterin' about?"

Bad comment! *Bad comment!*

And then I do hear something. Everyone hears it. *Blaaaa!* Portia's mobile phone. And then I hear her giggle, and say sorry, and then I hear, "Jenn-ee! Hi! Yeah – all over. No – no pain at all. The guy who did it – he was *so-oo* gentle." There's a pause, another giggle. "It looks *fab*. The sweetest little diamond stud. Look – gotta go – I'm still in the shop, Jenny! Talk to you later, OK?"

I don't say much to Portia on the way home on the bus. I feel sort of shattered. I sit beside her and listen as she runs through a description of all her summer crop-tops and all her revealing evening-wear and how she's going to look so much cuter in each and every one of them now she's had her belly-button done.

"What's up?" she says at last.

"Nothing."

"Yes there is. You still don't like it, do you?"

"You know I don't."

"You wait till you see it with the bandage off. Honestly, Rich, it's gorgeous. All sparkly."

"I thought your belly-button was gorgeous before. Unpierced."

"You think it's vulgar, don't you?"

"No."

"Yes you do. It isn't, honestly. I wouldn't have a ring or anything. It's like a jewel, and it's tiny. And tasteful. Really."

I shrug, and she pushes me and calls me an idiot, and then we both kind of stare out of the window, and her phone goes again, and she answers it in this completely phoney voice. I've realized something about mobile phones and the way people like Portia answer them in public. Even if the most dull and boring person in the world gives you a call, you have to go into a kind of overdrive of squealing ecstasy when you answer it. Kind of: "Well, *hi*! How are *you*? What are you *doing*? Wow! You *are*? *Wow!*" This is because you have to make it clear to everyone within earshot that the most hip and fascinating person in the universe is breaking off from their hip and fascinating life just to give *you* a bell.

I seem to be realizing a lot about Portia these days. It's sort of tiring.

Chapter 24

Portia refuses to come back to the flat with me. She says if she does we'll get "carried away" and that could endanger her new belly-button stud. I say we could be really, really careful but she isn't having it. She tells me I'm obsessed with sex. She tells me she'll see me in college the next day.

I stooge back to the flat and worry over what she said. Maybe she's right. Maybe I am obsessed. But I only want sex all the time because that's when we're closest. Well, closer.

Close at all.

We're going off the boil, aren't we? Since we slept together. I don't understand it. We've only made it twice. But it was good. It was brilliant. For her too, she said so. So how come it's gone all flat and we don't even kiss properly any more and . . . shit. It's my fault, it has to be. I don't understand women. Not at all.

I can feel that I'm heading for another long, brooding, depressed session as I let myself in the big office doors, but then something good happens. As I'm legging it up the stairs Nick sticks his head out of his office door and barks, "You busy?"

"Not especially, why?"

"That work I offered you. I need it done *now*. Whole set of storyboards to get done by this time tomorrow. Needs your rough style, darling. Yes? Double time. Yes?"

I'm in there like a rat up a drainpipe. And the Abacus offices, all flash and style, work on me like a tonic. I sit down with Nick and we work out the sharpest, most economical way to sketch out the frames and then I get down to it. Camilla, Nick's long-suffering PA, pats me on the shoulder as she passes, then gives me a cup of coffee and a doughnut and then (because I swallow that in two bites) another doughnut. I'm drawing hard, I'm whamming through it. I only wish the Porsche could see me, all ad-agency sharp, in this colour-crazy office, with this trendy bird *waiting* on me.

I call her that evening, on Abacus's phone bill, but she doesn't pick up, so I just leave a message: "Hey, Portia? How's the belly stud? I won't be in college tomorrow, I've got some work on for Nick. Drop by if you want to. See you." Then almost immediately

I redial and leave a second message: "That last message was from Rich, by the way. Just in case you didn't recognize me." Then I spend about five minutes wishing I could delete the second message, then I phone Chris and tell him to tell them I'm ill tomorrow. Got to be official, can't blot my copy book when I'm still on remand.

Then I get back to work.

I go to bed very late and get up late but I'm still back at Abacus at ten a.m. "The beauty of sleeping above the office, eh, darling?" says Nick. "Look – you get it done by five tonight so I'm in time to bike it round to them and it's not only double time, there's a bonus in it too."

And I work like a slave, storyboard after storyboard, fuelled by hot chocolate and tea from the chrome machine in the corner of the office. At eleven o'clock there's bacon sarnies, ordered in from one of the caffs near town. At one-thirty Camilla fetches up a load of well-stuffed baguettes. I'm measuring my time out by eating, drinking, finishing each storyboard. I think how I couldn't stand this grind for ever, how I definitely want to go to art college. I brood about Portia, wonder if she'll come round, hope she'll come round. I think of the money waiting for me at five o'clock.

There's a brief, welcome, noisy, hairy break at three-thirty when Barb turns up with Scarlett and

Freddie and both the lurchers. "What the bloody hell you bought *them* in for, doll?" squawks Nick, as the dogs scritch frantically across the floor towards him, towing Barb behind.

"What, the dogs or the kids?"

"The *dogs*."

"Oh, come on, you know what they do to the car if you leave them shut up in it."

"OK, OK – but why are you all *here*?"

"*Listen* – there's this *huge* ginger cat on the stairs!" shouts Freddie, before Barb can answer.

"It wouldn't let us past!" says Scarlett. "It was all arched up and spitting – the dogs were terrified!"

"And it nearly sprang at my face!" puts in Freddie.

"No it didn't," snaps Scarlett. "Where's it from, Daddy?"

"That's Petal," I say, and I realize I'm smirking with something like *pride*. "He's a real bruiser. Bonny got him."

"He can't be called Petal, that's ridiculous," says Scarlett. "That's like calling Hercules Sweetiepie, or something." And she goes a bit red, as if she's not sure her joke works.

I laugh loudly. "You're right. He's actually called Pitbull. Were the dogs really scared?"

"They were *terrified*," repeats Scarlett. "They were *cowering*."

"What does cowering mean?" demands Freddie.

"Bonny got a cat?" asks Nick.

"Yeah. That OK? To keep the rats away."

"Sure it's OK. Brilliant. I've told you – you do what you want up there."

One of the lurchers has its head rammed in a wastepaper basket, pulling out old sarnie wrappers. "So why are you *here*, Barb?" Nick repeats tetchily. "With those monsters?"

"I was just driving everyone out to Bannerby Park and I needed to call in and see Rich." She turns to me, smiling, and my stomach sinks a bit 'cos I know just what she's going to say. "Rich – I phoned Tigger. She was quite sane, for her. I took my *life* into my hands and said Bonny wanted to meet her at our place 'cos it's neutral ground. She was all icy and monosyllabic, but she agreed. We fixed on Sunday. For lunch. Late-ish. That OK?

"You want me to be there?"

"Yeah. You know I do."

"Bonny want me to be there?"

"Bonny *really* wants you to be there, Rich."

"OK. Don't leave me alone with Tigger though, OK?"

"I won't. I promise."

"Barb, stop holding him up," Nick calls out. "He's got just over an hour to finish or he misses his *jackpot* bonus. Now get those hairy mutts out of here!"

"Bye, Daddy," says Scarlett icily. "Nice to see you too." Then she trots over and cranes up and kisses him disapprovingly on the cheek, and the five of them disappear.

I do it, I get it done. I'm putting the last finishing lines to the last storyboard when the motorbike guy arrives like some last-century spaceman. Camilla parcels everything up and then Nick's handing round beers and going on about how, with his *dynamic but concise* proposal, the account is as good as in the bag.

And then he pays me.

I run up the stairs, wealthier by two hundred and fifty quid. For just over a day's work. It feels like an absolute fortune and a couple of short weeks ago just as soon as I'd stuffed it in my wallet I'd've been out shopping and getting bladdered. But I'm mature now, aren't I. In charge of my life. A householder. What one of my uncles calls a Mensch. I'm going to go into town tomorrow and I'm going to put *all* – well, *most* – well, *a good slice* of it in that account Mum opened for me. I'm going to pace myself. When I left Nick said he'd have some more work for me soon, but it's not like it's in the bag.

Bonny's in the main room when I get in, just standing in front of the wide open window, and for once my territorial hackles don't go up. I'm quite glad to see her in fact. I tell her all about the cash I've just made, and she says "Great, Rich! That's fantastic!" and we kind of grin at each other, then she laughs and says "We need butter, teabags, bog cleaner and cereal, OK?" and I say "OK, OK." Then I tell her about Pitbull's stand-off on the stairs with the lurchers, and she *really* loves that, says "That cat is so *brave*", and then raps on about how she hasn't seen or heard a single canal rat since he moved in.

"Not a live one anyway," I say. "The little bastard left half of one on the bottom of my bed last night."

"Oh, but that means he *likes* you!" she goes. "It's an offering." And then she frowns and says, "He's never left me anything!"

"Bonny, I can't believe you're jealous of a bit of mauled rat!"

She laughs and goes into the kitchen and forks out some food for Pitbull, and as soon as the sound of the fork on the dish sounds out, his hard-nut head appears over the window-sill and soon he's face down in his nosh. "He's getting used to being here, isn't he?" says Bonny proudly. "*And* he slept on my bed most of last night."

"Yeah? I thought I got off easily."

"I reckon he likes you best though. You got the rat. Maybe he'll sleep on you tonight."

"Bonny, I don't want the little shit to like me. *Or* sleep on me."

"Yes you do. You say that, but you do."

She tells me she's made spag bol, if I want some. Which I do, of course. I even offer to run out and get some red wine to go with it but she says no, she's got to keep a clear head to work on an essay tonight.

While we eat I'm waiting for her to say something about the impending meeting with her mum, so I can tell her I've agreed to come too, but she doesn't, so I don't say anything about it either, and we just chat about all and everything. When she wanders off and shuts herself in her room I think about running out to the phone box and giving Portia another call, but that looks too eager so I don't.

I try not to spend the rest of the evening waiting for her just to turn up.

I fail.

Chapter 25

I've only just got through the door at college the next day when I'm surrounded by Chris, Ollie, Ryan and Andy. They have that kind of energetic, threatening feel to them they get on when they're about to bludgeon me into a game of five-a-side. "Yeah?" I say suspiciously. "What's up?"

"Last weekend was *crap*," says Chris, genially.

"Speak for yourself," I say. "I had a fantastic time. You should get your own flat, lads, you should you know. Portia and I stayed in bed most of the time. We—"

Chris slings his arm round my neck, cutting off further chat. "Yeah, yeah. We know all about it, mate. We just think you should share it, OK?"

"Like tomorrow night," puts in Ollie.

"A party!" shouts Ryan, and Andy goes: "*Yeah!*"

"A party," I repeat coldly. "Tomorrow night."

"*Yeah!*"

"That leaves a hell of a lot of time to get organized, doesn't it?"

"What's there to get *organized*?" demands Chris, giving my neck an encouraging squeeze. "Ollie's got the decks and the speakers. We tell everyone today. They turn up tomorrow night. That way there's no way for the word to get round and gatecrashers to start lining up."

"Chris, mate, there's more to a party than that. . ."

"Yeah? Like what? I'm not planning on a fucking *finger* buffet, Rich. We ask our mates, Bonny asks hers –"

"Bonny?"

"Well, yeah. You'd ask her, wouldn't you? I mean – she's the one possible hitch, mate. She's got to agree, hasn't she?"

"Well, I might not see her. I might not see her tonight."

"So leave a note on her pillow. Just so's she's got time to ask all her friends tomorrow. Oh, come on, mate – it'll be brilliant."

"What're her friends like?" puts in Ryan.

"Private-school girls," says Ollie. "Rich and sex-starved."

"Yeah?" squeals Ryan. "They're not dogs though, are they? I'm not interested if they're dogs."

"Face it, Ry, you'd be interested in anything that might say yes."

"That is not bloody true. I—"

"We're getting off the point here," says Andy. "I mean – if Rich has got to ask this bird Bonny before he can have a party up there. . ."

"I didn't say I had to ask her," I say indignantly.

"No?"

"No. She's just *staying* there. She knows the score. I mean – we might have to keep out of her room, but –"

"So it's *yes* then!" says Chris, heartily. He gives my neck one last squeeze and detaches himself. "Well, that's a relief, 'cos I've already asked a load of people. Brilliant!"

I'm half thinking I'll go into one, lay into them for setting this up without me. But then I think I'll save my energy. After all, why not have a party? I think about Nick saying I could do what I liked up there. I think about how I'm owed, 'cos I'm going along to Bonny's showdown with her mum. I think about all the cash I've just made, how I feel like celebrating. I think about how cool it's going to make me look in front of Portia. "OK," I say. "You bastards. It's on. But everyone brings booze, OK?"

"*Great*," says Andy. "I'll spread the word."

"Not too many, for Christ's sake," I say. "I'd better tell Portia."

"Get her to bring *her* friends, yeah?" says Ryan

plaintively, while Ollie says, "Hey, she's up, man. Up on the wall."

"What, the – ?!"

"Yup. Those *am-aaazing* horny pictures you drew of the Porsche. They made it into the exhibition."

I leg it along to Huw's art room at top speed. And practically cannon into the principal's back. He doesn't notice, though, 'cos he's having a stand-off with Huw. Huw has stand-offs with everyone from the cleaning staff upwards, and he nearly always wins. I slide sideways behind the doorway to enjoy the show.

"You don't seem to realize, Mr Morgan, that this is the kind of thing that can lead us straight into a court case," the principal's intoning. "Suppose the girl's parents complain?"

"Why SHOULD they?" roars Huw, even more Welsh than usual. "She's over sixteen! Sex is legal so presumably posing NUDE is legal! Look – I wouldn't have dreamt of putting the damn things up without checking with her first. She loved the idea. Far as she was concerned, she'd be happy to have bloody spotlights playing over them!"

"Well. Perhaps. But setting the question of a court case aside, you *also* don't seem to realize that this is the kind of thing that unsettles the college. It leads to gossip, and salacious conjecture, and—"

"Oh, for the love of GOD. When did YOU last

walk these corridors? They're crammed to the bloody rafters with *salacious bloody conjecture*."

"Look, Mr Morgan," hisses the principal tetchily, "you don't have to descend to sarcasm. I just feel that displaying such sketches of a girl who attends this college . . . well. It's unnecessarily titillating."

"D'you know the girl in question? She makes a hobby out of being unnecessarily titillating."

"That is beside the point. She's *here*. A real person, here."

"Well, when you draw a nude, it does tend to be a real person. Not a bloody hologram. *Unnecessarily titillating.* You think no one thinks about girls without their clothes on until I shove a few sketches up on the wall?"

"Of course not. I'm just saying—"

"Look – I'm teaching art here. Underfunded and underappreciated as I am. And art has this strange tradition of drawing the human form. Now these pictures – they're good. They could be better, but they're good. That's why they're in my bloody exhibition. And that's why they're staying."

There's a pause. Huw is beetling up at the principal, and the principal's looking down with loathing at Huw. "So your final word is that they're staying?" the principal frosts out.

"Absolutely they're bloody staying. I won't be censored by PETTY-MINDED PRUDERY!"

There's a thunderous silence. Then the principal

turns on his heel with enormous dignity, and stalks off down the corridor.

I leave it a second or so for him to stalk round the corner, then I bound into the art room. "*All right*, Huw! Defending the right to make real art!"

"Ah, don't give me that crap, lad," he says, beaming at me. "Real art – bollocks! You were just showing off about your sex life, weren't you, you nasty little hound!"

"Oh, come on, Huw – they're erotic."

"Erotic my arse."

"So why d'you defend them?"

"Because I won't be dictated to by some bureaucratic, narrow-minded bastard like him! *God*, I enjoyed that. Haven't had a good run in with the authorities for months."

"You want to watch it, Huw," I say, wandering over to the wall where the exhibition's been pegged up. "You'll end up losing your job."

"Never. They'd never get anyone anywhere near to my genius with the pitiful salary they pay. People come here to do art 'cos of me and they know it."

It doesn't take me long to scan the wall and count up nine of my pictures. "Hey," I say, "I'm well represented."

"Don't get too pleased with yourself. Just about everything else was crap."

I stop in front of the three Porsche sketches, and

get immediate groin-clench. The night I drew them floods back into me. "*Woooah*," I breathe.

"Don't get turned on by your own stuff, lad. It's tantamount to self-abuse. Mind you, all the boys've been making those kind of noises. I've never had so many in to look at an exhibition before. But they don't only look at those three, see? That's the magic. They come in after some grubby thrill, they leave lifted and expanded by their encounter with art. It gets through to them. It gets to them."

I laugh, and turn to face him. "You know, Huw, I think you might be barking mad as well as a genius."

"Quite possibly, lad. Quite possibly. Now bugger off, I've got work to do."

I run into the Porsche at lunchtime, and somehow all the waiting and the angst over the waiting doesn't matter any more. She greets me like she answers her mobile phone, all loud, jealousy-inducing passion and enthusiasm. "Boy-*friend*! *Missed* you!"

"Missed you too, darlin'," I say as she winds herself round me like a barracuda. I can feel my brain switching off, lust taking over. "Did you get that message I left you?"

"Yeah! *Sweet!*"

"So why didn't you come over?"

"Oh – I didn't have time. Honestly. So much work piling up. And my mum – she made me babysit my little brother *again*. For no money. *Again*."

"Aw, *poor* baby," I say, appeased. "*I* got paid."

"Yeah? Lots?"

"Yeah. You had lunch? You want me to buy you some?"

"Oh, *love*-ly!" she carols. "Yeah!"

"So," I say as, wrapped round each other, we make our way over to the cafeteria, "you seen Huw's exhibition yet?"

"Of course I have! I went first thing, with Jenny and Mattie. Don't they look *faa*-bulous?"

"Yeah. Great. Did you see that factory one of mine he put up, the one with all machines and—"

"Jenny's seen them before of course but she *looves* them. Mattie didn't say much though. It was *so obvious* she was jealous. Then these boys came in and started making all these comments, and as we left I was blowing up about how immature they were and she said – *What do you expect?* Honestly. She's so jealous. It's pathetic."

We walk into the cafeteria and over to the serving bar, and as half a dozen or so heads turn to look at us the Porsche goes into overdrive. "It's 'cos of your pictures," she breathes as she winds herself even more sinuously round me and presses her mouth to my neck. "That's why they're staring. Let them. Don't let them bother you."

They don't bother me. They don't bother me at all. What bothers me is I'm as turned on as a tap and we're in a bloody public queue for food. I want to go somewhere where we're not centre stage. Where we might be able to follow through.

Portia, though, is lapping it all up. "Jenny told me those pictures are *all* anyone can talk about," she mouths at me. "It's *all over* the college!"

We order our lunch and pick up our trays and she sashays over to a table on the very farthest side of the caff, shimmying her way between the tables like an exotic dancer. Just about everyone's ogling her. "Sit *down*," I hiss. "Here's fine."

Finally, we sit down. "Mmm, thanks for treating me, Richy," she coos, forking into her salad. "So how much money did you make then?"

Without missing a beat I find myself rounding it down by a hundred quid, then I say: "Big news. You up for a party? You up to being hostess of a party?"

"What?"

"The guys've bullied me into having a party. Round at the flat."

"When?"

"Tomorrow night."

"*Tomorrow night?*"

"I know. The bastards just kind of went ahead and organized it."

"Oh, *honestly*, Richy, you ought to stand up for yourself more. Ollie and Chris – you let them push you around, you know."

"What? No I don't."

"You do. The way they *talk* to you."

"But that's just guys, Portia. I talk like that to them."

"The way Chris makes you play football all the time."

"I like playing football!"

"And that ghastly girlfriend Chris's got. She's like some kind of drill sergeant. I s'pose they're coming, are they? To the party?"

"Well, yeah. . ."

"Hmmm," she sniffs.

"Look, Portia, that's just the way we are together, me and the lads. If I didn't want a party, I'd just say so and that'd be it."

"It might've been nice if you and *I* could've organized it. Now they'll just take over."

"What's there to take over? It's just a matter of loud music and making sure everyone brings beer."

"Exactly," she says darkly. "Honestly, I don't really enjoy these student bash things."

"Oh, come on, Portia. I don't want a party if you're not there." I reach over, take hold of her hand across the table. "You'll come, won't you?"

She shrugs peevishly, and I say, "How's the belly-button?"

"Sore," she says accusingly, as though that's somehow my fault. "And Mum and I had this horrible row about it. She hates it. Honestly, I just *do not believe* that woman. It's *my* body, I think I have the right to do *exactly* what I want with it, don't you?"

"*Yeah!*" I say, fervently.

"She went on and on about how I should've discussed it with her first. Then she went on and on about how selfish I am, about how I never think about anyone but myself – I mean – *honestly*! It's just not true. And if it *was* true I don't see what the hell's so bad about it. I mean – why *should* I think about other people all the time – it's *my* life I'm living, not theirs, right?"

"Right," I echo.

"And then – about *ten minutes* later – we had another row about the washing."

"What about the washing?"

"She's *ruined* one of my tops, 'cos she didn't read the label properly. It clearly said delicate, and she just threw it in with everything else . . . and when I had a go about it to her, she starts saying I can do my own washing if I feel like that. Honestly. When do I get time to do my own washing?"

Portia rants on and on, forgetting to eat. I'm only half listening but even so I find myself siding with her poor old mum. I know better than to say anything, though.

"I'm going to have to move out, seriously I am. Jenny's so *wet*, though, she keeps making all these *problems* when I talk about getting a place together. I can't wait to go to art school. I can't *wait* to leave home."

223

"You need a party to cheer you up," I say cunningly.

"Hmmmm."

"You can ask Jenny, and Mattie, and everyone. . ."

"Mattie? I'm not asking that bitch. I'll ask Chloe though. And Sondra. I'm *pretty* sure there's nothing else happening."

And so it's *pretty* settled. Party on.

We head off (after a long and very public snog) to our separate classes. I try to get her to meet me that evening, but she says she can't. She says she'll see me at the party if she doesn't bump into me in college on Friday. I want to arrange something more definite than that, but I also don't want to look over-anxious and possessive and keen, so I don't.

"You want to turn up a bit early?" I ask.

"I'll try," she says, then adds waspishly, "but you'll have all your mates there, won't you, to help set it up?" and swans off down the corridor.

As I'm heading down the steps at the end of the day, Jenny darts out and touches my arm. "Sorry," she says. "Have you got a moment?"

"Yeah, sure. What's up?"

"I just – well, it's probably nothing. But I thought I should tell you."

"Tell me what?"

"Well, it's probably nothing. I'm probably just panicking over nothing."

"*What*, for Chrissake?" Jenny is one of these chronically apologetic people who make you want to smack them in the face. Plus I'm imagining the worst by this time. Such as Portia's got three other boyfriends apart from me.

"Oh, *sorry*, I'm burbling! Look – it's Tony. I've seen his car. Twice, now. Parked in one of the side roads by the college. Just kind of – you know – *sitting there*."

"What – for Portia?"

"Oh, she doesn't know he's there. Well – I'm pretty sure she doesn't. But he'd be able to see her go past to the bus stop."

"She did finish with him, didn't she?"

"Oh, yes. She told me all about it."

I take in a relieved breath, and say, "Have you told her you've seen him?"

"No. And I don't want to. Well – you know how easily upset she gets. She'd start thinking he was stalking her. She got in such a *state* before, you know – after that night he *lay in wait* for her, outside her house, the night she said she wanted a break from him. I mean – she gets so twitched so easily, she's so *emotionally sensitive. . .*"

In my opinion the Porsche is about as emotionally sensitive as a plastic toilet brush, but, of course, I don't announce this. "I wonder what he's up to?" I say. "Maybe he just wants to talk to her again?"

"Maybe. I just think it's *so sinister*. Just the way he sits in his car and everything. So I thought I'd let you know."

"OK. Well, thanks, Jenny. See you, OK?"

Chapter 26

I wander away from college a bit disgruntled and deflated, on account of Tony being back on the scene as a stalker and Portia not wanting to meet up with me that night. Still, if I have a night in I can get some more work done, can't I. I'm on target with all my outstanding Art and Graphics stuff, halfway through the General Studies, and I've only got another five Eng. Lit. essays to go. This morning Nick shoved a big envelope under my door with the last draft essay I'd given to Barb inside, plus a new version of it all typed up with her suggestions and comments, and a note that said:

This is on disk. Make your changes, and bung it back, and I'll print it out for you. Luv Barb.

What a star that lady is. It's like having my own private correspondence course. Yep, I'll be a good boy tonight and do some work. And while I'm in good boy mode I'll drop by the bank on the way back and feed a sizeable chunk of my storyboards money into my new account. I might even give Mum a quick bell. And *then* – Jesus I'll attain sainthood if I carry on like this – I'll pick up the teabags and cereal and whatever it was Bonny said we were out of.

I do all this (Mum is delighted to hear from me, more delighted I'm earning and working) and while I'm in the supermarket I see sirloin steaks are on offer, and before I can have second thoughts I pick up a packet with two in and then I get some potatoes and I head back to the flat meaning to cook for Bonny for once.

She absolutely can't believe it when she gets back and finds me peeling spuds. "I thought you said you couldn't *cook*?" she says.

"I can do a bit," I say.

"So what's happening – is Portia coming round?"

"No. This is for you."

I'm not prepared for her reaction. Her eyes go all googly and her face kind of *floods* with colour, and it's sweet, she pretends nothing's up and looks away and starts putting the kettle on and stuff.

"I'm going to do chips," I say.

"What in? We haven't got a chip pan."

"I can use a saucepan."

"You'll set the whole place on fire."

"No I won't. Trust me."

"OK," she says, "the cooking oil's up there." Then she disappears. Two minutes later she's back with a bottle of red wine.

"Where did that come from?" I ask.

"I had it in my room."

"What are you, a secret alcoholic?"

"No. I just knew it wouldn't be all that safe if I left it in the kitchen."

I laugh, and say, "Fair cop."

"It's OK. I've been nicking your tins of soup from that box under the sink."

"*Have* you? You cow. My mum gave me those. So I wouldn't starve."

Bonny goes all googly-eyed again. "Your mum gave them to you?" she echoes.

"Yeah. I think she thought it'd be more . . . you know . . . *nutritious* to give me tins of tuna and stuff, rather than just the dosh that'd get spent on beer."

"I think that's really lovely. God, I'd never've taken that tin of soup if I'd known it was from your *mum*."

"Don't be stupid. Now – how d'you cook steak?"

The meal, as it turns out, is not bad. Bonny sniggers at me 'cos I've forgotten to get any vegetables, which she says is typically *male*, but she gets together a bit of salad from stuff she finds in the fridge and hands me two squashy tomatoes to grill with the steaks. And my chips are a triumph. Nice and crispy, almost burnt but not quite.

I wait until we're sitting on the floor in front of the open window, with Pitbull sitting between us intimidating us into giving him bits of steak, to hit her with the news of the party. "What you doing tomorrow night?" I ask.

She looks at me weirdly. "Why?"

"'Cos Chris and Ollie – they're turning up here with decks and speakers. To have a party."

"And you want me out the way."

"No. Did I say that? I want you to *be* here. Bring some friends. What d'you reckon?"

And she's all glowy again. *Jesus,* I wish the Porsche was as easy to please as Bonny seems to be. "God, you believe in short notice, don't you?" she laughs.

"Well, it was Chris who was the prime mover. He was on about how nothing ever happens at the weekends and how this place is ideal for a party. And as I'm in Nick's good books right now – well, I thought it'd be OK. Long as you were OK about it."

"I think it's a great idea!" she says. "There's a group of us, about nine, meeting up at the pub Friday – is nine too many?"

"Not too many at all," I say, thinking fondly of Ryan's little face as nine unattached girls hit the party.

"Great. Well – I'll just bring 'em along here afterwards. Everyone's been saying they want to see where I'm staying."

"Great. Don't leave it too late, will you."

"Sure."

"And don't worry, we won't go in your room."

"What about shifting your bed in there?" she says. "Stop it getting jumped on."

"Yeah, good idea."

"And we can leave coats in there and stuff—" Then she suddenly breaks off and her face falls and she says "Oh. . ."

"What?"

"Petal. I'd forgotten about Petal. He'll be *traumatized* – all the noise and people and stuff. . ."

We both focus on Pitbull, who is engaged in extending a long, sharp claw and hooking the last of my steak off my plate. "Bonny," I say, "it would take a nuclear war to traumatize that cat."

She watches him as he gags down the bit of meat whole, and laughs. "Yeah. You're right, he's a survivor. OK – brilliant! What time they all coming?"

Friday evening seven o'clock. Two hours or so to go and I find myself ridiculously up about the party. Bonny and I shift my bed into her room and it won't fit unless we lay it on top of hers. I don't think the sexual symbolism of this is lost on either of us but neither of us – thank God – make a crack about it. Then we clear out the kitchen a bit, hiding breakable stuff away, and Bonny produces half a dozen French sticks and a big slab of Cheddar cheese from a

Sainsbury's carrier propped against the side of the fridge.

"This is my contribution," she says, a bit embarrassed. "I just thought fewer people might throw up if they have something in their stomachs. Other than beer, I mean."

"A party *with food*," I say approvingly. I cut myself off a big wedge of cheese and add: "This is getting slicker by the minute."

Bonny disappears into the bathroom to tart herself up and I have a roam round the main room, which is all echoing and exciting now, like it's waiting for the action. Then Bonny reappears, looking gorgeous, and without thinking twice I tell her so. And she goes red again and races out the door like a fiend's after her, shouting back, "See you in an hour or so, OK!"

I've only got time to open one of the six cans I brought for my own personal party consumption before Ollie, Ryan, Chris, Natalie and Andy roll up, laden with booze, decks and speakers. The next hour is spent plugging them in, moving them around, adjusting, tweaking. We have this brainwave of setting everything up in front of the big open window, so Ollie is silhouetted dramatically against the night sky and more importantly so he can act as a barrier between the party and the long drop to the ground. We give it a trial run and the sound, as Ollie says, is slammin'. The acoustics are ace. The floor vibrates. Everyone starts moving, even Ryan. "You know, I was right, we could run a club up here," he shouts above the noise. "We could *charge*."

"You won't be able to afford me, man," says Ollie. "Not soon."

"Oh, piss off, Oll. Just 'cos you've had a couple of poxy semi-demi-professional gigs—"

"Those were *real*! I got *paid*!"

"They were *birthday parties*! For *twelve-year-olds*!"

"They were turning thirteen, man!" squawks Ollie, then he jabs the finger up at Ryan, and gets back to mixing. Then Andy takes over as DJ and Ollie starts on his MC thing. He's good, he's hilarious. And just as he's really getting into it, the first guests arrive.

Chapter 27

Three quarters of an hour on, and the room isn't completely crowded out but we already know it's going to be a great night. I'm on edge because Portia isn't here yet, but not too on edge. There's stacks of beer piled up in the kitchen, and only a couple of gatecrashers who aren't really gatecrashers 'cos they used to go to Andy's school and people know them from seeing them around. And Ollie's mixing like he's inspired – everyone's moving about to it. Natalie gives up trying to get Chris to dance long enough to collar me in the kitchen where you can just about get heard without yelling and demands, "So where is she then?"

"Portia?"

"No, Minnie Mouse. *Yeah*, Portia."

"She'll get here. She's bringing some friends."

"*Oh* great. That'll be fun."

"Don't be a cow, Natalie."

"I'm not. I meant it."

"Like shit you did."

Natalie laughs, and says, "I thought she'd be here from the start, Rich. As your squeeze and all. Hostessing big time."

"She's not like that."

"Yeah she is."

"Well, maybe she is, but so what?"

"So long as she's letting you get what you want, eh?" sneers Natalie, and stomps back into the main room. I follow her, thinking I might have a go back, when I look up and see Portia framed in the doorway like some sexy strip-cartoon heroine. I'm through the crowd and in front of her in seconds flat.

"*Hi*, baby!" she squeals, and in what feels like slow-motion she flings her arms round my neck. She's not wearing such an extreme dress as she wore to Sondra's party, but bloody nearly. And behind her, Jenny, Chloe and Sondra are like carbon copies only not, of course, anywhere near as hot as the real thing.

"*Sowwy* we're late," gushes the Porsche, fixing her mouth briefly to mine. "Only we all got ready together, and that's disastrous, innit girls?"

The girls all giggle in agreement, and Chloe says, "Especially when we got through *all three* bottles of sparkly!"

"I know," agrees Portia, mournfully. "You going to let us in wivout drink?"

And they all giggle again at the very idea of them *not* being let in. Already, various guys are craning their necks round, sizing them up. One of the first things you learn when you hit puberty is that fabulous-looking girls freeload with ease.

They all sashay in, and gather in front of Ollie, who instantaneously pumps up his act, mixing and moving like crazy. "Is Ollie taken?" Portia husks up at me.

"*What?*"

"Only Sondra's got it *ba-ad* for him. D'you think she's in with a chance?"

I shrug. "Maybe."

"Will you have a word with him?"

"Oh, Jesus. Can't she manage to pull on her own?"

"Don't be *miserable*, Richy! What are friends for?"

"OK, OK. I'll have a word with him."

Portia pivots round then, and sizes up the other guests. I can tell she's torn between wanting to sneer and wanting to take the floor and show off. The desire to take the floor wins. She starts her pole-dancing routine again, and the girls start moving about behind her. All I have to do is stand there in the middle, with my unblinking eyes fixed on her fabulous body, jerking my head about a bit.

They're kind of *seeping out* ego, the girls.

Especially Portia. They're out of step with everyone else here. And they keep doing girly things like cupping their hands over each other's ears and screeching things, and giggling ostentatiously. I catch Ollie's face a couple of times – he's grinning, but his eyes have dismissed them.

Portia suddenly stops ignoring me and hooks her hands round my waist. "Going to get me a beer, Richy?" she squeals.

"Sure," I say, and bull my way through to the kitchen. I'm quite glad to move off if you want the truth. About ten people say "Hi!" and "All right?" and "Good party!" to me on the way through, which feels great. And it is a good party – it's fantastic, really jelling. I reckon two-thirds of the people we invited are here, and there'll be a few more after the pubs shut down. Which is just crowded enough. In the kitchen doorway, I grab two cans off the nearest pile. I'm the host after all, aren't I? I'm owed. But when I get to the main room something's shifted.

I look around and pretty soon I see what it is. Four guys who aren't from our college are standing over by the door. They're all tall, and chunky, and they look like they might play rugby. And nobody in the room has ever seen them before and that fact is being spread around the room by osmosis, and suddenly they're The Enemy.

I move closer to them, and see Bonny. "Rich!" she shouts, over all the heads. "This is *amazing*!" I push my way through to her. "Wow!" she goes, "I thought we'd be some of the first to get here! It's heaving!" And then she introduces me to five OK-looking girls standing around her.

And then she introduces me to the four chunky guys.

For some reason, now I know they're with her, I feel even more hostile. They all smile, a bit dazed, a bit thrown off-balance by the crush, and one of the guys says something about dumping his beer, and I noticed that at least they've bought a stash of liquor, the bastards, and Bonny points them jovially in the direction of the kitchen. They make their way through, copping a few malignant stares as they go.

"What d'you bring *them* along for Bonny?" I hiss.

"What d'you *mean*?" she bridles, mega-indignant. "You *told* me to bring some mates!"

"Yeah, but . . . you know. I thought they'd all be *girl* mates."

"Oh, *don't* be so *pathetic*! What difference does it make?"

"Well, it's like – it's a guy's party. So new girls are fine but new blokes aren't."

"That is just about the most *pathetic* thing I have ever heard!"

"Bonny, you don't seem to realize – them coming here – it's like they're moving in on our territory!"

"*Oh – my – God*. How *tribal*. I don't believe I'm

hearing this. I thought we'd moved on a bit since the Stone Age."

"Look – it's just a thing blokes feel!"

"And you think girls *don't*?" She nods over at Portia, Jenny, Chloe and Sondra, standing in a poisonous group in the centre of the room. Bonny's five girlfriends have congregated in front of Ollie, and Portia and co. keep casting sidelong glances at them, and snickering. "It's just we – well *some* of us," Bonny goes on, all sarcastic, "try and rise above it. Try and pretend we've *evolved* a bit. You know. Since the primal swamp."

"So who are they?" I ask grumpily. "Those guys?"

"It's May's older brother and his mates. We see them sometimes. And Rebecca and Harry are going out. It's no big *deal*. Look – I wouldn't've asked them if I thought it'd start World War Three – *Jesus!*"

I look over to where the four chunky guys are standing in a loud group, taking up too much space, and I decide it's up to me as host and all to be mature. Gracious even. Ollie is in the throes of handing the DJ job over to Andy again to take a break, and I know from experience that Ollie can be the most tribal of the lot. I head over to the inter-lopers, and reach them just as Oll is pushing past.

"Hi," I say gruffly. "All right?"

"Yeah," one of them says, while another raises his can to me. "Good party," grunts a third.

It's not a lot, but it's enough.

"Who the fuck are they?" growls Ollie, as we head for the kitchen once more.

"They're kosher," I say. "They're with Bonny."

"Hmmm. OK. Pass me some of that bread. And which is their beer, man?"

Two hours on, and some people have left, a few others have arrived late, the party's mellowed, but it's still ace. Ollie and Andy have left a few records on to run, and most people are sitting around now, backs against the walls, and just about everyone who isn't directly involved in talking or snogging is gazing happily out at the starry night sky through the enormous arched windows. I'm kind of *basking* in how good it's been. 'Cos of *my flat*. And in the last hour or so, since the music slowed, Portia has been all over me. Dead attentive. Which is nice.

"Isn't there another *room* we can go to?" she breathes into my ear. "I kind of grew out of making out in public when I was about fourteen."

Could've fooled me, I think, while I say, "Well, darlin', there's always the lift."

"Oh, ha, ha," she snaps. "What about Bonny's room? Is it out of bounds or something?"

"No but it's . . . well, it's kind of Bonny's. And she's here."

"Yes, but it doesn't look like she's going to be getting round to using it, does it?" the Porsche says cattily, and nods over to the other side of the room, where Bonny's sitting with both arms clasped round her knees. Ryan is on one side of her, and a couple of her girlfriends are lounging in front, and they're all chatting away a bit bored and sleepy.

"No, but she's still *here*. . ." I repeat limply.

"Oh well, *fine*. If you don't want to go somewhere private with me, *fine*."

It's a test, I know it. It's – *You must want me more than you don't want to piss off Bonny*. And I do, of course. Want her, I mean. I look at her luminous, sexy cat-face and I want her so much I don't care who I piss off.

I pull her to her feet, and we jiggle through the groups of people everywhere all over the floor, and get to Bonny's door. Then I pull it open very quickly and we slide inside. Two seconds later I've got Portia pinned against the back of the door, and we're going for it like crazy.

"Richy – *mmmm*," she murmurs. "Let's get on the bed."

Normally I'd be all for this, but being jammed against the door is cunningly stopping anyone else getting in. So I just hone in on her again like I'm so transfixed by lust my ears have cut out. "Mind my tummy-button!" she squeals, then she says – "Hey – want to see it?"

"Sure," I say eagerly, and drop my arms.

She reaches behind, unzips her dress. "I've only

just taken the bandage off. I nearly wore a crop-top tonight, to flash it off – but it's still weeping a bit."

"Oh, *yuck*," I blurt out, before I can stop myself, then I say, *very* quickly, as her dress slides down to her waist, "*OhmyGod*, Portia, that is *gorgeous*, that is properly *exquisite*, that really is." It is quite sweet. All sparkly, like a belly dancer's.

And I'm zoned in on her again before she can do her dress up or start telling me all over again how incredibly glad she is she had the piercing done. I'm thinking – we could make it standing up. We *could*. Except I'm not exactly sure how to achieve this, especially with having to be careful about her belly-button and everything. I glance around, and spot Bonny's holdall down on the floor, and I reach out with my foot and shove it over towards us. Then I jam it against the door, and then I kind of lurch backwards taking Portia with me and soon we're half off and half on my bed on top of Bonny's bed and everything in me is focused and primal and we're shedding what clothes we have to, and then it's happening, brilliant, *brilliant*, and Portia's making fabulous moaning noises, and it's *fantastic*, every movement's ecstasy, and I'm breathing like a marathon, and then I can't hold off any longer and it's over and I collapse on top of her pushing my nose into her hair and she goes: "Oh, this is *awful*!"

"*What?*" I sob out, devastated.

"Just – having to be all rushed and . . . and *sordid* like this."

"Rushed? God – *sorry* – I just—"

"Not *you*. Just – at a *party*, and everything. I wish we had more privacy. So we can take our *time*."

"We will, Portia, we will," I say, all relieved and emotional and desperate. "Bonny's gonna move out soon, and when she does, it'll be just me here, and you can come round whenever you want, and we can spend all *night* just—"

"When's she moving out?" Portia interrupts crisply.

"I don't know exactly. Soon."

"Only . . . well. . ." Portia trails off and suddenly goes all seductive. She puts her hand up and strokes my cheek; she pushes her finger slowly into my mouth. "Only I had another row with Mum last night. I can't *stand* it at home, Rich, it's really doing my head in. She's on at me the whole time, nagging and bitching at me. And I thought . . . well. When Bonny goes, I could move in here with *you*, couldn't I?"

Chapter 28

You know sometimes you're walking along a road you walk down every day, and it's a bit dark, and you're miles away, mind on something else, and then something – a big bit of cardboard flapping or something – just catches the edge of your eye, and you *jump*, some deep, instinctive, animal part of you *jumps*, clear out the way, in case it's dangerous?

That's what happens to me now, when Portia says about moving in with me. I *jump*. It feels like my stomach has disappeared and my primitive animal self is screaming *Woah – no! Danger, peril! Run! Save yourself!*

But at the same time my *mind* is going *wow* she wants to live with me, this is amazing we've only slept together three times and she wants to *live* with me, hey that must mean I'm a *brilliant lover*, and if she moves in we can do *this* all the time, any time, and I'm flattered and excited and I get hold of her amazing unreal face in my hands and say, "Blimey, Portia, I don't know what to say."

"How about yeth?" she lisps, smooching up at me.

"I mean – you sure about this? It's not like we've been together all that long, and. . ."

"Sure I'm sure," she says. "I told you – I've got to move out. And . . . and . . . I *really like you*, Richy. I want some *space* with you."

Outside the room, someone suddenly collapses against the door, and we both spin off the bed and start clambering back into our clothes. "You *see*?" mouths Portia. "It's awful, like this. Or with you out in that room and Bonny walking in on us any time she wants."

I straighten out the bed and pocket the condom – "Can't let *Bonny* stumble on *that*, can we?" Portia sneers – then we slide out to the main room, where nothing much seems to have changed, except the door to the tiny junk room is standing open and a great avalanche of junk has spewed out on to the floor. Chris grins up at me all sarky from his space next to Natalie on the floor, nods towards it and says, "Someone went looking for an empty bedroom. Seeing as the other one was taken."

"Who? You?"

"Me? Na. I knew it was full of crap, didn't I? Na – one of Andy's friends copped off with some bird and pulled open the door and *whooosh* – it was like *back-draught*, man, all this rubbish got *sucked out* and he was nearly *buried* in it. He could've *died*!" And he starts hiccuping with laughter.

There's a joint making its way slowly along the line of people slumped against the wall, which explains Chris's loopy cackle. Ryan's sitting next to Chris, and I know Bonny's the other side of Ryan, but I don't look straight at her, I daren't.

Chris hands the joint to Ryan, who offers it to Bonny first. "No thanks," she says.

"Why not?" murmurs Ryan, all smooth. "Try it!"

"I've *tried* it. I'm just not into it."

"Why not?" he says, bringing his face even closer to hers.

She moves back, and says, "Look, I just don't want any, OK?"

He cranes towards her again. "Go *on*! It'll help your head *expand*!"

There's a pause, during which I make a mental note to give Ry a few hints on his pulling technique, then Bonny says, "Look, Ryan, I don't want my head to expand, OK? It's all I can do to cope with it the way it *is*. The last few weeks I've been feeling things so much, so *strong* I . . . well. I just don't need any other stuff in there to deal with, all right?" She glares down at the floor then, and I find myself staring at her. That was quite an answer she gave. Boy, has she changed.

On the other side of the room, a load of people are heaving themselves to their feet and lurching towards the door, calling out "Bye" and "Thanks" and "See you, OK?". I can't see Bonny's friends, they must've left while we were in her room. Portia takes hold of my hand, and says, "Let's see if there's any booze left, hm?"

"Sure," I say, and she hauls me into the kitchen. It's a scene of complete wreckage. Knee-deep in bottles and cans, with the last of the block of cheese squatting like some malformed maggot right on the edge of the counter, a couple of fag-ends stubbed out on its back. "Oh, *gross*," says Portia, in icy disgust. I spot a bottle of lager still with its top on in the sink, and I pull it out and knock the lid off. Portia takes it out of my hand. "Thanks, darlin'," she says. "I'm *parched*." Then she walks out of the kitchen.

I look around for another one, but there's no joy. I clamber up on the counter and force the skinny skylight window open as far as it'll go, to let some of the fug and smoke out, then I jump down, scattering cans, and follow Portia out to the main room. The party is in its final death-throes. Andy's passed out on the floor, next to a few other slumped shapes. Bonny's disappeared, and Ryan's hunched against the wall staring ahead of him with his mouth open. Chris and Natalie are nose to nose, arms around each other, and Ollie's dancing slowly and sexily by himself by the decks, watched avidly by Sondra.

I look around longingly for Portia, and see she's rejoined her mates. She's giggling, swigging lager, and she has her mobile out.

"Oi, wake up, git face," I say to Andy, toeing him, but he doesn't.

"You want me to get a bin bag?" Ollie calls over.

"No," I say. I suddenly feel shattered. I just want to *sleep*. Curl up with my face in Portia's neck and sleep.

And then she's back by my side again. I put my arms round her and she says, "Richy – I've just ordered a cab. So we'd better go now – make our way down to the road, yeah?"

"What – you going?" I ask stupidly.

"Yeah. It's three in the morning! We're all staying the night at Jenny's."

"Oh. Right. Well – *thanks* for telling me."

"Oh, come on, Richy! You didn't expect me to stay *here*, did you?"

"Well – yeah, I did actually. I thought we'd kind of crash out together."

"What – with all this shit everywhere?" she squawks. "No thanks."

"Well, I've got to!"

"Oh, don't be *sour*, Richy! We had it all arranged – about Jenny's and everything."

"I thought you'd stay here, that's all."

There's a silence, then Jenny calls out, "Porshy – come on! We'd better get down there, the cabby said he'd only be ten minutes didn't he?"

"Coming!" carols Portia. Then she grabs me and kisses me on the side of the mouth and says, "Phone me tomorrow, yeah? When you get up."

I shrug, and she says, "Oh, come on, Richy. Think how fab it's going to be soon. *You* know. When you swap flatmates!" Then she high-heels it off out the door with the other three harpies.

Ryan looks up from his squat on the floor. "What's that about flatmates?" he groans.

I shrug, and say, "She wants to move in with me."

"*Woah*," breathes Ryan. "What about Bonny?"

"When Bonny moves out."

"*Woah*," he says again. "Properly shacked up."

And you can see written all over his face – *bloody hell how amazing, sex whenever you want it, in the shower, in the afternoon, every night . . . sex on tap.* But then his face changes, and he mutters, "Living together, though. That's serious, man. That's like comment – commet – *commitment*."

"Yeah," I mutter. "It is." It's then that I spot my mattress leaning up against the wall outside Bonny's bedroom. "Oh," I say.

"Bonny shoved it out there," Ryan said. "I helped her. Said she was going to bed. I want to go to bed, man."

"So go to bed. Right there."

"I can't sleep *here*," he moans, then he crumples down full length on to the floor and passes out.

Chris and Natalie help each other to an almost-standing position and weave their way towards the door. "That was an amazing party, mate," Chris says. He claps me on the shoulder, then he leans on me for a second or two. "*Really* amazing."

"You going?"

"Yeah. I'm going to see Nat home. But we'll be back in the morning to help clear up, yeah Natalie?"

"Like shit we will," she mutters, and they stagger out.

I look blearily over at Ollie, who's tidying away some of his records. "Thanks, man," I say. "That was great. You staying?"

"Yeah. My brother – he said he'll bring the van over in the morning, pick up the gear."

I kick away the cans and bottles cluttering the floor, clear a space, and heave my mattress down. "Luxury," comments Ollie. "You got room for two on that?"

"Not if one of the two is you, mate. No."

"Your bird gone?"

"Yeah. So – what about Sondra?" I didn't have a chance to prime Oll about her, but the way she was acting around him I didn't exactly need to.

"What about her?"

"She was mad for you."

"Yeah, well. She don't precisely flick my switch,

man. I mean – she's a looker, yeah, but when I spend some time around her, and her *voice*, and some of the shit she comes out with – no. I think no, man."

I look at Ollie, and I know, without asking him, I know he'd say the exact same thing about Portia now.

And I think maybe deep down I'd agree with him.

I wake up at about six in the morning as the first light's coming through, register that I have Ollie on one side of me and Pitbull on the other, and pass out again.

Chapter 29

Ollie is first up, smug as hell because he's not as wasted as the rest of us seeing as he didn't get so bladdered the night before because he was *working*. He brings me over a big mug of sweet tea and starts chatting to me very loudly all about how ace his mixing was and how two people asked for his number for parties they had coming up – "Proper gigs, man! One was an eighteenth!"

He won't let me sleep any more. "My bruv'll be here soon," he says. "You want some work out of me, let's get going now."

So in the end I crawl off my mattress and into the kitchen, and between us we start shovelling all the cans and bottles into bin bags. The noise we make wakes Andy and the others all crashed out on the bare boards, and one by one they get to their feet, all stooped and groaning like mutants, demanding tea and aspirin. I make them pick up the last of the cans, and Ollie puts the kettle on, and I walk over to the windows and swing them back against the wall. Clean air with a tang of the canal comes in, and everyone groans and shivers but no one asks for them to be shut again. Already, the sun's warm where it touches you. Andy fetches the broom, offers to sweep up; someone else jams the overspill from the junk room back behind the closed door.

After a bit, Bonny slides out of her bedroom in her silky kimono, closely followed by one of her girl-friends from last night and they both go "Hi" without looking up and together they lock themselves in the bathroom.

Ryan's gawping at the closed door. "D'you reckon they're lesbians?" he hisses at me.

"No, you sad bastard. Bonny didn't get off with you 'cos she didn't fancy you. OK?"

"Yeah, but – that girl – she had her in her room all night!"

"So? We were all out here all night. Ollie got into *bed* with me. That make us queer?"

"No. Well – you and Ollie, maybe."

Everyone votes Ryan to be the one to hump the full bags down to the dumpsters in the car park, and when he comes back up, Chris and Natalie are with him. They're looking all fresh and scrubbed and showered and that's really irritating so we tell them to piss off again because all the work's done. "All right then," says Chris. "You don't want us to cook you breakfast – fine."

"*Cook* us *breakfast*?" groans Andy. "I think I'm gonna throw up."

"You say that," says Natalie, heading bossily for the kitchen, "but a fried brekky is actually one of the best hangover cures known to man. It's the grease – it lines your stomach." ("*Ble-uegh*," from Ryan.) "Chris's mum gave us some bacon. And some bread. She is *so nice*."

And once the bacon's sizzling in the pan everyone wants some. Pitbull jumps in through the open windows, glares round at everyone, and sits down to wait. Bonny and her friend emerge from the bathroom, all damp-haired and sweet-smelling, and Ryan says, "There's bacon sarnies coming up, but only if you've done some *work*," and Bonny says, "We *have* done some work. We had to scour the whole bathroom before we could use it." Then she finds the ketchup, and I donate two cans of baked beans from my private store and heat them up, and Chris finds plates, saucers, anything, and soon we're all sitting there in the sun on the floor, eating and throwing bits to Pitbull and beginning to feel better, and we start joking and reminiscing about the party last night, the way you do when it's been really, really good.

"Where's the Princess?" Natalie suddenly raps out.

"Leave it, Nat," says Chris.

"Why? Just wondering why Portia isn't here, that's all."

"She's coming over later," I say, through a mouthful.

"Yeah?"

"Yeah. Said she'd clean up the kitchen."

Natalie sneers out a laugh at this, and I say, "No, really Nat – she's looking forward to giving the oven a really good seeing to," and Chris bursts out laughing and I join in. Then we wipe our plates with the last of the bread, and soon everyone's standing up and making their way off, and in the end it's me who cleans up in the kitchen, while Bonny gets a rag and attacks all the beery sticky patches out in the main room.

"Well – was it worth it?" I ask, when we've finally finished and the flat is almost back to normal and the fug of beer and fag smoke has all but disappeared.

"The party? Yeah, it was great."

"Your mates enjoy it?"

"Yeah. Ollie's fantastic. May wants him to do her party."

"Brilliant. He should pay me an agent's fee, I reckon."

We're still not quite looking at each other. It's hanging there between us, the fact that I sloped off into her room with Portia and barricaded her out. I think maybe I should apologize but I don't want to bring it up. I mean – it's not such a big deal, is it? The other thing we're not bringing up is the fact that we're both supposed to be having the Sunday Lunch from Hell tomorrow, over at Barb's house with Tigger there. Well, I'm not going to mention it. Not until she does. Not until this hangover's subsided a bit anyway.

It's now getting on for two in the afternoon and I decide I really have to haul all my disgusting clothes down to the laundrette. Mum had said I could take stuff home and this is seriously tempting, but I know if I bump into Dad with a load of dirty clothes under my arm it'll only confirm his lowest opinion of me, that I'm an exploitative, uncaring git. So I do the laundrette, and I pick up some milk and choccy biccies and bananas from the shops, and when I get back to the flat it's empty. And I find what I most want to do is sleep. That's the thing about hangovers. You think you've got over the worst, but they lie in wait and pounce again, roughly two hours after you think you're coming out the other side.

When I wake up the sun's just beginning to set. I run down to the phone box on the corner and dial Portia's number, and she answers, right away.

"So how's the hangover?" I ask.

"*Gha-astly*. That's why I didn't come over this morning."

"Yeah, right."

"Honestly, I was *so ill*."

"You had all that wine first, didn't you? That you should've brought to the party. Wine and beer make you feel queer, beer and wine make you feel fine."

"*What?*"

"Old saying. Never mind. My money's gonna go. What about tonight?"

"Well. . ."

"You wanna go somewhere?"

"What, a club or something? I'm *tired*."

"Or a pub."

"I don't really like pubs. I mean – what are they *for*?"

"Well, you could come round. Bonny's out."

"Oh, I don't know, Richy. Jen's all depressed at the moment – I said we might get a video out. You know – have a girls' night in."

Portia actually uses phrases like "girls' night in". Non-ironically. I knew I wouldn't see her tonight though, even before I phoned.

Call it instinct.

Chapter 30

Sunday lunchtime, Bonny and I are seated side by side on the bus heading over to Barb and Nick's place. It was all arranged in a very low-key, very civilized fashion. Bonny told me she was going to leave about one o'clock, and asked if I was still coming. And I said yes, sure, and she said thank you, and that was that.

Bonny's wearing her new outfit, the rusty jacket Portia was jealous of, and the trousers and the high-heeled boots. She's got this weird, frozen look about her. She doesn't want to talk on the bus. I can't think of anything to say or anything to ask her anyway.

We bump along, and reach our stop, and just as we're getting off the bus, she says, "Oh – I'm staying the night at Dad's tonight. Sorry – I should've told you."

The first thing I do is get this flash-vision of
Portia on my bed, the second thing is say: "OK, fine.
Does that mean you're getting on a bit better with –
what's she called? Your stepmum?"

Bonny looks taken aback. "Ellie? I've never
thought about her being my stepmum. I s'pose she
is, though, isn't she."

"Yup. She OK about you now?"

"Yeah. We've done all this talking. She's really
understanding, it's . . . it's . . . *anyway*, Dad said to
phone him when Mum's gone, and he'll come and
get me."

Bonny's voice is coming out all thin and tight, like
she's choking. I wish I could think of something to
say, something to cheer her up. "So – you thought
what you're going to say to your mum and everything?" I mutter.

"Sort of. Well – it depends. On how she *is*. You
know."

We're at the house. Bonny takes in a deep,
raggedy, panicky breath, and we walk up to the front
door and I knock. Barb opens the door straight away
and hisses, "She's not here yet!"

As we shuffle into the hall, she says, "The kids are
round with my mum for the day. I thought it was
best – it'll just be the four of us."

"What about Nick?"

"He's going out too. He works with Tigger, so he
thought it'd be—" She breaks off as Nick rounds

the bend in the stairs, looking all groomed and glossy. "Nick! You said you were going to the gym! How come you've got your Armani on if you're going to the gym!"

"I never said I was going to the gym, Barb."

"Yes you did! You said you were going to get some exercise!"

"I am," says Nick, peering in the hall mirror, licking his fingers and flicking his hair back. "I'm power-walking."

"Yeah?" she scoffs. "So why are you all tarted up?"

"'Cos I'm power-walking to a wine bar, OK? I'm meeting Jed."

"Power-walking to a *wine bar*? Bloody *typical*!" she explodes. "There's no point exercising if you get pissed up straight after!"

"Yes there is, Barb. First I exercise, then I indulge. It's called balance, OK? I'm leading a highly balanced existence." And with that he flounces out of the door, turns back, says "Good luck, all right? *Everyone*." And he heads down the path.

"I'll give him balanced existence," mutters Barb, as he disappears from view. Bonny stutters out this nervy little laugh, and Barb goes on, "Look, sorry for shouting. I'm a bit on edge, that's all."

"Thanks for doing this, Barb," chokes out Bonny. "I feel awful about landing you with –"

"Stop it," says Barb. "It's OK. Now come on – let's get a glass of wine down you."

It's weird, just the three of us standing around in the savoury-smelling kitchen, waiting for the vampire to arrive. Bonny's so tense she's practically vibrating with it, and Barb's making a lot of noise at the stove. I feel OK, considering. I'll be able to take a back seat, after all.

"You don't think she'll . . . *not turn up*, do you?" whispers Bonny.

"No. No way," says Barb. "She phoned last night. Confirmed."

"Oh. Right."

"Look – I thought we'd eat in here – less formal – d'you think that's OK? I can be – you know – busy with the lunch, but not actually leave the room – d'you think Tigger'll be offended we're eating in the kitchen?"

"No. Well – no."

There's a pause, then Barb puts her hand on Bonny's arm and says, "Just remember what we talked about, Bonny, OK? No matter how much she cries, you're not going back."

"I know, I know."

"Your mum needs help. And you're not the one who can help her, not in that way."

"I know."

"OK. Right." Barb turns, smiles at me, and just as I'm smiling bravely back the doorbell goes and

Barb grits her teeth, mutters "OK, this is it" and scoots off to answer it. Bonny's face is white. I think about putting my arm round her and giving her a quick squeeze but there isn't time, because the kitchen door's swinging open and Tigger's rushing in and bearing down on her daughter with both scary arms reaching out and wide open. "Oh – *darling*!" she wails. She grabs Bonny, and then there's a squeaky, snuffly thirty seconds or so while they both hang on to each other.

Barb and I look on anxiously. Bonny's the first to pull back. "I'm sorry, Mum," she gasps. "I'm really sorry you've been so upset by all this it's the – *last* thing I wanted but I *had* – I had to do it I had to go – *OK*?"

It comes out like a prepared speech, only it's all rushed and the spacing's all wrong. Tigger pats her arm and sobs, "It's OK, darling. It's behind us now. Don't get upset."

There's a kind of breathless pause, then Barb steps forward and puts a glass of wine in Tigger's hand, who takes it without so much as a glance at her and lifts it to her mouth. She's looking good, Tigger. All her old polish back. I bet she's taken hours to get ready. But just then she glances up and catches me staring. "Richy! What are *you* doing here?"

I glance over at Barb. Who says: "Tell her, Rich." Oh, *great*. Chuck me in the snake pit why don't you.

"Um. . ." I say.

"I wanted him to come, Mum," whispers Bonny. "We're –"

"You're an *item*, aren't you?" Tigger squeals. "Oh – how *lovely*."

"No we're not!" cries Bonny, and I take a deep breath and say, "I'm afraid I wasn't exactly honest with you before, Tigger. That mate Bonny's staying with, in his flat? It's me."

"But why didn't you *tell* me?" she demands. "When you came round? Why did you have to lie to me?"

"I think Rich felt—" starts Barb.

"I'm asking *him*," snaps Tigger.

"Um . . . *well*. It was all a bit heated, wasn't it, back then, and you were upset, and Bonny was in a state, and I thought maybe everyone needed a bit of space, you know, and it wasn't down to me anyway, to tell you, it was down to Bonny. . ."

This garbled crap seems to satisfy Tigger. "Look, let's all go and sit down," she quavers. "I haven't come here to start making accusations about what happened, or make people feel guilty or anything." She turns to Bonny, pastes a brilliant, brittle smile across her face, and says, "You look lovely, darling. New clothes?"

"Yes."

Her gaze travels downwards. "And boots." She lets out a splintery laugh. "Oh, honestly, darling, look at the size of your *feet* in those *boots*! I sometimes wonder how I ever produced a daughter with feet that size! Still, you look lovely. You really do."

There's a kind of stunned pause, then Tigger repeats, "Let's go through and sit down shall we? I've got something to tell you."

"Er – go through to the other room if you want, Tigger," says Barb, "but I thought we'd eat in here and it'll be ready in a minute. . ."

"In *here*?" says Tigger, scathingly. "Oh well, OK. Let's sit down *in here* then. Come on everyone."

Barb turns away to the stove, probably to avoid decking Tigger with a heavy frying pan. Tigger is making it massively clear by all the means at her disposal that Barb is not included in the "everyone". I'm included though, and I wish I wasn't. I think about offering to help Barb with lunch but it would be so obviously fake that I don't, I pull out a chair and sit down instead.

We're all opposite each other round the black kitchen table with one space left for Barb. It's kind of intense.

"What's your news, Mum?" ventures Bonny. You can see all this hope flickering over Bonny's face. Hope that Tigger's going to announce she's emigrating or something.

"Well," smirks Tigger, taking another little sip of wine, "after that dreadful falling out we had I thought – we just can't let this go on. Someone's got to do something to turn it around. So I booked myself into therapy."

"Oh – *Mum!*" says Bonny, eyes glowing, and Barb turns round from the stove and says, "Tigger, that's *marvellous*!"

"Aren't you proud of me, darling?" twinkles Tigger, ignoring Barb. "Well – one of us had to break the pattern, start to heal the . . . the *distance* between us. The *misunderstanding*. I'd've got you to come with me, only obviously I couldn't get hold of you, could I?"

Bonny's face kind of falls a little. "Me?" she croaks.

"Yes, darling. It's – well – *family* therapy. And it's not nearly as good if just *one* of you goes. Obviously."

There's a stricken silence. Then Bonny whispers, "How did you get on?"

"The first therapist was *hopeless*, she didn't under-stand at all. Really aggressive, on about *me* the whole time, asking all these ridiculous questions about my past. I told her it was the *present* I was interested in. I said – 'Look, I know my daughter isn't here, but this is about our *relationship*, it has to be balanced between both of us.' Honestly, she didn't seem to know a *thing*. I ditched her after that very first session." Tigger sits back, proudly. "But I didn't give up. I tried another therapist a friend of mine recommended. And she was *much* better. Much better all round."

"What did she say?" asks Bonny faintly.

"Well, for the first couple of sessions she just listened, and let me have a little cry when I wanted to – she was *so sweet*. She understood how much I was hurting, over what you'd – over what had happened." Tigger dabs at her eye, glances over at Bonny. "I think she's going to be a real help. It's awfully difficult to just put it in a few words, darling, but basically she thinks we have an overly *symbiotic* relationship. That's when people are too dependant on each other, too close. She says it's *completely* natural, because of how terrible it was when your father walked out on us. We would've naturally clung together, and she says it's actually quite a lovely thing, that we care so much for each other. But now you're growing up, we need to . . . *draw back* a little from each other. Without losing the closeness and support, and the love. That's what she said, without losing the support and *love*."

There's another ghastly silence. Barb walks quietly over and refills everyone's glass, and as she passes, she squeezes Bonny's shoulder briefly.

"Is that all she says?" asks Bonny, in a dead voice.

"Oh, she says all kinds of things. And *listens*. I told her all about the way you ran off, how you wouldn't communicate with me. I had to, darling. That rage you flew into just before you ran off."

"It wasn't me in the rage, it was you," croaks Bonny.

"Oh, sweetheart, it doesn't *matter*! Don't you see? We've got to move *beyond* blaming each other. We've got to break the cycle, make something *new*. My lady says that you took a very damaging, severing step, running off, and now it's going to be very hard for you to turn around and come back. Because you'll see it as an admission of defeat. But she says it isn't defeat. She says you've got to look beyond all that – see it as moving forward yet again, not going back. Do you think you can do that, darling?"

I look over at Bonny, and see she's drowning. She'd prepared herself for tantrums, tears, torture – but not for this. Not for this analysed *reasonableness*. I watch her sinking, and I don't know what to do.

Somehow Tigger, with the help of her therapist, has managed to twist and pervert everything we know to be true.

"Don't look so stricken, darling," Tigger goes on. "Nobody's blaming *you*. There's no damage done. My therapist said how strong I'd been, living through that time when you didn't get in touch with me. And strength is what we need now, to make it work."

"I'm not moving back in with you, Mum," whispers Bonny. "I'm not going back to how it was."

"But that's just the point, Bonny darling! It won't be 'how it was'. We've got to make a new start! My therapist has given me so much help on that. Little things, little strategies. Like – I've always got to knock before I come in your room. And maybe getting you a mobile phone, for privacy. And even if we want to, we don't go out together so much in the evening."

"Shall I dish up?" asks Barb, faintly.

Tigger slams her glass irritably down on the table and I shoot to my feet to help Barb carry the stuff over. She's done roast beef and about three different veggies, and being able to hand round the potatoes and pour out the gravy helps me take a few steps back to normality.

"Oh, isn't this fabulous," gushes Tigger, to no one in particular. "A real *family* meal. Oh, I've missed this. We used to have lovely roasts, didn't we, Bonny?"

Bonny's eating like the food is iron filings in her mouth. Her eyes look glazed, dead, helpless. I glance over at Tigger and all I can see is her ruthless determination and I think: vampires get you by doing something unexpected. By coming at you from a different angle.

I should've remembered that.

Chapter 31

"There's absolutely no rush, Bonny darling," Tigger's going, "I mean – come and stay for a few days first. For the weekend or something. And we can try out our 'new way'. It's not going to be easy, Bonny. For me most of all, my lady said that. You're not my baby any more and I've got to accept that. It'll take *work*. But I think it's worth it, don't you?" And she kind of dimples over at Bonny, like it's all been settled.

"I – I really don't think it'll work, Mum," Bonny whispers.

Tigger looks up from her plate all tragic, and says, "It's not like you to be so defeatist, darling! What are you saying? That you won't make even a tiny little effort to work things out?"

"No, I'm not saying that, I'm—"

"I can't believe you'd be that cruel. I *know* you're not that cruel. Not after all I've been through. The fight I've had just to . . . just to *face each day* and begin to *trust* again." And she dabs at her eyes once more.

We all wait for Bonny's reply, but it doesn't come. She's staring down at her plate, not eating, not moving.

Barb's biting her lip, anxiously, moving a bit of meat around on her plate. Then she clears her throat a bit and says, softly, "Maybe it's all a bit soon still, maybe—"

"I'm talking to my *daughter*, Barbara, thank you!" snaps Tigger. "Don't you think you've done enough damage? Encouraging her to run away in the first place?"

"Mum, it *wasn't* her. . ."

"Look, darling, I've said I don't want to rake over the past and I *don't*. I just want you to come home. Is that too much to ask? For me to want my only daughter to *come home*?"

There's a horrible silence. Tigger's got this putrid, saintly smirk on her face, like she knows she's won. I can't stand it. I take a frantic swig of wine and blurt out, "Oh, come on, Tigger, you can't take my flatmate away from me just as we've got it all sorted!"

"*What?*" snarls Tigger.

"Not now we've worked out a cleaning rota and everything!"

"Richard, I really don't see what—"

"It took us a while to get used to each other, but we've really got it sorted now. *Really* sorted – you should see us. *Food* – we take food in turns. We shop and stuff, in turns. And *cook*. She's showing me how to cook. And whoever cooks doesn't wash up, the other one does. We got it properly sorted, we really have."

Bonny's looking up from her plate now. Barb's watching me with her mouth open. And then I risk a glance at Tigger and see that if they could, her eyes would *fry* me. "Well, that's really sweet, Richard," she grits out, "but—"

"*And* we've got a cat! Seriously, we joint-own this cat 'cos of all the rats near the canal. We take it in turns to feed him an' all. I don't wanna be a single parent, do I, if Bonny goes."

Barb lets out this little burst of nervous laughter, and Tigger slams her knife and fork down. "Stop *trivializing* this!" she spits.

"I'm not! I swear to God I'm not! Look – Bonny's nearly eighteen, isn't she. Seems to me that's not such a bad time to leave. I mean, your 'new way' – it could be sorting it out living apart, couldn't it? I mean she's gonna have to leave soon anyway, isn't she. Another year. Get her A levels, go on to uni."

"Bonny couldn't cope at university," snaps Tigger.

"Why d'you say that? Course she could. Bonny is one of the most sorted out, capable people I know. Jesus."

"Look, Richard – I appreciate the fact you've been kind to Bonny and—"

"I haven't been kind. We're sharing a flat, that's all. It's worked out brilliantly."

"You don't know the situation. You don't really know *her*."

"Yes I do. I know her and I really like her. And I know what I'm talking about 'cos I've just left home too and it's the best thing I could've done. It was time for me to go. Now what I've got to do is go back and make peace with my old man, get us off on a better footing. Like Bonny's trying to do with you. But I couldn't go back to live there."

Tigger throws herself back in her chair with her eyes shut. "Thing is, Tigger," I charge on, "I've thought about it a lot and I reckon my dad couldn't handle me being an adult in the same house as him. You know – not a little kid any more he could push around. Not that I'm saying you push Bonny around. But she's an adult now. Properly an adult. She's got her own ideas on things and maybe it's time for her to have her own space." Then I pause for breath.

Tigger snaps her eyes open and hisses, "Have you *finished*?"

"Yeah," I say genially. "Sure. But you want to think of the advantages to you too, Tigger. I mean – isn't it time for you to have some space too? That guy you were telling me about – I mean, you can hardly have guys there if your daughter's in the next room, can you? Any more than she can. All *far* too inhibiting." And I smile at her, daring her to answer. She doesn't. So I sit back, arms folded.

No one's saying anything but the atmosphere's vibrating like a bow string when the arrow's just been shot. Barb stands up and starts slowly to gather the plates in, then she says, "I've made a chocolate mousse if anyone's—"

"Oh, for *Christ's sake!*" Tigger screeches. "Will you *stop* going on about *food!*"

"I'm just trying to—"

"My heart's being broken here, and all you can talk about is *food!*"

"Why's your heart being broken, Tigger?" I ask, loudly. "You're not losing Bonny. It's just she's grown up. You should be proud of that. Isn't that what being a parent's all about? Letting go and stuff?"

"He's right," says Barb, softly.

"Oh, *shut up!* It's all your fault! If she hadn't had you to run to, she'd've *had* to stay put!"

There's a beat of silence, then Barb says, quietly, "Tigger, can you hear what you just said?"

"Oh, *shut up! Shut up!*"

"Mum – you've got to listen. You've got to." Everyone turns, looks at Bonny. "It's nothing to do with Barb. If you keep blaming her, you'll miss the point, and you'll miss . . . you'll miss any chance for us to sort things out between us."

"But darling I—"

"Mum, just listen. I'm not coming back, and I am going to university. And if you want to work things out between us, you've got to accept that. You've got to."

Tigger crumples her napkin and drops it on the table. Then she says, "Barbara, would you call me a cab, please?"

Barb stands up without a word and goes into the hall. Tigger pushes her chair back and stands up too.

Bonny leans pleadingly across the table. "Mum, don't just walk out like this. . ."

"*Shhhh*," I say.

Ten glacier-cold minutes later, and Tigger's left, and Bonny's crying, and Barb's got her arm round her saying, "You did the right thing, sweetheart, you did the right thing."

I help myself to a Coke from the fridge. I feel absolutely wasted with all this emotional stuff. I'm just not used to it. I've got this nagging thought that maybe I interfered too much, but I reckon it's just too bad if I did. Bonny stood up to her after all. She *escaped*.

"I phoned your dad when I phoned for a cab," Barb's saying. "He'll be here any minute."

Bonny can't seem to speak. She just keeps hanging on to Barb, and then the door goes, and I let her dad in, and he says "Hi" all anxious, and pushes past me and races into the kitchen, then he just kind of detaches Bonny from Barb and half carries her out to the front door. I can hear Barb talking to him in a low voice. Then I hear the front door shut, and then I hear Barb pelting down the hall again, and just as I'm worrying what the hell she's going to say to me she bursts in with this huge grin and shouts "All *right*!"

"*What?*"

"She's done it! She stood up to her! And you were *bloody amazing*, Rich! God! Gimme a hug!" She launches herself at me and squeezes me so hard I can't breathe for a second or two. "Mr White Knight riding in like that, oh God, Bonny's going to be more in love with you than ever now, oh *Jesus* forget I said that, Jesus I'm so *proud of her*!" Then she whirls over to the table, picks up the wine bottle, empties it into her glass and grins at me again.

I laugh, delighted, and say, "You really reckon it's going to be all right? I mean – she looked so *wasted*, she looked—"

"*Course* she was wasted. Drained, _out_ of it. She's been so screwed up, having that manipulating cow as a mother. Standing up to her like that was probably the hardest thing she's had to do, ever." Then Barb raises her glass to me and chants,

"*They fuck you up, your mum and dad,*
They may not mean to, but they do."

"What?"

"It's a poem. Kind of stating the obvious, wouldn't you say? You think about it – you're programmed to love your folks unquestioningly, aren't you – those big people who feed you and pick you up – however mean they are, you're programmed to love them. And with Bonny – all that baby love for her mum's still there. She's full of regret, longing – the works. But she did it! She faced her mum and all the worst emotional blackmail she could throw at her and she remembered what she was about and she didn't back down. *Brilliant.*"

"D'you think she'll be OK? Tonight?"

"Yeah. Yeah, I do. Her dad's a good bloke. I thought he was a bit of a prat at first, but he really has got Bonny's interests at heart."

We both kind of sigh then, in unison, all the tension gone, and I say, "I don't know how you kept your temper, the way Tigger kept jumping down your throat."

"Oh, I was prepared for that. But you were *brilliant*, Rich! Whatever possessed you to come out with all that bullshit, the stuff about cooking and the cat and everything?"

"I dunno."

"Instinct. You're a genius. It just – *caught* Tigger off guard, you blasting off like that. I could see Bonny getting stronger with every word you came out with. It kind of let her get her breath back and . . . *well*. She did it. She'll sleep like the dead tonight, I promise you. So will I. Come to think of it."

We sit contentedly down at the table once more. "Barb?" I say, lazily.

"Yeah?"

"Did you say you'd made a chocolate mousse?"

She laughs, stands up, heads for their enormous fridge.

"Only it seems a shame to waste it, if you made it specially and everything . . ."

The mousse lands in front of me, followed by a bowl and a spoon. "Eat as much as you want, matey. You deserve it. *God*, I feel good. I'm so glad that's over. That woman's lethal. The one thing Bonny wanted her to do was get some kind of professional help. And she does, but she uses it to try and trap Bonny into moving back with her! That second therapist sounds like a real sap. I'd love to know what the first one said, though."

"Probably told her she was a total psycho, ought to be locked up."

"Yeah. *Wooo*. Well, that was great, wasn't it. Sunday lunch. Beef and bile."

"Sprouts and savagery."

"Gravy and . . . and. . ."

"Grousing."

"Crap, Rich. That's crap. *Uuurgh*. I'm exhausted."

"How can she live like that, though," I muse, spooning out some more mousse. "Tigger. Being so fake. Shoehorning Bonny into what she wants."

"Lots of people are like that, Rich. The trick is to seek out the ones that aren't."

"But she's totally out of touch with what's real. And so *selfish*. It's like she doesn't care at all about finding out who Bonny really is, just. . ." I trail off. I'm describing Tigger but it hits me I could be describing Portia. In fact the similarity between the two is downright terrifying.

"How's your girlfriend?" Barb asks suddenly, like some kind of scary mind-reader. And because I'm so strung out by everything that's gone on I blurt out, "Dunno. We're sleeping together. Which is – *amazing*. But she wants to move in with me. Into the flat. . . Dunno. Dunno what to do. What d'you think I should do?"

Barb laughs, a bit embarrassed. "Oh, blimey, Rich – if *you* don't know, I don't know how you expect *me* to! It's serious stuff, living together."

"Yeah, it is."

"Do you want to live with her?"

"No."

"You sound pretty definite."

"I am. The thing is – I don't think I like her all that much."

"*Oh.*"

"Why d'you say 'oh' like that?"

Barb drains her glass, then she looks straight at me and says, "Because I think it sucks to sleep with people you don't like all that much. OK?"

Chapter 32

It's only five-thirty by the time I make it back to the canal. My head's buzzing with thoughts, not just about Bonny and everything that's going on for her, but about me too. Bonny standing up to Tigger made me think of the situation with my old man, how I had to fight him to be who I am, just like Bonny fought her mum. And how that's all unfinished business too. I owe Mum, I even owe that little jerk Sam. I can't opt out just 'cos Dad and I had a rough time.

The thing Barb said about me and Portia I'm not so keen to look at. Early evening is one of my horniest times. I head straight for the phone box on the corner and punch in Portia's mobile number. And get her "leave a message" message, complete with cutesy background music. So I say – "Portia – we got the flat to ourselves tonight. Come round, any time. Yeah?"

Then I head back there to wait.

First I do a couple of hours' work on yet another English essay. Then I crash out for a bit, then I wake up and mooch into the kitchen and make a big mug of sweet tea.

It's beginning to get dark. How long ago did I leave the message on Portia's mobile? Three hours maybe. Where is she? Why doesn't she come round?

I mooch back into the main room, and prowl over to the window, and think about starting work again, but I reject that right away. I'm stale and I need a break. It'd be nice to go round and knock up Chris, or Ollie, get them to come out for a pint, but I don't want to leave the flat because Portia could turn up any time.

I get my pad out then, and start sketching, just some vague ideas I've had circulating, but even that doesn't grab me. I'm restless. Like a cat on a hot tin roof. And I'm thinking Portia and I could be on our own here, all night maybe. She complains about not having any privacy but as soon as it's guaranteed she's nowhere to be found. Where is she? Why doesn't she come round?

My eyes skid round the room again and land on the junk-room door. Whoever crammed everything back in and forced it shut after the party didn't exactly do a brilliant job. It looks like it's bulging, ready to break its bonds any minute, and a great big bit of orange card is sliding out from under it. I walk over, and pull the door open, and just like at the party, an avalanche of stuff slides out. I curse loudly, which is pretty stupid because I knew this would happen. Then I kick aside some of the rubbish and make my way into the room. It's bigger than I thought it would be. The last of the sunset light is slanting in from the one high window. The window's quite long, and all you can see through it is sky – no bricks, no buildings, just sky.

I stand there for a minute looking round about me, wondering what to do, and I find myself thinking about Bonny, about everything that happened today. I remember how it seemed to drain everything out of her just having to be in the same room as Tigger; the wasted, washed-up way her face looked when she'd finally left. And suddenly everything kind of falls into place, and I know exactly what I'm going to do.

I'm not going to try and kick Bonny out of the flat any more. I'm going to clear this room out so one of us can sleep in it. Bonny and I are going to be like proper flatmates, with a bedroom each, and she can have a safe haven away from the evil vampire for as long as she likes. No more awkwardness, no more trying to claim the big room as mine – we can share it.

And then Portia can't move in, can she? Not to live with me. Not if Bonny's still here, she wouldn't want to. I'm safe. Portia can sleep with me behind a closed door, but not live with me.

Win both ways. *Perfect*.

I leg it into the kitchen, grab the roll of black rubbish sacks left over from the party, leg it back. Then I start at the door and cram armload after armload of boards and photos and papers into sack after sack. I'm all excited, working like a dog. I tie the sacks up and haul them out to the landing, where I dump them by the lift. Back when I moved in Barb told me to chuck everything, but if I leave it all out here I can double check with Nick before consigning it all to the dumpsters.

Once twelve sacks are out the door, I can really move about in the little room. It's nice. Not anything like the size of the bedroom Bonny's in, but nice and square and substantial. And I make a discovery. One wall isn't a wall but a series of sliding doors and on the other side of them is some very neat cupboard space, totally empty apart from a couple of wooden hangers. This is *brilliant*. I had a vague idea I might try and shift Bonny in here but now I've seen the cupboards *I* want the room. I can shove everything, all my clothes and junk, behind these sliding doors and the room will just be a window and a bed. Total minimalism. And a door. Total privacy.

Me and Portia, with the moon shining down on us from above.

I scoop up the last of the rubbish and sack it up, and drag it out to the landing. Then I notice the lift's in place. I could've sworn it was down below, when I was out here last.

Portia. It has to be Portia.

I spin round, all eager to show her our new private space, and this guy steps out right in front of me. He's early twenties, hard-looking, shorter than me but broad, strong. He comes up very nastily close and says, "*Are you Richard Steele?*"

And I've never seen him before but I know exactly who he is.

Chapter 33

"Are you gonna answer me or what? I said *are you Richard Steele?*"

"Yeah," I mutter guardedly.

"I was down your college the other day. I saw some very interesting stuff up on your art-room wall." And without warning his right arm shoots out and grabs my neck and pins me up against the wall.

My fist snaps up, knocks his hand away. "What the *fuck* d'you do that for?" I shout. "What the *fuck* are you playing at?"

He's about ten centimetres away from my face now, glaring, and I glare back, fists ready. "You know what pictures I'm talking about, you dirty-minded bastard," he snarls. "My girlfriend. Without her clothes on."

285

"*Yeah*? She wasn't your girlfriend when I drew those. She was *mine*."

Tony sucks in a breath hard, mad, and then he lifts his fist and drives it into my face, and I twist back, fast, so it just catches my cheekbone. I swing round, drive my fist into his stomach. He bellows, lurches at me, and I grab his arms, shove him back. He stumbles, squares up again. And for a few crazy seconds we're both just standing there facing each other, gurgling with pain.

"She told me you'd finished," I gasp out. "She got in touch with me, said you'd finished."

"We were on a *break*. Not finished."

"Yeah but – after that. She said she'd *finished* with you!"

"Well, she didn't. We got back together."

"How long ago?"

"Never you fucking *mind* how long ago! I'm telling you to lay off my girlfriend!"

"*Yeah*? Well, I'd like to hear that from her mouth, OK? Friday night – she was *with me*."

Tony's face screws up with rage and hate and he pitches himself at me, full force. I crash backwards into the iron gate of the lift; all my breath slams out of me. I slide sideways and he's on to me like a wolf, smashing his fist down into my forehead, and this red fug fills my brain, and I twist and buck like a madman and we crash over sideways. And then somehow I'm on top of him, and I grip his shoulders and slam his head down, hard, on to the floor. "What you *fucking* playing at?" I shout, and smash his head down again.

He's gone white. I've killed him. *I've killed him.*

His eyes open and roll back. "You all right?" I mutter.

There's a pause, then he suddenly lurches upwards, grappling, trying to throw me. I hang on, slam myself back down on him. "You fucking stay put or I'll smash your head in proper this time," I grit out. "You *listen*. I had no fucking idea you and Portia were still together. She lied. OK?"

"You stay away from her," he groans.

"I'll stay away from her if that's what *she* wants. *OK?*"

Tony makes a sudden heave, pitches me sideways. I scramble to my feet and we square up to each other again, fists ready.

And suddenly I don't want to fight. Not any more. Not over Portia. She's not worth it.

"She's been stringing us both along," I say. "Hasn't she?"

Tony glares at me, head down, ready.

"You think about it. She *let* me do those pictures."

He's balling and unballing his fists now.

"She's been busy a lot, hasn't she, over the last week or so. Well – when she can't see you, it's me she's with. And when she can't see me – it's you. Last night – she was with you. Wasn't she?"

He takes a step forward and I tense myself, ready, then he turns, walks to the top of the stairs, starts walking down. I know it's a point of honour with him to go slow and not look back, and I let him go.

Half an hour later I'm in the pub with Ollie, getting bladdered and showing off the two bruises on my face. He's really into hearing about the fight, wants to make sure I came off best, and the way I tell it, I did. Although at the time it felt like we were both losers. And I spill out all the anger and hurt about Portia two-timing me, and Ollie says, "Yeah, but it's not really a surprise, is it, man?"

He lets me rabbit on, though. Talking it through. "I'm just glad I haven't got it as bad as that poor sod, that's all," I say. "You should've seen his *face*. He was gutted. It was like – I could've broken his *head* off and it wouldn't have damaged him as bad as finding out about Portia."

"You reckon he's finished with her now?"

"Dunno. Probably not. I am though. I'm through."

Ollie's shaking his head. "You say that, man, but I seen you around her. You're addicted. You're addicted *bad*."

"Not any more I'm not."

"You say that, but she'll come slithering up to you and it's like she puts a spell on you –"

"Oll, mate, have some faith in me, OK? It's *over.*"

"Good. That's good. I'll hold you to that, mate. That girl is bad news. Lying. Two-timing you. Using you."

"Yup."

"Not exactly a nice person, is she?"

I laugh, and finish my beer. I'm thinking – in the end, all I really wanted from her was sex. Maybe I'm not exactly a nice person either.

That night I shift all my stuff into the new room. My bed fits really well right in the middle, with just enough space to walk down on either side and open the door. I lay down and look straight up at the three stars I can see through the skylight window and I get this sick, sad jolt when I think how it was supposed to be me and Portia in here, how good that would've been. I make myself conjure her up, how she looks, how she feels, to test myself on how miserable I really am underneath.

I'm OK though. Or maybe I'm just numb. Anyway I go off to sleep feeling more peace than I can explain.

I make it into college early next day. I've got no plans about what I'm going to do when I see Portia. A big part of me doesn't care, much. It's over, the worst has happened, what can happen now? But I don't see her. I reckon she's taken the day off. At lunchtime I

catch Jenny looking over at me and whispering to
Chloe and that's all.

I get back to the flat early. I'm looking forward to
Bonny walking in and seeing the great empty space
in the main room and then showing her the new
room, and her being all pleased with me because it
means I want her to stay and everything.

But when I've ridden up in the old clanking lift
there's a note waiting for me, tucked in the door-
frame. It's in Nick's ebullient writing, and it says:

*Rich – just use me as an answering service why
don't you – Bonny phoned – she's going to
stay at her dad's for another night. I've
got some more storyboards waiting – drop by.
Luv Nick.*

I'm pleased about the storyboards and surprised
how pissed off I feel about Bonny. Still, she'll see it
all tomorrow, won't she. I go in, and the great room
swallows me up like a barn. It's fantastic, but very,
very empty. I picture Bonny laughing when she
walks in, and think: maybe we can get some furniture together. Daddy's the kind of guy who'd buy
new sofas every few years – maybe we can scrounge
one of his old ones. And a table, maybe. A table to
eat off and work at and stuff.

It's still early. And I'm hungry. I think about
Bonny, talking everything over with her old man,

and without stopping to think further I go and strip the grubby sheet and duvet-cover off my bed and pick up my grimy towel from the bathroom and set off to my old home.

Chapter 34

I don't feel nervous, as I walk up the front path. There's something gritty and flinty inside me now, 'cos of what happened with Tigger and Bonny, and then Tony turning up, and finding out about Portia. Things are as they are, I reckon. You just have to deal with them.

It's Mum who opens the door to me. She doesn't say anything, just flies at me and wraps her arms round me, practically squeezes the living breath out of me. Then she stands back and says, "Oh, God, look at your *face* – you're bruised!"

"Footy," I say. "It got a bit rough. More like rugby really."

Mum frowns, and says, "Well – that apart, you look pretty well, Rich!"

"Yeah, well, take the tone of surprise out of your

voice, Mum. I am well. I'm eating, and sleeping, and wearing clean clothes. And sleeping on clean sheets too. Well, I would be if you'd just run these through the machine for me." She laughs, and reaches out her hand for the bag, and I say, "I forgot to do them when I went to the laundrette. You did offer."

"I know, I know, it's fine. Come on, come and have a cup of tea."

As soon as she's got the washing-machine running and we're sitting down at the kitchen table she says, "It was good of you to phone, the other day, Rich. I just – I know I can reach you through Chris, but I don't like to."

"Well, if things keep going well, Mum, I'll get myself a mobile. Then you can get hold of me anytime."

She laughs, and asks me about college, and I tell her, and she's really pleased. She asks me how my money's going and I tell her OK, and that Nick's offered me some more work. Then she tells me that Sam and Dad went out to kick a ball around while it's still light, and they'll be back soon.

"What you got in the oven?" I ask. "Smells like lasagne."

"It is."

"Got enough for me?"

"Um –"

"*Look*, Mum – I can do this now. Let me see him."

There's a long pause. Then she says, "All right, dear."

We make small talk for the next ten minutes, waiting. And then I hear the front door go. Mum gets to her feet, all jumpy, but the kitchen door's flung open before she can reach it. "I *sco-ored* –" Sam shouts, but he breaks off when he sees me. Then he immediately turns and looks up at Dad, coming through the door behind him, to see how he's going to react.

"Hello, son," says Dad, all expressionless. "Thought you'd drop by did you?"

"Yeah. I thought it was time we saw each other again."

"What've you done to your face?"

"Rugby," says Mum.

Dad walks over to the table, picks up the teapot.

"I'll make some fresh," says Mum.

"No need," says Dad.

There's a long, painful silence, while Mum fetches another mug and Dad pours himself the dregs of the tea. Mum sits down at the table again, but Dad stays standing.

"So," I say. "How you been?"

"All right."

"I'd've come round sooner, only –"

"Your mum told me you'd phoned, said you were OK."

"I am."

"College?"

"It's fine. I'm back in."

"Caught up on your work, have you?"

"Nearly. It's fine."

There's a long pause. Mum gets up from the table, goes over to the cutlery drawer, gets out some knives and forks. And lays some in front of me.

"You staying to eat, are you?" asks Dad.

"Yes," Mum says, firmly. "He is."

She puts her oven gloves on, pulls the old brown lasagne dish with the cracked corner out of the oven and plonks it down in the middle of the table. Sam scoots over from the doorway, takes his seat. And then at last Dad sits down as well. He stares over at me with that look that used to scare the shit out of me when I was a kid, half-frowning, eyes narrowed a bit, like he's weighing you up and finding you lacking. I stare back for a bit, then I stare at the lasagne. And this thought goes through my head that he's finding this reunion harder than I am.

Mum starts dishing up big platefuls. She gives one first to Dad, then to me, then Sam, then herself, just like the old days. Then we all pick up our forks and start eating simultaneously.

"God, this is good, Mum," I say, through my first mouthful. "I've missed your cooking."

"Sure you have," she says ruefully.

"No, honest, I have. Mind you, this girl I'm sharing with, Bonny, she cooks all right –"

Dad glares at me. "You living with someone?"

"Only like a flatmate."

"Yes? That why you draw naked pictures of her is it?"

"*What?*"

"We went to your exhibition," murmurs Mum, all embarrassed, looking at Sam, who's sniggering into his hand. "Mr Morgan – your teacher – he sent us an invitation to the open evening."

"*Did* he? Blimey. What did you think?"

"We thought they were very good," says Dad, heavily. "But when we saw those nudes –"

"They threw us a bit," finishes Mum in a rush. "Sam – *stop that*!"

"Well, that's not Bonny," I say, and I look over at Dad, who isn't looking back at me. I'm not embarrassed, not exactly, that he saw those sketches of Portia. I'm more amazed – amazed that he went to see my pictures. He's never done anything like that before.

"Bonny and I are just good mates, *flat*mates," I go on. "You'll have to meet her one day – you'd like her." I tuck into my lasagne and think – they would like her, too. Not like Portia. They'd see through the Porsche in five seconds flat.

Sam suddenly can't hold it any more and he kind of chokes with hilarity and squawks, "*So is the one in the pictures your girlfriend?*"

"Be quiet, Sam," says Dad. "That's none of our business."

Mum looks over at Dad and smiles at him, all approving, and I say, "Yeah, mind your own business, Sam. But for the record – no. Not any more."

There's a bit of an embarrassed pause then, and we all carry on eating. And then I say, "So you liked my stuff, did you?"

I'm expecting Mum to pitch in, but it's Dad who says, "Yes. It's excellent. And Mr Morgan – he obviously thinks you've got a real talent. He spent some time talking to us. Says it would be a crime if you didn't get to art college."

Good old Huw, I think, a bit choked. "Well, I am going to art college, Dad," I mutter. "I'm determined."

"Good," he says. Then he stands up and starts clearing the plates away.

"So – how did you end up with a flatmate then?" asks Mum.

"Oh, well, she knows Nick and Barb too. And she was like – a refugee."

"Like you, you mean," says Dad.

"No," I say. "Not like me. A whole lot worse than me. But it's working out, this flat. It's great. You'll have to come and see it."

"We'd like to," Dad says.

"I mean – I don't know how long it'll last, whether Nick'll need it for someone else or something. But for the moment he's cool about it, and it's great. He says he likes having someone there. And we've sorted out the rat problem. And it means I'm on the spot for emergency storyboards, and there's quite a few of those, 'cos Nick does everything at the last minute, which is great for my bank balance, and ... and everything." I finish up, and I realize I'm trembling, somewhere deep inside. It means so much to be talking to them again like this. To be back part of it.

"Well," says Dad, "that all sounds really good, son. But look – if it doesn't work out, you know you can move back here, don't you?"

"Can I?" I say. "Thanks."

Chapter 35

I get back to the flat not too late, and Pitbull meets me yowling furiously because I forgot to feed him before I went out. So I find a tin of gunk for him and spoon it out, and soon he's purring like a steam engine, then he settles down in the middle of my bed just as soon as I've got the clean sheets back on it and starts licking his arse.

I sleep like the dead that night, and as I drift off I go over how good it was to see my folks again, how Dad and I are on a new footing now, how I don't think I'll ever move back home but somehow that's OK, somehow it's the best solution all round. I think – I'll tell Bonny all about it. She'll understand.

I'm into college really early the next day 'cos I have an appointment with the principal. Being the untrusting sort, he wants to check I'm up to speed on my backlog of work. Which I reckon I am. In fact if I keep this rate up I'll only be a couple of weeks late for the final deadline. Which is all-round impressive by anyone's standards.

At nine-thirty-five sharp I knock on his door with my third English essay in draft form clutched in my mitt, all geared up to convincing him to tick off my "objectives achieved" box.

"Ah, Mr Steele," he says unenthusiastically, as I stick my head round. "Yes. Come in, come in. What's happened to your face?"

"Nothing sir. A bit of a fight."

"You haven't been brawling, have you?"

"No sir. I was attacked."

"Hm." He draws a folder towards him, and peers down at the list attached to it. "It's Ms Reardon's report I'm concerned with. You're still several essays down."

"Yes, but I've brought another one of them along," I say, brandishing my sheets of screwed up paper. "In draft. I want to word-process it properly, you know, like the other two."

"Hm." He glances down again. "Yes, Ms Reardon does state here that the standard of your recent essays was a significant improvement on your previous efforts. She gives the *Macbeth* one an A-minus, I see." He shoots a suspicious look at me. "Have you been getting help with them?"

"Just a bit of private tuition," I smirk.

"And your current work? I see you're falling behind somewhat on that. . ."

"Well, a bit, sir, obviously. As I've been working on all the late stuff." I flash a smile at him, and lie, "I've got a plan worked out though. To catch up."

"Hm. Well. Your Art and Graphic reports are glowing, of course. As usual. So I think we can agree that at this stage, you've met the targets required."

And even though I wasn't expecting anything else, I heave a massive sigh of relief. "Thank you, sir," I go, all grateful.

"Don't let this make you complacent, Mr Steele. Don't ease up on yourself."

"I won't."

"You must keep on track for the final deadline. Which will bring us up nearly to the end of term, of course."

I gawp at him. Over these last few amazing weeks, I've almost lost touch with time. But he's right. Summer's coming. All those weeks off. Time to catch my breath. Time to relax. Time to put in some work for Nick – covering for people wanting to have holidays. Get a stash of cash ready to see me through next year. *Brilliant*.

The principal shuts my folder and sits back, and something almost like a smile twitches his lips. "I must say I am quite impressed with you for once, Mr Steele. I didn't think you'd do it. I know you've had a certain amount of personal upheaval."

For one insane minute I think he must know about the Porsche messing me around, but then it dawns on me he means leaving home and everything. "It's fine, sir," I say. "Everything's fine. You know – now."

"You know we're here to help, don't you? If you have problems you need to discuss."

I get this flash-picture of me sobbing on to the shoulder of his immaculate grey suit. "Thank you, sir," I say, and leave.

I head straight for the cafeteria after that, hoping to bump into some of my mates. I can't see anyone when I get there though. I just notice Jenny sidling out at top speed. I get myself a mug of tea and a roll, kind of a late breakfast, and sit down by the window. I'm about halfway through it when the chair opposite me is suddenly jerked out from underneath the table.

I look up. It's Portia. Sitting down, face about ten centimetres away from mine, crying, "Richy, I've been looking for you *everywhere*! Why haven't you *phoned* me?"

I'm working on a crushing reply when she breaks in with, "Oh, your *face*! Did Tony do that to you?"

"Yes."

"He had this great lump on the back of his head

– you really *went* at each other, didn't you?" Then she widens her eyes at me, like the thought turns her on a bit.

"What d'you want, Portia?" I demand.

"What do I *want*? I want to *talk* to you! I want to *explain*!"

"*Explain*. Explain what? That your ex didn't *know* he was an ex so he came round and tried to beat seven shades of shit out of me?"

"Oh, *Richy* –"

"That the reason he didn't *know* he was an ex was you were still going out with him?"

"Richy, *let* me explain –"

"No. I don't care."

"Yes you do. Look. You know he sent me those freesias?"

I shrug.

"And I was going to phone him up and thank him then break it off for good?"

I shrug again.

"Well, I *couldn't*. When it came to it, I *couldn't*. He was so upset, said it nearly killed him just to hear my voice again . . . and he was so desperate to see me . . . I . . . I *couldn't*." And she gazes over at me, all tearful and meaningful.

I'm not fooled for a minute. The tender, tragic girl in front of me isn't the real Portia, no way. I sit back, fold my arms and say, "So you saw him again."

"Yes. I thought I could tell him face to face."

"But you couldn't."

"No. If you'd seen his *face* –"

"OK, Portia, I've got the point, you're all heart. But in that case, why didn't you let *me* in on it?"

"What?"

"Why didn't you tell me you were seeing him again? That you had two of us on the go?"

"Oh, *Richy* – it wasn't like that!"

"Yes it was. It was exactly like that. Why didn't you tell me?"

"I thought – if I told you, you'd fly into one of your strops, and . . . and I don't know, it was so good between us, I didn't want to spoil things."

"Well, Portia, I hate to disappoint you, but Tony ramming his fist in my face did actually spoil things. Just a bit."

She flings herself back in her chair. "Why are you *being* like this?"

"Like what?"

"All kind of cold and sarcastic. It's horrible."

"Well, hey, I'm *so sorry*! I find out you've been two-timing me and I'm meant to be nice?"

"It wasn't two-timing."

"What was it then? Three-timing? You got someone else on the go as well?"

Portia glares at me icily, then gets to her feet, all dignified. "If you can't talk about this properly, I'm going," she says.

"Fine."

She turns and sweeps over to the cafeteria door. Then she does a dramatic U-turn, speeds back over, sits down, leans over towards me, and says, "Richy, I understand how pissed off you are! I really do! But look at it from Tony's side. He was *desperate*. He told me he started coming up to the college, just on the off chance he'd see me. And when I phoned him he – he *begged* me to give him another chance."

"Well, I'm not going to do any begging, Portia."

"I know. I know you're not. That's one of the reasons I like you so much."

"Oh, for *God's* sake – look, you stick with Tony. Since he's so desperate to have you."

"But what about *me*? What about what *I* want?"

"Seems to me you've had exactly what you want up till now!"

There's a silence, while Portia ponders this, then I say, "When did Tony see the drawings?"

She shakes her head. "I . . . I dunno. I'd arranged to meet him. And when I was late he drove straight here to the college, and looked for me, and. . ."

"Found them instead."

"Yes. He only ripped up two of them."

"*What?*"

"Before Huw slung him out. Then he found me. And we had this horrendous showdown. He *made* me tell him who you were, Richy. Your address and everything."

"He didn't smack you around too, did he?"

"No. Of course not. I just – I was scared. I thought he *might*."

She's lying again, I can tell. From what I know of old Tony he'd yank out his own eyes with a corkscrew before he hurt a hair of her head.

"He *threw* the bits of picture at me," she adds.

"Must've hurt."

"And I know he nearly got into a fight with Huw. Tony was telling me about it later. He thinks Huw's *mad*. He kept kind of – *crowing*, and laughing, and going on about the ferocious power of art."

Despite what's going on inside me, I smile. "Huw isn't mad," I say.

"He's left the space on the wall. Where the pictures were. And in the gap he's pinned up this insane note about an unknown terrorist attack, and art creating havoc, and stuff like that."

"Oh, great. So it's all over the college again, eh? Jealous rival rips up sketches. Portia drives two guys to half kill each other. I bet you love it."

"Oh, don't be so *stupid*! Can't you see how much all this *hurts* me?"

"You want the truth? No."

She lets out an indignant sob, and I repeat, "I don't think you're hurting at all, Portia."

"Well, you don't know me then."

"Maybe I don't. I know all I want to."

"Look – I know it can't go on like this. I know I can't have both of you."

"Oh, you've worked that one out have you?" I say, all sarcastic. "Why? Has Tony given you an ultimatum?"

"Yes. Yes, he has, actually. Finish with you or that's it, it's over between us. And I s'pose you're going to say the same."

"No."

"Why not?"

"Because it's over anyway."

And for the first time since I've known her, I see a look of real distress, even panic, cross Portia's features. "What d'you mean? If I choose *you* – if I tell Tony he and I are finished –"

"Like you did before? No. I don't trust you. Not an inch."

Suddenly, she's spitting. "Who the hell d'you think you are, all on the moral high ground? Talking about trust? You were after me when you *knew* I was with him. . . You . . . you *seduced* me. . ."

I burst out laughing. "Oh, come *off* it, Portia. Yeah, I was crazy about you, I admit it. I didn't care about your boyfriend, not if you didn't. I was absolutely obsessed by you."

She leans towards me, lower lip trembling. "*Was?*"

"Yes, *was*. It's over, Portia. And you're right, I've got no right to come on all morally superior. I think we've both been pretty shitty. The point is, it didn't matter then, and it does now."

"*Why?*"

She's stunning. Looking across the table at me, all huge-eyed, she's stunning. But somehow her face doesn't draw me any more, nothing like it used to. Maybe you can only ignore what's behind a face for so long.

"'Cos I don't like who I am with you," I say. "I don't like who we are together."

"Richy – we're great together!"

"No we're not. It's all tense and sexy and . . . and *on one level* and we can't talk and it never goes anywhere. And you *used* me. You used me and you used Tony."

"You saying you didn't use *me*?" she spits.

"No. Maybe I did. But I was blown away by you, Portia. Even though you *pissed me off* a lot of the time, I really wanted it to work. Which looking back was pretty stupid of me, because it can't, can it."

She covers her eyes with her hands when I say that, comes out with this grotesque sobbing, and I suddenly feel really sick, sick at myself, her, everything. "Look – you just don't do it for me any more, OK? It's over," I say, and I stand up and walk out.

Chapter 36

The flat's still empty when I get back there. Still no Bonny, and no sign of her in the kitchen or anywhere else. But there's no note, either, so I reckon she'll be back.

Over to the left of the great arched windows, the sun's starting to go down, and the glass looks like it's on fire. I feed Pitbull and go and sprawl on the floor in front of them. I can feel my brain wanting to replay that scene with Portia, but I put a block on it. I've had enough of it, all of it. I look out of the window, and concentrate on the sunset.

Pitbull finishes his grub, and disappears out of the window like usual, and I lean over the ledge to watch him. He's got his own little route all worked out – I bet the rats think of it as the road to hell. He makes his way along the ledge and then hops on to the fire escape ladder that runs down the side of the building. His stubby ginger tail is the last thing to disappear from sight; I watch it go and I have this sudden desire to follow him.

Nick told me about the fire escape soon after I moved in. It'd have to be tested, regularly, wouldn't it? It'd have to be safe. I crouch on the window ledge, get hold of the fire escape railing nearest to me, and give it a hard rattle. This knocks me off balance, though, and I find myself tipping terrifyingly forward and before I can scream I'm flat out against the ladder, hanging on for dear life. One foot's on a rung. The other isn't. I move my dangling foot on, and start breathing again.

Once my heart rate's slowed from *immobilized with terror* to just plain *scared*, I start to descend. Six rungs down, and there's a little platform where the ladder shifts from the back to the side of the building. I keep going down, past Abacus's offices (I can see Camilla working late and I think about shouting to her but I reckon she might faint) and then down again to the second storey, the one that's empty.

And here the fire escape stops off. At the most fantastic big old balcony you can imagine. I'd clocked it from ground level before, but never realized I could reach it from the fire escape. It's wide, and generous, and it runs the whole length of the side of the mill, overlooking the canal on one side and the town on the other. The sun's setting right over it. It's all gold and glowing.

I step on to the floor and Pitbull mews at me. He's crouched on one of the stone urns either side of the big glass doors leading to the balcony. Judging by his scratching movements he's turned it into a toilet.

I walk over to the doors and peer in at the derelict room beyond, just in time to spot a rat disappearing into a packing case. I go "Fetch it – *rat*!" to Pitbull, who gives me a withering look and disappears. Then I head over to the stone railing, and I'm just leaning my elbows on it to bask in the sunset, when I hear shouting from up above.

It's Bonny. It has to be. She's come in and found the windows wide open and me not there and she probably thinks I've topped myself. I swing back over the balcony edge and swarm up the fire escape, and as I appear outside the flat window Bonny nearly falls backwards with shock.

"You have to see this!" I crow. "You have to!"

She barely hesitates. I go down a couple of rungs and she follows me out. "Don't go too *fast*," she breathes.

"Don't worry, I'm right behind you. See – here's a platform. Now round the corner . . . OK, we're here!"

Bonny's face is a picture as she steps on to the balcony. "Isn't it *fantastic*?" I cry.

"Whose is it?"

"Ours. That floor's empty. We can use it whenever we want – who's going to care? We can
sunbathe here. I only just twigged today that
summer's coming. And I can draw here – I'd *love* to
draw here. Hey – I wonder if we can get one of those
little barbecue thingies down that ladder, that'd be
brilliant. . ."

Bonny's laughing as she walks over and looks
at the view. "This is great," she says. "This is
amazing."

"You could plant up those pots, couldn't you?" I
say. "You like plants. They've been well manured by
Pitbull."

Bonny grimaces, then she kind of peers at me and
says, "Rich – what you done to your *face*?"

"Ah, that. Portia's boyfriend beat me up."

"Portia's *boyfriend*?"

"The one I thought she'd finished with. I beat
him up too."

"Blimey. When was this?"

"Sunday night."

"Christ. Does Portia know?"

"Yep. She liked the idea of her two blokes kicking
the shit out of each other."

"Oh, God. What's going to happen?"

"Nothing. We're finished."

"You said that last time."

"Yeah, but this time it's true. Don't look like that,
it's *true*. What I don't understand is how I let myself

get drawn back in. I mean – I knew what she was like. Right from the start."

Bonny laughs, and says, "Oh, well, you know that joke about men, don't you?"

"What joke?" I ask, suspiciously.

"That God gave them enough blood to operate their brains and their penises but not both at the same time."

"Oh, yeah, ha bloody ha."

"Barb told me it."

"She would."

"So are you all right?"

"Yeah. Yeah, I am. It's just left a bit of a bad taste, you know? I feel like an idiot."

The sun's sinking out of sight, and without saying anything we both slide down and sit with our backs against the wall, watching it go. "Anyway," I say. "What about you? You look a hell of a lot better than the last time I saw you."

"I am," she says. "I was *wasted* when I left Barb's."

"Has Tigger been in touch?"

"No. I sent her a letter. It was Ellie's idea. Just to . . . reaffirm what I'd said when I saw her, that I still love her but I'm not moving back home and so on. Ellie's been *great*, Rich. Dad's got all this anger still, about Mum, but Ellie just let me talk and she was more objective and . . . and kind of *practical* . . . and . . . anyway."

We rap on. I tell her all about seeing my folks, and

she really listens, she's glad for me. She thanks me
for how I laid into Tigger and we have a laugh about
me saying I didn't want to be a single parent with
Pitbull. We talk and talk, and finally the sun drops
right down and disappears, and the glow's gone, and
Bonny says she's getting cold. And I stand up and
say, "Jesus *Christ*, Bonny!"

"What?"

"I've been so wrapped up in this balcony and
everything, I've forgotten what I've really got to
show you!"

"What?"

"Come on, let's go back up!"

"Is it something you've drawn?"

"I'm not saying. Come on!"

Five minutes later we're standing in the doorway of
my new box room, and Bonny's admiring it and
saying, "Well, I did wonder what the hell had
happened to your bed when I walked in – only I
forgot about it when I thought you might've fallen
out of the window."

"Isn't it fantastic?"

"It's *small*."

"Yeah, but look at that skylight. And *these*." And
I jump over to the cupboards and yank them open,
making one of those corny "ta-DA!" sounds. "I was
going to get you to shift in here, but I wanted these.
Sorry."

Bonny's looking at me, smiling this lopsided smile.

"And I like the main room dead bare," I go on. "Don't you? I wouldn't mind getting hold of a big old sofa or something, but let's keep it dead bare, yeah? Maybe in the summer we can paint it out . . . we can. . . Bonny, are you all right?"

"Did you do this so I could stay on?" she whispers.

"Yeah. Well . . . basically yeah."

She looks almost as though she's going to start crying, then she croaks, "I don't know what to say, Rich."

"Say – thank you. You are one hell of a brilliant great bloke and I don't know how I'll ever repay you."

But this doesn't make her smile. And then I see she actually has got tears in her eyes.

"Bonny – what's up?"

"It's just – it's . . . oh, *Jesus*. You've done all this and I'm . . . I've been trying to get up the courage to tell you ever since I got back, Rich."

"Tell me *what*?"

"I'm – I'm moving *out*."

Chapter 37

"*W*hat? Where to?"

"To Dad's."

I feel *massively* pissed off when she says this. So pissed off I don't stop and think, I just pitch in with, "Look – OK – I know I wanted you out when you first got here and I was a bit of a bastard to you and everything, but *Jesus*, Bonny, that's behind us now isn't it?"

"Well –"

"I've just *proved* I've changed. I've just shifted into this *room*."

"I know, Rich, that's great, it's just—"

"*Don't* tell me you're gonna move out now I've done all this work shifting into this room."

"Well . . . it's just that . . . Ellie and I get on much better than I thought we would, and . . . you know,

I'll get my meals cooked and . . . and . . . I've got a really nice bedroom, and . . . there's a washing-machine and. . ." She kind of limps to a stop and looks at me.

"They're not proper reasons," I say. "Come on."

She looks down, doesn't answer.

"*You* don't need someone to cook and wash your clothes for you. You've been doing that since you could *walk*."

She shrugs. "Well – it'd be nice to have a rest, get looked after for a change –"

"Oh, *bollocks*. What sort of rest you gonna get with two little kids in the house? God – it'll be *awful*!"

"Well – I want to see more of Daddy. I want—"

"You don't have to move in with him to see more of him!" There's a pause, and I glare at her bowed head. Then I say, "It's me, isn't it. You've decided you can't stand me."

"*No!*" she hisses.

"So what is it? God, Bonny – I can't *believe* you're giving up all the freedom you've got here!"

At last, her head comes up. "I don't see why you're so pissed off, Rich! You can get someone else to move in with you! They'd move in like a shot!"

"I don't want someone else! I've just got used to you! I mean – come on, Bonny, now I've stopped being such a bastard to you, now we've got a room each, and we're getting on better than ever – what's the *problem*?"

There's a silence, then she croaks out something I don't catch.

"What?" I snap.

"I said – maybe that *is* the problem."

"I don't get you."

And suddenly she's blazing. "Oh, for *Christ's sake*! I wish I was a lesbian, I really do. Barb's right – men are so *stupid*."

"Yeah?"

"*Yeah!* Jesus, Rich – I'm – I'm – *shit*. You remember I asked you out, don't you?"

"Yes," I say. "To the cinema."

"To anywhere. Well – I was *crazy* about you."

Inside, I do this cartoon double take. "*Were* you?"

"Yes. From the first time I saw you."

"At Nick's party."

"No. Before. You didn't see me. It was in Smiths. You were crouched down in front of the pencil racks, picking up one pencil after the other. You'd got your art tin open, balanced on one knee, and all your pencils were down to little stubs, and you looked completely pissed off, like you couldn't afford to replace what you needed, and I thought – I thought you were *completely gorgeous* and I'd give *anything* to see the drawings you'd done, getting your pencils down to stubs like that."

I'm just staring at her, amazed, not even pleased,

too amazed to be pleased. Then I think I ought to say something, so I croak out, "Blimey."

Bonny's firing at me from all cylinders now, hardly blinking. "Then it was Nick's party. And you'd had your hair cut, and you looked even more . . . I thought you looked great. And we *got on* great, d'you remember? You had all these ideas, you knew what you wanted to do, you talked like you were going to do it, and I did too, I talked like you could make what you want to happen just *happen*. And I just – you just *swallowed* me up. And then you did this *thing*, with my mum. You started criticizing her, and me for doing too much with her. I felt like you'd smashed me round the head, only it wasn't bad, it was good, it was like you'd smashed a band round my head, a band squeezing my brain in, and it was like I felt my mind spreading out, and I could *breathe. . .*" She breaks off and looks at me, huge-eyed. "Do you realize what that did for me?" she whispers.

I shake my head. I feel almost completely gob-smacked but I have to hear more, I have to hear it all, I can't move.

"It was the start of me getting away. You were the one who – you showed me what we were like, me and Mum. D'you remember later – telling me she was like a vampire?"

"Yeah. That was out of order. I—"

"No it wasn't. It was *right*. You were right. And

then when everything came to a head – you let me move in here. And *then* – you went round and saw her for me. I mean – come on, Rich – who wouldn't *fucking fall for you*?"

There's a pause. I'm completely at a loss, and Bonny's just standing there, staring at the floor, breathing hard. Then just as I'm racking my brain for how to deal with all this she says, "Although you're right, you did behave like a complete bastard after I'd moved in. I felt about as welcome as one of the canal rats. And of course there was *Portia*. You didn't even see me, not really, just as someone in the way in your flat. I knew it was hopeless so I got used to living alongside someone I was *besotted* with and just . . . *relaxed* with you, opened up with you – I knew I had absolutely no chance of getting anywhere with you. And we – we kind of became friends, didn't we?"

"Yeah, we did."

"We got on OK."

"We got on great."

"I thought so," she says, looking down again. "Really great. Not just for an hour or so but day after day, really great. And that just made it all a lot worse 'cos that's when I *really* fell for you. OK? I spend all my time looking forward to seeing you, even just five minutes of you. OK? Now I'm going."

And she turns on her heel and stamps into her room, slamming the door behind her.

* * *

Well – what do you do? What would *you* do? If this was a crap American teen sitcom, I'd see the light and realize it was her I'd loved all along and rush into the room and sweep her up into my arms and everyone would go *Aaaaaah*.

But this isn't an American teen sitcom, so I just stand here with my mind all mushed up and my mouth hanging open like an idiot and everything she's said just kind of hanging in the air in front of me and I've no idea what to do with it. And within seconds, it feels like seconds, she's stomped back out with her holdall all bulging with stuff and she starts firing words at me again.

"You know, I was ashamed at first. Of feeling all this when you obviously felt nothing much for me. But then I stopped feeling ashamed. Why should I? It's good – feeling this much. It hurts but it's good. And if I can feel this for you, well, I can feel it for someone else too, can't I? I was moaning on to one of my friends about it all the other night. And she really made me think. She was all sympathy and you'll-meet-someone-else, you know, the usual stuff, and then she went all quiet. And when I asked her what was up she said, 'I dunno, maybe I'm missing out. I've never felt anything *like* what you're talking about.'

Then Bonny stops talking, and stomps towards the door.

"Bonny!" I wail.

"*What?*"

"Don't just leave like this!"

She turns on me again. "Rich, *I've got to*. I can't carry on living alongside you, feeling like this — I *can't*. It's just about *killing* me."

And then she's really gone.

Chapter 38

And then I'm on my own and all the drama's stopped. After the most amazing, mind-boggling month – the dream of big money, Portia, this flat, *Bonny* – everything exciting stops, and one day just starts running into another.

Barb turns up to collect the rest of Bonny's stuff and leaves a great boxful of cat food for Pitbull. I ask her how Bonny is and she just says "Fine" and I don't feel like I can ask any more.

I see Portia occasionally, getting into Tony's car, or flirting with a new victim. It doesn't touch me. Week runs into week, all very flat, all very calm. The weather gets hotter and I sunbathe on the balcony, and I work there too, fighting Pitbull for the ever-moving strip of shade. I complete all my work only ten days late and the principal tells me I can come back next term.

And then the college year's finished and it's really summer. Andy gets a bar job up near the trendy end of the canal and he stays over in Bonny's old room so often that by the end of July we reckon he's properly moved in. We get on fine. He doesn't pay me any rent 'cos I'm still not paying rent, but he's pretty generous with food and beer and stuff, so life gets easier. Like I hoped, I'm doing lots of storyboards for Nick, and I'm saving a fair bit of my dosh for next year. And I'm drawing, too. Stuff for me. Out on the balcony, in front of the big arched windows, down on the canal edge, anywhere. The best stuff I pin up on the walls in the main room, and I look at it and learn from it, and take it down when I do something better.

One day I run into Huw and he drags me off back to his workshed to see the sculpture he's working on. It's a man, naked, seated, big broad head, huge arms lying on his knees, big blind stone eyes staring ahead. Huw's working on his feet and they're massive, half-formed. He's so powerful, the man, he makes me feel weak just to look at him. He's brilliant. "Can I draw him?" I ask.

"Long as you don't get under m'feet, boy," Huw answers.

We spend the rest of the afternoon there together, working in silence. It's weird, it's one of the best afternoons of the summer so far. I draw the man, and I draw Huw working on him, and we both keep on until the light starts going and Huw says we'd better stop. He inspects my sketches and pulls out one of the best and asks can he keep it, and I say sure.

"Maybe I'll get a catalogue together," he says. "Use this to advertise my stuff, eh? Maybe I'll get myself a website." And I say "You don't even know how to switch a computer on, Huw," and we both laugh.

He tells me I can call round anytime, he'll be in his shed, enjoying the freedom of the summer. That's what that shed is to him, freedom. I doubt I'll go round again, but I'm glad the invite's there. I wander back to the flat and pin all the sculpture pictures up around the walls in the main room, and Andy rolls in and says it looks like a sodding art gallery, but I can tell he likes it.

Mum, Dad and Sam come round and see the flat, and they're all highly impressed, especially Sam. Mum brings another cardboard box full of tins of soup and tuna, and Dad presses twenty quid on me before he goes. I tell Sam he can sleep over some time. It's like the bad times are really behind us. I know it's easier at home without me there, and I don't mind, not now. Any time I want, I can turn up and see them and get fed.

I hardly think about what happened with Portia at all, but I do think about Bonny. What I can't get over is what she said she felt for me. That it was *me* she felt all that for. Me. Not an act, not a look – *me*.

I can't get it out of my head. And I miss her.

Andy's great, and the lads are round a lot, but I miss the way she and I talked together, the way it was so easy to be with her, but kind of exciting too, the way she pulled my leg and understood what I felt. I even miss the stupid jokes we used to have about Pitbull. I think about what she said – If I can feel this for you, I can feel it for someone else too, can't I? And I realize something. I'm jealous of the someone else. This is crazy. Bonny hasn't met him yet and I'm jealous of him. This guy who's going to respond to her, like I was too stupid to do, the guy who's going to talk to her with his mind and his body, with everything in him, and she's going to talk back, *God* is she going to talk back.

I don't know what to make of it, when I think like that.

I see quite a bit of Nick and Barb and the kids – Nick'll shout up the stairs that they're having a barbie that night, and take me back with him, or Barb'll leave a message telling me to meet them all for a picnic. It's good, and not only 'cos I get a really big feed. I play football with Freddie and try and stop Scarlett painting my nails and stuff. Every time I go round to their house I'm hoping Bonny might be there too, but she never is. Then one Saturday I'm round there, and Barb's decided I need another haircut ("shorter for the heat") and while she's snipping away I hear myself asking her for Bonny's phone number.

And what she says is – "No."

Just like that.

"What you mean *no*?" I demand. "I want to talk to her. Ask her how she is and stuff. Like a mate."

"You're not a mate," Barb says.

"Barb – what you on about?"

"I'm on about the fact that she's still not over you and I know she's started seeing someone else and you can just leave her alone, OK?"

I shrug and sulk for a bit, but I don't argue, because you don't, with Barb.

I think about the someone else, though.

The bastard.

I bet he isn't a patch on me.

Halfway through August, Chris and Natalie head off to Morocco together, Ollie's dragged off screaming and kicking with his family to Cornwall, and Andy and I talk about "just taking off somewhere" but in the end we stay put, earning money. I'm doing a couple of nights at Andy's bar as well now, and I meet this girl Carol there. For two weeks she's there every night I've got a shift. We're at the stage where we're joking and flirting and a bit special together, and then one night it's closing time and she comes halfway round behind the bar to say goodbye, and we end up kissing, a bit more than just goodbye. Then the next night I'm there she comes back in with her friend, and invites me and Andy to a party that Saturday.

Andy's up for it. He loves parties. And I'm aiming to go too. I shave and shower and pull open my cupboard doors to get my good gear out. Only I just stand there and look at it. I feel like I can't be bothered.

I wander into the main room, still wrapped in my towel, and Andy says, "Christ, aren't you ready yet?"

"I'm not going," I say. "You go on your own, yeah, mate? You know where it is."

"Oh, come on, Rich," he groans. "What's up with you? You never want to go out, nowadays."

"Yes I do," I snap. "What you saying that for? It's just – if I go, I'll have to get off with Carol, won't I?"

"Yeah. But I thought you were up for that. You looked well up for it the other night."

"Yeah, well, that was the other night. It's just – *uuuurgh*. I don't want to get into going out with her and everything, do I. She's nice but she's not that nice. And if I get off with her I'll have to ask her out and she'll keep coming to the bar and. . ."

Andy's halfway out the door, bored by my excuses. "Next time, mate!" I shout after him.

And I spend that Saturday night on my own, just sitting there listening to music and drinking the three beers left in the fridge as the sun sinks down and the blackness comes in. I feel kind of strange, floating, empty. Like I'm missing something, but I'm not sure

what it is. Andy staggers in about two in the morning and staggers past me. He doesn't realize I'm
there in the dark and I don't say anything. I don't
want him thinking I'm weirder than he does already.

A couple of days after that I leave the flat just feeling like I've got to walk, and I wind up mooching
through the centre of town. I'm turning into the
main square with its pavement cafés full up in the
sunshine when I see two gorgeous, unbelievably
brown legs swinging on the wall ahead of me. And
I look up and there's Bonny, sitting all alone on the
Town Hall wall with a can of lemonade in her
hand.

Only it's a different Bonny. I can't explain it but
she's completely different, she's moved on. And it's
like something starts hammering at me, hammering
at my head, *doof*, *doof*, *doof*, and it's like something's
slotted into place at last.

"Hi!" I say.

"Hi," she says back, and her face splits into the
best smile you can imagine.

"Where have you been?" I ask. "You're *black*!"

"Spain," she says.

"Yeah? Who . . . with?"

"Oh, just the family. I went along to help look
after the kids so Dad and Ellie got some time on
their own."

"Was it good?"

"It was *shattering*. They don't *stop*. Spain is great, though. The colours there – it's great."

There's a bit of a pause then, and I look at her, at how she's changed. She's all free and easy, just shorts and a little top, and she really fits who she is now, she fits her skin, she's *shining*.

"God, it's good to see you again, Bonny," I say. "I was wondering how you were."

She just shrugs, keeps smiling, swinging her legs, all at ease.

"You want to get a drink?" I ask, awkwardly. "At one of the cafés?"

"You'll never get a seat," she says. "That's why I bought this." Then she jumps down from the wall, and she's standing right in front of me, holding out her can. "Want some?"

I take it, and swig some, and she says, "So what about you, Rich? You been away?"

I say no, and then I tell her what's been happening, all about Andy moving in and the work being good. She listens, and asks a few things, and I ask about Tigger, and she tells me it hasn't moved on much, but she's seen her a couple of times, and we're *talking*, really talking like we used to.

And I realize something. It's not just Bonny who's changed, it's me. It's the way I'm seeing her. She's gorgeous. She's all warm and open and *real*.

We talk on, and then I say, "You might've come round. To the flat. To see Pitbull at least."

She gives me a weird look. "I hear about him," she says. "I pay for his food."

"Yeah, you keep the maintenance up, but it's not like proper caring is it?" As soon as this is out of my mouth I know it's wrong. It's wrong to try and tease her. Bonny looks away, shifts her feet. I think she's going to go, and I feel like I'll do anything to keep her there.

"How's the new man?" I ask loudly. "Barb told me you were seeing someone."

"Did she? Oh – it didn't work. He was all . . . *anyway*, I dumped him." Then she looks at me hard and says, "You get back with Portia?"

"Nope. I've been celibate all summer."

"Hah!"

"Bonny –"

"Yes?"

"D'you want to come to the cinema or something?"

There's a long, long pause, and I feel like my heart's pumping loud enough to be heard, and then she says: "No."

Just that – "No."

"Why not?" I go. "Just the *cinema* – it's not a major big deal is it?"

"That's why not," she says. "Look – I gotta go."

And she turns, and starts legging it down the street, and I leg it after her. I grab her arm and make her stop. "What d'you mean 'That's why not'?" I demand.

She yanks her arm away like she'd like to smash it

back in my face. "Just leave me alone, Rich, OK? What're you on, some kind of sick ego trip? I can't *believe* you asked me out after what I told you!"

"I thought maybe you'd got over that."

"Well, I *haven't*."

"Well, *good*. Neither have I!"

There's a long, long silence. Then she says, "That doesn't make sense. What you said – it doesn't make sense."

I move in closer to her. I dip my head so it's almost touching hers. She's breathing in as I breathe out.

"It does make sense," I say. "Come out with me. Please, Bonny."

She doesn't answer – I can't think of anything to say to make her answer. I get my head on one side and move in even closer and she doesn't pull back so I put my mouth on hers and kiss her.

She shuts her eyes and hardly moves. It's like she's listening to something I'm trying to tell her.

I stop, pull back, and she says, "All right."

"All right?"

"Yeah. But not the cinema. It's too hot for the cinema. What about that pub by the canal."

"*Yeah?*"

"We can sit outside and –"

"Talk."

"Yeah," she says, and then her face kind of crumples up and she leans her head against my chest and I put my arms round her, and I feel so good I could die.